Jamil nodded his dismissal and turned towards Lady Cassandra's tent. Over the last few days he had constructed his own mental image of his daughter's new governess—that of a rather frumpy, slightly forbidding bluestocking, austere and businesslike. He hoped he would not be disappointed.

He pulled back the door curtain of the tent and stepped through into the main room. The vision which greeted him was so far from the one he had imagined that Jamil stopped in his tracks.

Her long hair, a dark golden colour with fiery tints, rippled over the cushions. Her face had all the classical proportions of beauty, but it was not that which made her beautiful. It was the way her mouth curved naturally upwards. It was the hint of upturn on her nose which made it not quite perfect. And it was her curves.

A sharp pang of desire jagged through him. This woman had the type of _____ which turned heads. T_____ _____ inevitably spelled t_____

D1135786

AUTHOR NOTE

When I was asked to write my first ever sheikh story for the Mills & Boon *Summer Sheikhs* anthology, I assumed it would be a one-off. But the exotic magic of the desert cast its spell over me. The allure of an all-powerful prince, master and commander of a fantastical kingdom steeped in sensuality and set in the midst of a starkly beautiful and totally alien landscape, proved irresistible. I had to return.

Cassandra, heroine of this book, made her first appearance in INNOCENT IN THE SHEIKH'S HAREM, which tells the story of Prince Ramiz of A'Qadiz and Lady Celia, Cassie's elder sister. English Rose meets Desert Prince, and in the process eminently sensible Celia discovers her true passionate nature, while autocratic, invulnerable Ramiz finds that ruling in splendid isolation can be a very lonely business. The enclosed world of the harem, the wild beauty of hot desert nights, the intervention of not only Celia's father but her formidable aunt and Cassie, too, are the ingredients for a denouement in which Regency England meets exotic Arabia. Of course, true love ultimately bridges the cultural divide.

Cassie was smitten, as was I, with the intoxicating atmosphere of Arabia. Her story was begging to be told, and I was as eager as she to return to the sultry world of the desert in order to tell it. Two years after Celia and Ramiz are married Cassie has her opportunity, when she visits Celia in an effort to heal her broken heart. She swears she will never love again, but of course she's never met anyone like Prince Jamil al-Nazarri, one of Ramiz's closest allies. And Jamil has never met anyone like Cassie. Sparks fly from that first meeting. Their encounters are as scorching as the desert sun, as tumultuous as a desert storm.

I hope you enjoy reading Cassie and Jamil's story as much as I loved telling it. Here in Scotland, as I write this, we're having our usual damp and *driech* summer. Outside my window the rain is falling steadily, and the sea is iron-grey. Something tells me it won't be long before I am transported back to the desert again.

THE GOVERNESS AND THE SHEIKH

Marguerite Kaye

MILLS & BOON

All the characters in this book have no existence outside the imagination of the author, and have no relation whatsoever to anyone bearing the same name or names. They are not even distantly inspired by any individual known or unknown to the author, and all the incidents are pure invention.

First published in Great Britain 2011
by Mills & Boon, an imprint of Harlequin (UK) Limited,
Eton House, 18-24 Paradise Road, Richmond, Surrey TW9 1SR

© Marguerite Kaye 2011

ISBN: 978 0 263 88297 1

Harlequin (UK) policy is to use papers that are natural, renewable and recyclable products and made from wood grown in sustainable forests. The logging and manufacturing process conform to the legal environmental regulations of the country of origin.

Printed and bound in Spain
by Blackprint CPI, Barcelona

In loving memory of W,
who helped make me the person I am
and whose spirit, hopefully, lives on in me

Previous novels by the same author:

THE WICKED LORD RASENBY
THE RAKE AND THE HEIRESS
INNOCENT IN THE SHEIKH'S HAREM
  (part of *Summer Sheikhs* anthology)

and in Mills & Boon® Historical eBook *Undone!*:

THE CAPTAIN'S WICKED WAGER
THE HIGHLANDER AND THE SEA SIREN
BITTEN BY DESIRE

Look for
THE CAPTAIN'S WICKED WAGER,
now part of the
***Scandalous Regency Nights* anthology.**
First time in print format.
Available now.

Born and educated in Scotland, **Marguerite Kaye** originally qualified as a lawyer but chose not to practise—a decision which was a relief both to her and to the Scottish legal establishment. While carving out a successful career in IT, she occupied herself with her twin passions of studying history and reading, picking up first-class honours and a Masters degree along the way.

The course of her life changed dramatically when she found her soul mate. After an idyllic year out, spent travelling round the Mediterranean, Marguerite decided to take the plunge and pursue her life-long ambition to write for a living—a dream she had cherished ever since winning a national poetry competition at the age of nine.

Just like one of her fictional heroines, Marguerite's fantasy has become reality. She has published history and travel articles, as well as short stories, but romances are her passion. Marguerite describes Georgette Heyer and Doris Day as her biggest early influences, and her partner as her inspiration.

Marguerite would love to hear from you. You can contact her at Marguerite_Kaye@hotmail.co.uk

Chapter One

Daar-el-Abbah, Arabia—1820

Sheikh Jamil al-Nazarri, Prince of Daar-el-Abbah, scrutinised the terms of the complex and detailed proposal laid out before him. A frown of concentration drew his dark brows together, but could not disguise the fact that his face, framed by the formal head dress of finest silk, was an extraordinarily handsome one. The soft golden folds of the cloth perfectly complemented the honeyed tones of his skin. His mouth was set in a firm, determined line, but there was just a hint of a curve at the corners, enough to indicate a sense of humour, even if it was seldom utilised. The sheikh's nose and jaw were well defined, his flawlessly autocratic profile seemingly perfectly designed for use on the insignia of his kingdom—though Jamil had, in fact, refused to consent to his Council's request to do so. But it was his eyes that were his most striking feature, for they were the strangest colour, burnished like autumn, with fiery glints and darker depths which seemed to reflect his changing mood. Those eyes transformed Jamil from a striking-looking man into an unforgettable one.

Not that the Prince of Daar-el-Abbah was easily over-looked at the best of times. His position as the most powerful sheikh in the eastern reaches of Arabia saw to that. Jamil had been born to reign and raised to rule. For the last eight years, since he had inherited the throne at the age of twenty-one following the death of his father, he had kept Daar-el-Abbah free from incursion, both maintaining its independence and enhancing its supremacy without the need for any significant bloodshed.

Jamil was a skilled diplomat. He was also a formidable enemy, a fact that significantly enhanced his negotiating position. Though he had not used it in anger for some time, the wicked scimitar with its diamond-and-emerald-encrusted golden hilt that hung at his waist was no mere ceremonial toy.

Still perusing the document in his hand, Jamil got to his feet. Pacing up and down the dais upon which the royal throne sat, his golden cloak, lined with satin and trimmed with *passementerie* twisted with gold thread and embedded with semi-precious stones, swung out behind him. The contrasting simple white silk of the long tunic he wore underneath revealed a slim figure, athletic and lithe, at the same time both graceful and subtly powerful, reminiscent of the panther, which was his emblem.

'Is there something wrong, your Highness?'

Halim, Jamil's trusted aide, spoke tentatively, rousing the prince from his reverie. Alone of the members of the Council of Elders, Halim dared to address Jamil without first asking permission, but he was still wary of doing so, conscious of that fact that, although he had the prince's confidence, there was no real closeness between them, nor any genuine bond of friendship.

'No,' Jamil replied curtly. 'The betrothal contract seems reasonable enough.'

'As you can see, all your terms and conditions have been met in full,' Halim continued carefully. 'The Princess Adira's family have been most generous.'

'With good reason,' Jamil said pointedly. 'The advantages this alliance will give them over their neighbours are worth far more than the rights to the few diamond mines I will receive in return.'

'Indeed, Highness.' Halim bowed. 'So, if you are satisfied, perhaps I may suggest we proceed with the signing?'

Jamil threw himself back down on to the throne, in essence a low stool with a scrolled velvet-padded seat. It was made of solid gold, the base perched upon two lions, while the back was in the shape of a sunburst. It was a venerable and venerated relic, proof of the kingdom's long and illustrious history. More than three hundred years old, it was said that any man who sat upon it who was not a true and destined ruler would fall victim to a curse and die within a year and a day. Jamil's father had cherished the throne and all it stood for, but Jamil loathed it as ostentatious and impractical—though, as with most things ceremonial, he continued to tolerate it.

He lolled on the unforgiving seat, resting his chin upon his hand, the long index finger of his other hand tapping the document that lay on the low table before him. The various members of his Council of Elders, seated in order of precedence on low stools facing the dais, gazed up at him anxiously.

Jamil sighed inwardly. Sometimes the burden of royalty was wearisome. Though the betrothal contract was important, it was not really uppermost in his mind right now. He recognised that the marriage his Council had for so long entreated him to enter into was a strategic and dynastic necessity, but it was of little personal interest to him. He would marry, and the union would seal the numerous political and commercial agreements that were the foundation of the contract. Daar-el-Abbah would gain a powerful ally and—once Jamil had done his duty—an heir. He personally would gain…

Nothing.

Absolutely nothing.

He had no wish to be married. Not again. Especially not again for the sake of Daar-el-Abbah, this kingdom of his, which owned him body and soul. He didn't want another wife, and he certainly didn't want another wife selected by his Council—though, truth be told, one royal princess was bound to be very much like another. He hadn't disliked his first wife, but poor Karida, who had died in childbirth not long after Jamil came to power, had seemed to prefer the comfits of the liquorice and crystallised ginger she ate with such relish over almost anyone or anything else.

Jamil could happily do without another such, as this Princess Whatever-her-name-was, to whom Halim and his Council were so keen to shackle him, would no doubt turn out to be. He was perfectly content with his single state, but his country needed an heir, therefore he must take a wife, and tradition decreed that the wife should be the choice of the Council. Though he railed against it, it didn't occur to Jamil to question the process. It was the way of things. Anyway, in principle he was as keen to beget a son as his people were for him to provide them with a crown prince. The problem he was having was in reconciling principle with practice. The fact was, Jamil was not at all sure he was ready for another child. At least not until he had the one he already had under some semblance of control. Which brought him back to the matter uppermost in his mind: his eight-year-old daughter, Linah.

Jamil sighed again, this time out loud. A rustle of unease spread through the assembled Elders in response. Twenty-four of them, excluding Halim, each man wearing the distinctive Council insignia, an al-Nazarri green checked head dress with a golden tie, or *igal*, to hold it in place, the sign of the panther embroidered on his tunic. Behind the Elders, the throne room stretched for almost a hundred feet, the floor made of polished white marble edged with green-and-gold tiles. Light flooded the chamber from the line of round windows set high into the walls, reflecting through the gold-plated iron grilles, bouncing off the teardrop crystals of the five enormous chandeliers.

Most of the men arrayed before Jamil had served on his father's Council, too. The majority were traditionalists, resistant to every attempt at change, with whom Jamil found himself becoming increasingly irked. If he could, he would retire the lot of them, but though he was coming to the end of his patience, the prince was not a foolish man. There were many ways to skin a goat. He would take Daar-el-Abbah into the modern world, and he would take his people with him whether they wanted to join him on the journey or not—though he preferred that they came of their own accord, just as he favoured diplomacy over warfare. This marriage now being proposed was his gesture towards appeasement, for the hand that gives is the hand that receives.

He should sign the contract. He had every reason to sign. It made no sense to postpone the inevitable.

So he would sign. Of course he would. Just not yet.

Jamil threw the papers at Halim. 'It won't do any harm to make them wait a little longer,' he said, getting so swiftly to his feet that the Elders were forced to throw themselves hurriedly on to their knees. 'We don't want them thinking they are getting too much of a bargain.' He growled impatiently at his Council. 'Get up! Get up!' No matter how many times he said he no longer wished them to show their obeisance in private meetings, they continued to do so. Only Halim stood his ground, following in his wake as Jamil took the two steps down from the dais in one and strode quickly up the long length of the throne room towards the huge double doors at the end.

'Highness, if I may suggest…?'

'Not now.' Jamil threw open the doors, taking the guards on the other side by surprise.

'But I don't understand, Highness. I thought we had agreed that—'

'I *said* not now!' Jamil exclaimed. 'I have another matter I wish to discuss. I've had a most interesting letter from Lady Celia.'

Halim hurried to keep pace as they headed along the wide corridor towards the private apartments. 'Prince Ramiz of A'Qadiz's English wife? What possible reason can she have for writing to you?'

'Her letter concerns Linah,' Jamil replied as they entered the courtyard around which his quarters were built.

'Indeed? And what precisely does she have to say on the matter?'

'She writes that she has heard I'm having some difficulty finding a female mentor up to the challenge of responding to my daughter's quite particular needs. Lady Celia's father is Lord Armstrong, a senior British diplomat, and she has clearly inherited his subtle way with words. What she really means is that she's heard Linah is out of control and has run rings around every single woman in whose charge I've placed her.'

Halim bristled. 'I hardly think that your daughter's behaviour is any business of Lady Celia's. Nor is it, if I may be so bold, the business of A'Qadiz, or its sheikh.'

'Prince Ramiz is an upstanding man and an excellent ruler who has forward-thinking views similar to my own. I would suggest, Halim, that any opportunity to bring our two kingdoms closer together is something to be encouraged rather than resented.'

Halim bowed. 'As ever, you make an excellent point, Highness. That is why you are a royal prince and I a mere servant.'

'Spare me the false modesty, Halim, we both know you are no mere servant.'

Jamil entered the first of the series of rooms that ran in a square round the courtyard, unfastened his formal cloak and threw it carelessly down on a divan. His head dress and scimitar followed. 'That's better,' he said, running his fingers through his short crop of hair. It was auburn, inherited from his Egyptian mother. Reaching into a drawer of the large ornate desk that dominated the room, he found the letter and scanned it again.

'May I ask, does Lady Celia offer a solution to our supposed problem?' Halim asked.

Jamil looked up from the elegantly worded missive and smiled one of his rare smiles, knowing full well that Lady Celia's proposal would shock his Council and drive a pack of camels through the dictates of convention relating to the upbringing of Arabian princesses. Today's Council meeting had bored him to tears, and he was sick of tradition. 'What Lady Celia offers,' he said, 'is her sister.'

'Her sister!'

'Lady Cassandra Armstrong.'

'To what purpose, precisely?'

'To act as Linah's governess. It is the perfect solution.'

'Perfect!' Halim looked appalled. 'Perfect how? She has no knowledge of our ways—how can you possibly think an English woman capable of training the Princess Linah for her future role?'

'It is precisely because she will be incapable of such a thing that she is perfect,' Jamil replied, his smile fading. 'A dose of English discipline and manners is exactly what Linah needs. Do not forget, the British are one of the world's great powers, renowned for their capacity for hard work and initiative. Exposure to their culture will challenge my daughter's cosy view of the world and her place in it. I don't want her to become some simpering miss who passes the time while I'm finding her a husband by lolling about on divans drinking sherbet and throwing tantrums every time she doesn't get her own way.' *Like her mother did.* He did not say it, but he did not have to. Princess Karida's tantrums were legendary. 'I want my daughter to be able to think for herself.'

'Highness!' Shock made Halim's soft brown eyes open wide, giving him the appearance of a startled hare. 'Princess Linah is Daar-el-Abbah's biggest asset; why, only the other day the Prince of—'

'I won't have my daughter labelled an asset,' Jamil interrupted fiercely. 'In the name of the gods, she's not even nine years old.'

Slightly taken aback at the force of his prince's response, for though Jamil was a dutiful parent, he was not prone to displays of parental affection, Halim continued with a little more caution. 'A good marriage takes time to plan, Highness, as you know yourself.'

'You can forget marrying Linah off, for the present. Until she learns some manners, no sane man would take her on.' Jamil threw himself on to the tooled leather chair that sat behind the desk. 'Come on, Halim, you know how appallingly she can behave. I'm at my wits' end with her. It is partly my own fault, I know, I've allowed her to become spoilt since she was deprived of her mother.'

'But now you are to be married, the Princess Adira will fill that role, surely.'

'I doubt it. In any case, you're missing the point. I don't want Linah to be raised in the traditional ways of an Arabian princess.' Any more than he would wish his son to be raised in the traditions of an Arabian prince. As he had been. A shadow flitted over Jamil's countenance as he recalled his father's harsh methods when it came to child-rearing. No, of a certainty he would not inflict those traditions on his son.

'You want her to behave like an English lady instead?' Halim's anxious face brought him back to the present.

'Yes. If Lady Celia is an example of an English lady, that is exactly what I want. If this Lady Cassandra is anything like her sister, then she will be perfect.' Jamil consulted the letter in his hand again. 'It says here that she's one-and-twenty. There are three other sisters, much

younger, and Lady Cassandra has shared responsibility
for their education. Three! If she can manage three girls,
then one will be—what is it the English say?—a piece
of cake.'

Halim's face remained resolutely sombre. Jamil
laughed. 'You don't agree, I take it? You disappoint me.
I knew the Council would not immediately perceive the
merits in such a proposition, but I thought better of you.
Think about it, Halim—the Armstrongs are a family
with an excellent pedigree, and, more importantly,
impeccable connections. The father is a diplomat with
influence in Egypt and India, and the uncle is a member
of the English government. It would do us no harm at
all to have one of the daughters in our household, and in
addition they would be in our debt. According to Lady
Celia, we would be doing them a favour.'

'How so?'

'Lady Cassandra is already in A'Qadiz and wishes
to extend her stay, to see more of our lands, our culture.
She is obviously the scholarly type.'

'One-and-twenty, you say?' Halim frowned. 'That is
rather old for a female to be unwed, even in England.'

'Quite. Reading between the lines, I suspect her to
be the spinsterish type. You know, the kind of women
the English seem to specialise in—plain, more at home
with their books than the opposite sex.' Jamil grinned.
'Once again, exactly what Linah needs. A dull female
with a good education and a strict sense of discipline.'

'But Highness, you cannot be sure that—'

'Enough. I will brook no more argument. I've tried

doing things the traditional way with Linah, and tradition has singularly failed. Now we'll do it my way, the modern way, and perhaps in doing so my people will see the merits in reaching out beyond the confines of our own culture.' Jamil got to his feet. 'I've already written to Lady Celia accepting her kind offer. I did not bring you here to discuss the merits of the proposal, merely to implement my decision. We meet at the border of A'Qadiz in three days. Lady Celia will bring her sister, and she will be accompanied by her husband, Prince Ramiz. We will cement our relationship with his kingdom and take delivery of Linah's new governess at the same time. I'm sure you understand the importance of my caravan being suitably impressive, so please see to it. Now you may go.'

Recognising the note of finality in his master's voice, Halim had no option but to obey. As the guards closed the doors to the courtyard behind him, he made for his own quarters with a sinking heart. He did not like the sound of this. There was going to be trouble ahead or his name wasn't Halim Mohammed Zarahh Akbar el-Akkrah.

At that moment in the kingdom of A'Qadiz, in another sunny courtyard in another royal palace, Ladies Celia and Cassandra were taking tea, sitting on mountainous heaps of cushions under the shade of a lemon tree. Beside them, lying contentedly in a basket, Celia's baby daughter made a snuffling noise, which had the sisters laughing with delight, for surely little Bashirah was the cleverest and most charming child in all of Arabia.

Cassie put her tea glass back on the heavy silver tray beside the samovar. 'May I hold her?'

'Of course you may.' Celia lifted the precious bundle out of the basket and handed her to Cassie, who balanced her niece confidently on her lap, smiling down at her besottedly.

'Bashirah,' Cassie said, stroking the baby's downy cheek with her finger, 'Such a lovely name. What does it mean?'

'Bringer of joy.'

Cassie smiled. 'How apt.'

'She likes you,' Celia replied with a tender smile, quite taken by the charming image her sister and her daughter presented. In the weeks since Cassie had arrived in A'Qadiz she seemed to have recovered some of her former sunny disposition, but it saddened Celia to see the stricken look that still made a regular appearance in her sister's big cornflower-blue eyes on occasions when she thought herself unobserved. The shadows that were testimony to the many sleepless nights since *that thing* had happened had faded now, and her skin had lost its unnatural pallor. In fact, to everyone else, Cassandra was the radiant beauty she had always been, with her dark golden crown of hair, and her lush curves, so different from Celia's own slim figure.

But Celia was not everyone else, she was Cassie's oldest sister, and she loved her dearly. It was a bond forged in adversity, for they had lost their mother when young, and though the gap between Cassie and their next sister, Cressida, was just a little more than three years, it was sufficient to split the family into two distinct camps, the two older ones who struggled to take Mama's place, and the three younger ones, who needed to be cared for.

'Poor Cassie,' Celia said now, leaning over to give her sister a quick hug, 'you've had such a hard time of it these last three months—are you sure you're ready for this challenge?'

'Don't pity me, Celia,' Cassie replied with a frown. 'Most of what I've been forced to endure has been of my own doing.'

'How can you say that! He as good as left you at the altar.'

Cassie bit her lip hard. 'You exaggerate a little. The wedding was still two weeks away.'

'The betrothal had been formally announced, people were sending gifts—we sent one ourselves—and the guests had been invited to the breakfast. I know you think you loved him, Cassie, but how you can defend him after that...'

'I'm not defending him.' Cassie opened her eyes wide to stop the tears from falling. 'I'm just saying that I'm as much to blame as Augustus.'

'How so?' Until now, Cassie had refused to discuss her broken betrothal, for she wanted only to forget it had ever happened, and Celia, who could see that the wound to her sister's pride was as deep as that to her heart, had tactfully refrained from questioning her. Now, it seemed, her patience was about to pay off, and she could not help but be curious. She leaned over to lift Bashirah from Cassie, for she was making that little impatient noise that preceded an aggressive demand for sustenance. Celia thought of Ramiz and smiled as she settled the baby at her breast. The child had clearly inherited her demanding temperament from her father. 'Won't you tell me, Cassie?' she said gently. 'Sometimes talking about things, however painful, helps, and I've been so worried about you.'

'I'm perfectly all right,' Cassie replied with a sniff.

She looked so patently not 'all right' that Celia laughed. 'Liar.'

Cassie managed a weak smile in return. 'Well, I may not be all right at the moment, but I will be, I promise. I just need to prove myself, make a success of something for a change, give everyone, myself included, something to be proud of.'

'Cassie, we all love you, no matter what. You know that.'

'Yes. But there's no getting away from it, Celia, I've behaved very foolishly indeed, and Papa is still furious with me. I can't go back to England, not until I've proved I'm not a complete nincompoop.'

'Cassie, Augustus failed you, not the other way round.'

'He was my choice.'

'You can't choose who you fall in love with, Cass.'

'I'll tell you something, Celia, I'm going to make very sure I choose not to fall in love ever again.'

'Oh, Cassie, you say the silliest things.' Celia patted her sister's knee. 'Of course you will fall in love again. The surprising thing is that you have not fallen in love before, for you are such a romantic.'

'Which is precisely the problem. So I'm not going to be, not anymore. I've learned a hard lesson, and I'm determined not to have to learn it again. If I tell you how it was, maybe then you'll understand.'

'Only if you're sure you want to.'

'Why not? You can't think worse of me than I already do. No, don't look like that, Celia, I don't deserve your pity.' Cassie toyed with the cerulean-blue ribbons that were laced up the full sleeves of her delicate-figured muslin dress. 'Augustus said these ribbons were the same colour as my eyes,' she said with a wistful smile. 'Then again, he also told me that my eyes were the colour of the sky at midnight, and that they put a field of lavender to shame. He brought me a posy of violets in a silver filigree holder and told me they were a hymn to my eyes, too, now I come to think about it. I didn't even question the veracity of it, though I know perfectly well what colour of blue my own eyes are. That should give you an idea of how deeply in love I thought I was.'

A pink flush stole up the elegant line of Cassie's throat. Even now, three months after it had all come to such a horrible end, the shame could still overwhelm her. Hindsight, as Aunt Sophia said, was a wonderful thing, but every time Cassie examined the course of events—and she examined them in minute detail most frequently—it was not Augustus's shockingly caddish behaviour, but her own singular lack of judgement that mortified her most.

'Augustus St John Marne.' The name, once so precious, felt bitter on her tongue. Cassie made a moue of distaste. 'I first met him at Almack's, where I was fresh from another run-in with Bella.'

'Bella Frobisher!' Celia exclaimed. 'Who would have believed Papa could stoop so low? I still can't believe she's taken Mama's place. I doubt I will ever be able to bring myself to address her as Lady Armstrong.'

'No, even Aunt Sophia stops short of that, and she has been pretty much won over since James was born. I have to say though, Celia, our half-brother is quite adorable.'

'A son and heir for Papa. So the auspicious event has mollified even our terrifying aunt?'

Cassie giggled. *'Bella Frobisher may be a witless flibberty-gibbet,'* she said in a fair imitation of their formidable Aunt Sophia's austere tone, *'but her breeding is sound, and she's come up trumps with young James. A fine lusty boy to secure the title and the line, just what the family needs.* And honestly, Celia, you should see Papa. He actually visits James in the nursery, which is far more than he did with any of us, I'm sure. He has him signed up for Harrow already. Bella thinks I'm jealous, of course.' Cassie frowned. 'I don't know, maybe I am, a little. Papa has only ever been interested in us girls as pawns in his diplomatic games—he and Bella had drawn up a short list of suitors for me, you know. I mean, I ask you, a short list! How unromantic can one get. It was what I was arguing with Bella about the night I met Augustus.'

'Ah,' Celia said.

'What does that mean?'

'Nothing. Only you must admit that when someone tells you to do something you are very much inclined to do the exact opposite.'

'That's not true!' Cassie's bosom heaved indignantly. 'I fell in love with Augustus because he was a poet, with a poet's soul. And because I thought he liked all the things I did. And because he is so very good-looking and most understanding and—'

'And exactly the sort of romantic hero you have always dreamed of falling in love with.' Celia kissed the now-sated and sleeping Bashirah and placed her carefully back into her basket. 'And partly, Cassie, you must admit, because you knew Bella and Papa would not approve.'

'I concede, that might have been a tiny part of the attraction.' Cassie frowned. Celia had merely articulated what she herself had long suspected. When Bella had handed her the list of suitors her father had compiled, Cassie had promptly torn it in two. The confrontation had ended, as most of her confrontations with Bella ended, in an impasse, but over dinner, and during the coach ride to King Street, Cassie had found her resentment growing. It was while in this rebellious mood that she had encountered Augustus, a singularly beautiful young man who was most gratifyingly disparaging of her stepmother's treatment of her.

'We danced a quadrille that night at Almack's,' she told Celia, forcing herself to continue with her confession, 'and during supper Augustus composed a quatrain comparing me to Aphrodite. He dashed it off right there on the table linen. I thought it was just the most romantic thing ever. Imagine, being a poet's muse. When he told me about his impoverished state, I positively encouraged myself to fall in love, and the more Papa and Bella protested against my betrothal, the more determined I was to go through with it.' Cassie brushed a stray tear away angrily. 'The terrible thing is, in a way I knew it wasn't real. I mean, there was a part of me that looked at Augustus sometimes and thought, *Are you seriously intending to marry this man, Cassandra*? Then I'd think about how much he loved me, and I'd feel guilty, and I'd think about how smug Bella would be if I changed my mind, for it would prove her right, and—and so I didn't do anything. And the funny thing is that, though there were times when I questioned my own heart, I never once doubted Augustus. He was so impassioned and so eloquent in his declarations. When he—when he jilted me it was such a shock. He did it in a letter, you know; he didn't even have the decency to tell me to my face.'

'What a coward!' Celia's elegant fingers curled into two small fists. 'Who was she, this heiress of his, whom he abandoned you for? Do I know her?'

'I don't think so. Millicent Redwood, the daughter of one of those coal magnates from somewhere up north. They say she has fifty thousand. I suppose it could have been worse,' Cassie replied, her voice wobbling, 'if it had been a mere twenty…'

'Oh, Cassie.' Celia enfolded her sister in a warm embrace and held her close as she wept, stroking her golden hair away from her cheeks, just as she had done when they were girls, mourning their poor departed mama.

For a few moments Cassie surrendered to the temptation to cry, allowing herself the comfort of thinking that Celia would make everything better, just as she always had. But only for a few moments, for she had resolved not to spill any more tears. Augustus did not deserve them. She had to stop wallowing in self-pity, and anyway, what good did tears do? She sat up, fumbling for her handkerchief, and hastily rubbed her cheeks dry, taking a big gulp of air, then another. 'So you see, Bella and Papa were right all along. I'm selfish, headstrong and foolish, and far too full of romantic notions that have no place in the real world. *"A heart that can be given so easily cannot be relied upon, and must never again be given free rein."* That's what Aunt Sophia said, and I have to say I agree with her. I have tasted love,' Cassie declared dramatically, temporarily forgetting that she had abandoned her romantic streak, 'and though the first sip was sweet, the aftertaste was bitter. I will not drink from that poisoned chalice again.'

Celia bit her lip in an effort not to smile, for Cassie in full unabridged Cassandra mode had always amused her terribly. It was reassuring that her sister wasn't so completely given over to the blue melancholy as to have lost her endearing qualities, and it gave her the tiniest bit of hope that perhaps her very tender heart would recover from the almost-fatal wound dealt it by Augustus St John Marne. Ramiz would have dispensed swift retribution if he ever got his hands on him. Celia toyed momentarily with the satisfying vision of the feckless poet staked out, his pale foppish skin blistering and desiccating under the fierce desert sun, a legendary punishment meted out to transgressors in bygone days in A'Qadiz. And then, as was her wont, she turned her mind to practicalities.

'You are expected at the border of Daar-el-Abbah in three days. Ramiz will escort you there, but Bashirah is too young to travel and I'm afraid I can't bear to leave her so I won't be coming with you. It's not too late to change your mind about all this though, Cassie. The city of Daar is five days' travel from here and you are likely to be the only European there. You will also have sole responsibility for the princess. She has a dreadful reputation, poor little mite, for she has been left to the care of a whole series of chaperons since her mother died in the process of giving birth to her. The prince will expect a lot from you.'

'And I won't let him down,' Cassie said, clasping her hands together. 'Who better than I to empathise with little Linah's plight—did I not lose my own mother? Have I not helped you to raise our three sisters?'

'Well, I suppose in a way, but…'

'I am sure all she needs is a little gentle leading in the right direction and a lot of understanding.'

'Perhaps, but…'

'And a lot of love. I have plenty of *that* to give, having no other outlet for it.'

'Cassie, you cannot be thinking to sacrifice your life to a little girl like Linah. This position cannot be of a permanent nature, you must think of it as an interlude only. It is an opportunity to allow yourself to recover, and to do some good along the way, nothing more. Then you must return to England, resume your life.'

'Why? You are content to stay here.'

'Because I fell in love with Ramiz. You, too, will fall in love one day, properly in love, with the right man. No matter what you think now, there will come a time when looking after someone else's child will not be enough.'

'Perhaps Prince Jamil will marry again, and have other children. Then he will need me to stay on as governess.'

'I don't think you understand how unusual it is, his taking you into the royal household in the first place. Daar-el-Abbah is a much more traditional kingdom than A'Qadiz. Should he take another wife—which he must, eventually, for he needs a son and heir—then he will resort to the tradition of the harem, I think. There will be no need for governesses then.'

'What is Prince Jamil like?'

Celia furrowed her brow. 'I don't know him very well. Ramiz has a huge respect for him so he must be an excellent ruler, but I've only met him briefly. In many ways he's a typical Arabian prince—haughty, distant, used to being revered.'

'You make him sound like a tyrant.'

'Oh, no, not at all. If I thought that, I'd hardly allow you to go and live in his household. His situation makes it difficult for him to be anything other than a bit remote, for his people idolise him, but Ramiz says he is one of the most honourable men of his acquaintance. He is anxious to forge an alliance with him.'

'Yes, yes, I'm sure he is, but what does Prince Jamil actually look like?'

'He's very good looking. There's something about him that draws attention. His eyes, I think—they are the most striking colour. And he's quite young, you know, he can't be any more than twenty-nine or thirty.'

'I didn't realise. I had assumed he would be older.'

'Though he has not married again, it is not for lack of opportunity. I don't know him well enough to like him—I doubt any woman does—but what's important is, I trust him. The thing is though…' Celia hesitated, and took Cassie's hand in her own '…he's not a man who will readily tolerate failure, and he's not a man to cross either. You must curb your tongue in his presence, Cassie, and try to think before you speak. Not that I expect you'll see very much of him—from what I've heard, one of the contributing factors to his daughter's bad behaviour is his complete lack of interest in her.'

'Oh, how awful. Why, no wonder she is a bit of a rebel.'

Celia laughed. 'There, you see, that is exactly what I have just cautioned you about. You must not allow your heart to rule your head, and you must wait until you understand the whole situation before leaping in with opinions and judgements. Prince Jamil is not a man to get on the wrong side of, and I am absolutely certain that should you do so he would have no hesitation in trampling you underfoot. The point of this exercise is to restore your confidence, not have it for ever shattered.'

'You need have no fear, I will be a model governess,' Cassie declared, her flagging spirits fortified by the touching nature of the challenge that lay ahead of her. She, who had resolved never to love again, would reunite this little family by showing Linah and her father how to love each other. It would be her sacred mission, her vocation. 'I promise you,' Cassandra said with a fervour that lit her eyes and flushed her cheeks and made Celia question her judgement in having ever suggested her sister as a sober, level-headed governess, 'I promise you, Celia, that Prince Jamil will be so delighted with my efforts that it will reflect well on both you and Ramiz.'

'I take it, then,' Celia said wryly, 'that you are not having second thoughts or falling prey to doubts?'

Cassie got to her feet, shook out her dress and tossed back her head. Her eyes shone with excitement. She looked, Celia could not help thinking, magnificent and quite beautiful, all the more so for being completely unaware of her appearance. Cassie had many faults, but vanity was not one of them. Celia felt a momentary pang of doubt. How much did she really know of Jamil al-Nazarri the man, as opposed to the prince? Cassie was so very lovely, and she would be very much alone and therefore potentially vulnerable. She stood up, placing a restraining hand on her sister's arm. 'Maybe it is best that you should take a little more time, stay here for a few more days before committing yourself.'

'I have decided. And in any case, it is all arranged. You are worried that Prince Jamil may have designs on me, I can see it in your face, but you need not, I assure you. Even if he did—which seems to me most unlikely, for though in England I pass for a beauty, here in Arabia they admire a very different kind of woman—it would come to nothing. I told you, I am done with men, and I am done for ever with love.'

'Then I must be done with trying to persuade you to reconsider,' Celia said lightly, realising that further protestations on her part would only unsettle Cassie further. 'Come then, let me help you pack, for the caravan must leave at first light.'

Chapter Two

At dawn the next day, Cassie bade Celia a rather tearful goodbye and set off, following closely behind Prince Ramiz, who led the caravan through the dark and empty streets of Balyrma and out into the desert. She wore the royal blue linen riding habit she'd had Papa's tailor make up especially for this trip, which she fervently hoped would not prove too stifling in the arid heat of the desert. The skirt was wide enough to ensure she could sit astride a camel with perfect modesty. The little jacket was cut in military style, with a high collar and a double row of buttons, but was otherwise quite plain, relying on the severity of the masculine cut to emphasise the femininity of the form beneath it. By the time the caravan began to make its way through the first mountain pass, however, the sun was rising and Cassie was wishing that a less clinging style was currently more fashionable. Though she wore only a thin chemise under her corset, and no other petticoats, she was already frightfully hot.

The first two days' travel took a toll on both her appearance and spirits. The heat seared her face through her veil so that her skin felt as if it were being baked in a bread oven. Her throat ached from the dust and constant thirst, and the unfamiliar sheen of perspiration made her chemise cling like an unpleasant second skin that had her longing to cast both stays and stockings to the winds.

The excitement of the journey was at first more than compensation for these discomforts. The dramatically shifting scenery of ochre-red mountains and undulating golden dunes, the small grey-green patches that marked the location of oases, the ever-changing blue of the sky and the complete otherness of the landscape all fascinated Cassie, appealing at an elemental level to her romantic heart.

Until, that is, she started to lose sensation in the lower half of her body. The camel's saddle, a high-backed wooden affair with a padded velvet seat that gave it a quite misleading air of comfort, began, on the second day, to feel like an instrument of torture. Renowned horsewoman that she was, Cassie was used to the relative comfort of a leather saddle with the security of a pommel, ridden for pleasure rather than used as a mode of long-distance transport. Six hours was the longest she'd ever spent on horseback. Counting up the time since she'd left Celia at the royal palace, she reckoned she'd been aboard the plodding camel for all but eight hours out of the last thirty-six. What had begun as a pleasant swaying motion when they had first started out, now felt more like a side-to-side lurching. Her bottom was numb and her legs ached. What's more, she was covered from head to toe in dust and sand, her lashes gritty with it, her mouth and nose equally so, for she had been forced to put up her veil in order to see her way as dusk fell and Ramiz urged his entourage on, anxious to make the pre-arranged meeting point by nightfall.

Sway left, sway right, sway forward. Sway left, sway right, sway forward, Cassie said over to herself, her exhausted and battered body automatically moving in the tortuous wooden saddle as she bid it. *Sway left, sway right, sway—'Oh!'*

The lights that she'd vaguely noticed twinkling in the distance now coalesced into a recognisable form. A camp had been set up around a large oasis. A line of flaming torches snaked out towards them, forming a pathway at the start of which Ramiz bid his own entourage to halt. Her aches and pains temporarily forgotten, Cassie dismounted stiffly from her camel, horribly conscious of her bedraggled state, even more conscious of her mounting excitement as she caught a glimpse of the regal-looking figure who awaited them at the end of the line of braziers. Prince Jamil al-Nazarri. It could only be him. Her heart began to pound as she made a futile attempt to shake the dust from her riding habit and, at Ramiz's bidding, communicated by a stern look and a flash of those intense eyes that had so beguiled her sister, put her veil firmly back in place.

Following a few paces behind her brother-in-law, Cassie saw Prince Jamil's camp take shape before her, making her desperate to lift her veil for just a few moments in order to admire it properly. She had never seen anything so magical—it looked exactly like a scene from *One Thousand and One Nights*.

The oasis itself was large, almost the size of a small lake, bordered by clumps of palm trees and the usual low shrubs. The water glittered, dark blue and utterly tempting. She longed to immerse her aching body in it. On the further reaches of the shore was a collection of small tents, typical of the ones she had slept in on her overland journey from the Red Sea to Balyrma. They were simple structures made of wool and goatskin blankets held up with two wooden poles and a series of guy ropes. The bleating of camels and the braying of mules carried on the soft night air. The scent of cooking also, the mouth-watering smell of meat roasting on an open spit, of fresh-baked flat bread and a delicious mixture of spices she couldn't begin to name. Two much larger tents stood slightly apart from the others, their perimeter lit by oil lamps. Their walls were constructed from what looked to Cassie like woven tapestries or carpets, topped by a pleated green-damask roof bordered with scalloped edges trimmed with gold and silver.

'Like little tent palaces,' she said to Ramiz, momentarily forgetting all he had told her about protocol and tugging on his sleeve to get his attention. She received what she called his sheikh look in return, and hastily fell back into place, chiding herself and praying that her lapse had not been noted.

Another few paces and Ramiz halted. Cassie dropped to her knees as she had been instructed, her view of the prince obscured by Ramiz's tall frame. She could see the open tent in front of which the prince stood. Four carved wooden poles supporting another scallop-edged green roof, the floating organdie curtains that would form the walls tied back to reveal a royal reception room with rich carpets, a myriad of oil lamps, two gold-painted divans and a plethora of silk and satin cushions scattered around.

Cassie craned her head, but Ramiz's cloak fluttered in the breeze and frustrated her attempts to see beyond him. He was bowing now, making formal greetings. She could hear Prince Jamil respond, his voice no more than a deep sonorous murmur. Then Ramiz stepped to one side and nodded. She got to her feet without her usual grace, made clumsy by her aching limbs, and made her curtsy. Low, as if to the Regent at her presentation, just as Celia had shown her, keeping her eyes lowered behind her veil.

He was tall, this prince, was her first impression. A perfectly plain white silk tunic beneath an unusual cloak, a vivid green that was almost emerald, bordered with gold and weighted with jewels. A wicked-looking scimitar hung at his waist. He certainly wasn't fat, which she'd been expecting simply because Celia told her that it was a sign of affluence, and she knew Prince Jamil to be exceedingly rich. But the thin tunic was unforgiving. Prince Jamil's body showed no sign of excess. He was more—lithe.

The word surprised Cassie. Apt as it was, she hadn't ever thought of a man in such a way before. It was his stance, maybe; the way he looked as if he was ready to pounce. A line of goose bumps formed themselves like sentries along Cassie's spine. Celia was right. Prince Jamil was not a man to cross. As he put his hands together in the traditional welcome, Cassie tried to sneak a quick look at his face, to no avail.

'Lady Cassandra. *As-salamu alaykum*,' Prince Jamil said. 'Peace be with you.'

'*Wa-alaykum as-salam*, Your Highness,' Cassie replied from behind her veil, her voice raspy with thirst, 'and with you also.' She caught a glimpse of white teeth as he smiled in response to her carefully rehearsed Arabic. Or to be more accurate, he made something approximating a smile, which lasted for about two seconds before he held out his hand in greeting to Ramiz, and then ushered him into the throne room, where a servant pulled the organdie curtains into place, thus effectively obscuring them from view. Cassie was left to follow another man who emerged from the shadows to lead her towards the smaller of the two large tents.

'I am Halim, Prince Jamil's man of business. The prince asks me to ensure you have all you require. Refreshments will be served to you in your tent.'

'But—I assumed I would dine with Prince Jamil and Ramiz—I mean Prince Ramiz.'

'What can you be thinking of to suggest such a thing?' Halim looked at the dusty-veiled female who was to be the Princess Linah's governess with horror, thinking that already his worst fears were being confirmed. She had no idea of the ways and customs of the East. 'You are not in London now, Lady Cassandra. We do things very differently here—Prince Jamil would be shocked to the core.' The latter statement was a lie, for Prince Jamil was forever lamenting the outmoded segregation of the sexes at meal times, but this upstart governess was not to know that, and the sooner she was put firmly in her place the better.

'Please, don't mention it to him,' Cassie said contritely. 'I did not mean to offend. I beg your pardon.'

'It shall be so, but you would do well to heed my warning, Lady Cassandra. Daar-el-Abbah is a very traditional kingdom. You must tread extremely carefully.' Halim bowed and held back the heavy tapestry that formed the door of the tent. Cassie stepped across the threshold and turned to thank him, but he was already gone. She stared in wide-eyed amazement at the carpets, the wall hangings, the divans and cushions, the carved chests and inlaid tables. Another heavy tapestry, depicting an exotic garden in which nymphs sported, split the tent into two. In the smaller of the compartments she found, to her astonishment, a bath of beaten copper filled with warm water and strewn with petals. It had a delightful fragrance, orange blossom, she thought. A selection of oils in pretty glass decanters stood beside

it on a little table, along with a tablet of soap and the
biggest sponge Cassie had ever seen.

She needed no further encouragement, stripping
herself of her travel-worn clothes and sinking with a
contented sigh into the bath. She lay luxuriating in it
for a long time, allowing the waters to ease her aching
muscles. Eventually she sat up and washed her hair, then
chose a jasmine oil with which to anoint herself before
donning one of her own nightgowns and a loose wrap-
per in her favourite shade of cerulean blue. Her hair she
brushed out and left loose to dry in its natural curl.

'Since I'm obviously surplus to requirements while
the men discuss weighty matters of state, I may as well
be comfortable,' she muttered to herself. Part of her
resented being so completely excluded, despite the fact
that she was perfectly well aware her presence would
be unprecedented in this deeply patriarchal society. As
Papa's daughter, playing a role, albeit a small one, in the
world of politicking and diplomatic shenanigans was
second nature to Cassie. Though she was not the trusted
confidante that Celia had been, she was used to pouring
oil on troubled waters and providing a sympathetic ear.
It irked her, though she knew it should not, that both
Ramiz and her new employer should so casually dismiss
her.

But as she emerged into the main room of the tent
and found a silver tray covered in a huge selection of
dainty dishes had been provided for her, along with a
jug of sherbet, Cassie's mood brightened significantly
and common sense reasserted itself. She was expecting

too much—and she would do well to remember that she was here to govern a small girl, not a country! The princes were welcome to their weighty affairs of state.

Stacking up a heap of cushions on the floor beside the tray, she set about making an excellent meal. Far better to enjoy her own company than to have to make polite conversation with the prince tonight, all the time on tenterhooks lest she overstep some invisible mark. Far better to have a good night's sleep, to be introduced to him formally in the morning when she was refreshed and able to make a better impression.

She washed her fingers in the bowl and lolled back on the cushions in a most satisfyingly un-ladylike manner, which would have immediately prompted Aunt Sophia into one of her lectures about posture and politesse. The thought made Cassie giggle. Despite the fact that Celia was inordinately happy in her marriage, and despite the fact that, having met Ramiz, her initial reservations were quickly assuaged by his charm and patent integrity, Aunt Sophia thought Arabia a decadent place. *For once a female has abandoned her corsets, there is no saying what else she will abandon*, had been her parting words to Cassie. *Firmly laced stays signify firmly laced morals. Remember that, and you will be safe.*

Safe from what? Cassie wondered idly now, yawning. She should go to bed, but instead settled back more comfortably on the mound of cushions and examined her surroundings. The ceiling of the tent was constructed from pleated silk, decorated with gold-and-silver tassels. It reminded her a little of one of the rooms at the

Brighton Pavilion, to which she, in the company of Papa, had been invited to take tea with the Prince Regent. Which room was it? Her eyes drooped closed as she tried to remember. Tea had been delayed for over an hour because Prinny was being bled. Papa was most upset, considering it very poor form. But at least she had been allowed to socialise with the prince, unlike here. Strange to think that Prinny was king now. Which room had it been?

Cassie fell fast asleep.

An hour later the princes, having concluded discussions to their mutual satisfaction, parted company. Ramiz, who had never before left Celia alone for more than one night since they were married, was anxious to return to Balyrma, and could not be persuaded to stay on, despite Jamil's entreaties.

'I won't disturb Cassandra,' Ramiz said to Prince Jamil, 'you will pass on my goodbyes, my friend, if you would be so kind.' Ramiz headed back to his own waiting caravan, glancing up at the night sky, reassured that the moon was full enough for him to be able to travel for a few hours before having to stop for the night.

Jamil waited until his new ally was beyond the torch-lit path, and turned to Halim. 'That went well, I think.'

'Indeed, Highness. Extremely well.'

'I'll see the Lady Cassandra now.'

'But, Highness, it's very late.'

'Nonsense. She'll be expecting me to welcome her

formally into my household, as is the custom. You know that until I do, she will not be considered under my protection. I hope you told her, as I instructed you, that I would call on her when my business with Prince Ramiz was concluded?'

Halim swallowed. 'Not in so many words, Highness. My English is not the best, perhaps something was lost in translation.'

'That is news to me. You speak, to my knowledge, seven languages fluently.' Jamil looked sharply at his aide. 'I hope, Halim, I can be assured that your enthusiasm for this endeavour matches my own? I would not like to contemplate the consequences, were it otherwise.'

'Highness! I promise you that—'

'I do not want promises, Halim, I want your unequivocal support. And now, whether she is expecting me or not, I intend to see Lady Cassandra. We start for home at first light. Make sure all is ready.'

Jamil nodded his dismissal and turned towards Lady Cassandra's tent. Over the last few days, he had constructed his own mental image of his daughter's new governess. His fleeting glimpse of her had done little to confirm or deny the figure that existed in his mind's eye, that of a rather frumpy, slightly forbidding bluestocking, austere and businesslike. He hoped he would not be disappointed.

He pulled back the door curtain of the tent and stepped through into the main room. The vision that greeted him was so far from the one he had imagined that Jamil stopped in his tracks. Was the sleeping beauty who lay before him some sort of offering or gift that Lady Cassandra had brought with her? It was a ridiculous notion, he realised almost immediately, but how else to explain the presence of this alluring female?

Her long hair, a dark golden colour with fiery tints, rippled over the cushions. Her face had all the classical proportions of beauty, but it was not that which made her beautiful. It was the way her mouth curved naturally upwards. It was the colour of her lips, like Red Sea coral. It was the hint of upturn on her nose, which made it not quite perfect. And it was her curves. There was something so pleasing, so tactile about a curve, which was why it was such a prominent feature of the Eastern architecture. Curves were sensual, and this female had them in plentiful supply, from the roundness of her full breasts, to the dip and swell from her waist to her hips.

She was wearing some sort of loose gown with long sleeves trimmed with lace, an absurdly feminine piece of clothing, obviously designed for the boudoir. The sash had come undone to reveal a thin garment that left little to the imagination. He could see the rise and fall of her breasts at the neckline. He could see the dark aureole of her nipples through the gauzy material. He could see all too clearly that underneath it she was completely naked. She gave off an aura of extreme femininity, the type of yielding softness that begged for a corresponding male hardness. A sharp pang of desire jagged through him. This woman had the type of beauty that turned heads. The type of beauty that inevitably spelled trouble.

'Lady Cassandra?'

The temptress opened her eyes. They were the blue of a turquoise gemstone, under heavy lids that gave her a slumberous appearance. A woman waiting to be woken, stirred into life.

'Yes?' Cassie gazed sleepily up at the man standing over her and rubbed her eyelids. Her surroundings came into focus. And then so did the man. The first thing she noticed was his eyes, which were the strangest colour she had ever seen, burnished like an English autumn, though his gaze was wintery. His mouth was set in a straight line, his brows in a frown. His skin, framed by the traditional white silk head dress, was the colour of honey.

A man of loneliness and mystery, scarce seen to smile, and seldom heard to sigh. Lord Byron's words popped into her head, as if they had been waiting for just this opportunity to be heard, so pertinent were they. Like the Corsair, this man was both intriguing and inscrutable. He had an imperious air about him, as if he surveyed the world from some higher, more exclusive plane. Intimidating, was the word which sprang to mind. *Who was he? And what was he doing in her tent in the middle of the night?*

Clutching at the neck of her nightgown, the sash of her robe, her unbound hair, Cassie tried to get up off the cluster of cushions upon which she had been lying and succeeded only in catching her bare foot on a particularly slippery satin one, which pitched her forwards. 'Oh!'

His reactions were lightning quick. Instead of falling on to the carpet, Cassie found herself held in a hard embrace. She had never, even dancing a waltz, been held this close to a man—not even by Augustus, that soul of propriety. She hadn't realised how very different was the male body. A sinewy arm, lightly tanned under the loose sleeve of his tunic, held her against his unyielding chest. Were all men this solid? She hadn't really realised either, until now, that she was so very pliant. Her waist seemed designed for his embrace. She felt helpless. The feeling was strange, because it should have made her feel scared, but she wasn't. Not completely.

'Unhand me at once, you fiend!'

The fiend, who was actually remarkably un-fiend-like, retained his vice-like hold. 'You are Lady Cassandra?' he said, gazing at her in something akin to dismay. 'Sister to Lady Celia, daughter of Lord Henry Armstrong?'

'Of course I am.' Cassie clutched her robe more firmly together. 'More to the point, who are you, and what, pray, are you doing in my tent in the middle of the night? I must warn you,' she declared dramatically, throwing herself with gusto into the role of innocent maiden, safe now in the knowledge that the stranger meant her no harm, 'I will fight to the death to protect my honour.'

To her intense irritation the man smiled, or made as if to smile, a slight curl of the mouth that she'd seen somewhere before. 'That will not be necessary, I assure you,' he said. He had a voice like treacle, rich and mellow, his English softly accented.

'I am here as Prince Jamil's guest, you know,' Cassie said warily. 'If any harm were to come to me and he were to hear of it, he would—he would...'

'What would he do, this Prince Jamil, who you seem to know so well?'

'He would have you beheaded and dragged through the desert by a team of wild horses,' Cassie said defiantly. She was sure she had read about that somewhere.

'Before or after the beheading?'

Cassie narrowed her eyes and set her jaw determinedly. 'You are clearly not taking me seriously. Perhaps I should scream.'

'I would prefer it if you did not. My apologies, Lady Cassandra, allow me to introduce myself. I am Sheikh Jamil al-Nazarri, Prince of Daar-el-Abbah. I did not intend to alarm you, I merely wished to formally welcome you into my protection. Protection,' he added sardonically, 'that you obviously feel in urgent need of.'

Prince Jamil! Dear heavens, this was Prince Jamil! Cassie stared aghast at his countenance, forgetting all about the heinous crime of meeting a prince's eyes, which Celia had warned her about. 'Prince Jamil! I'm sorry, I didn't realise, I thought...'

'You thought I was about to rip your nightclothes unceremoniously from you and ravish you,' Jamil finished for her, eyeing the luscious curves, barely concealed by her flimsy garment.

Cassie clutched her nightdress even tighter to her and

tried, not entirely successfully, to banish this shockingly exciting idea from her mind. 'I wasn't aware that you were going to call on me,' she said in what she hoped was an unflustered tone.

'Halim did not mention that I intended to visit you?'

'No.' She saw a fierce frown form on the prince's countenance. She would not like to be in Halim's shoes. Cassie bit her lip. 'I'm sure it was an oversight. He may even have mentioned it, but I didn't hear him. I was very tired.'

'Your generosity does you credit. Don't worry, I won't have him beheaded and dragged through the desert by wild horses.'

His words were accompanied by a half-smile that Cassie could not help but return. 'I'm afraid I let my imagination run away with me a bit.'

She was not the only one. Reality crashed down on Jamil's head with a vengeance, forcing him to bid a metaphorical goodbye to his cherished vision of a dowdy, sober, English aristocrat. He looked at the dishevelled female standing before him who apparently was Lady Cassandra Armstrong, Linah's new governess. This ravishing, curvaceous, luscious creature with lips that were made to cushion kisses was to stay at the royal palace and teach Linah manners. Respect. Discipline.

Jamil clutched at the golden band of his headdress and pulled it from his head along with the *gutrah* itself and threw both onto a nearby divan. He ran his hands through his short hair, which was already standing up in startled spikes, and tried to imagine the reception his Council would give her. Almost, it would be worth bringing her back to Daar just to see their stunned expressions. Then he imagined Linah's reaction and his mouth straightened into its familiar determined line. 'No,' he said decisively.

'No? No—what, may I ask?'

'I cannot permit you to be my daughter's governess.'

Cassie's face fell. 'But why not? What have I done?'

Jamil made a sweeping gesture. 'For a start you look like you belong in a harem, not a schoolroom.'

Dismay made Cassie forget all about the need for deference and the necessity of not speaking without thinking. 'That's not fair! You caught me unawares. I was prepared to go to my bed, not to receive a formal state visit. You talk as if I lie around half-naked on a divan all day, buffing my nails and eating sweetmeats.'

Jamil swallowed hard. The idea of her lying around half-naked was most distracting. To be fair, she was actually showing less flesh than if she had been clad in an evening gown. Except that he knew her to be naked underneath. And the folds of her robe clung so lovingly to her, he could not help but notice her contours. And there was something about her, the slumberous eyes, the full bottom lip, the fragrance of her skin, jasmine and something else, sensuous and utterly female.

'What I meant is, you don't look—strict enough to be a governess,' he said.

Despite the very awkward situation, Cassie's sense

of the ridiculous was tickled. She bit hard on her lower lip, but her smile quivered rebelliously.

'I don't know what you find in the situation to amuse you,' Jamil snapped.

'I beg your pardon,' Cassie said, trying very hard to sound contrite. 'If you would perhaps tell me how you expect me to look, I will endeavour to change my appearance accordingly. I have lots of perfectly demure dresses, I assure you.'

'It's not a matter of clothing. Or lack of it. It's—it's you. Look!' He took her by surprise, taking her by the arm and turning her towards the full-length mirror that stood in a corner of the tent.

Cassie looked at her reflection in the soft glow of the lamp that hung from the canopied ceiling. Her hair was burnished, more auburn than gold, curling wildly about her face, tangling with the lace at the neckline of her negligee. Her skin was flushed. Her eyes had a sparkle to them that had of late been missing. She had an air of disarray that made her look a little—wanton—there was no denying it. *How could that be?*

Behind her, Prince Jamil moved closer. She could feel the hardness of his body just barely touching her back. She could sense him, warm and male, hovering only inches away from her. He reached over her shoulder to brush her hair back from her face and his touch, for some reason, made her shiver, though she wasn't cold in the slightest.

'Look,' he said, gazing at her intently, straightening the lace at her neck, running a hand down her arm to twitch the lace straight there, too, to tighten the sash of her robe which kept coming undone despite her best efforts to knot it securely. 'Look,' he said, his hand brushing her waist. Their eyes met in the mirror, autumn gold and summer blue, and she looked—not at herself but at them, the two of them, close enough to almost merge into one—as he did, too, at precisely the same moment.

And at that precise moment something happened. The air seemed to crackle. Their gazes locked. Cassie's breath caught in her throat. Prince Jamil bent his head. She watched in the mirror as he lifted the fall of her hair from her shoulders, as if she were watching a play, as if it was happening to someone else, as if the sensual creature before her was not her.

But if it was not her, why was it that she could feel his lips on the bare skin of her neck? The tiniest touch, but it was searing. Her skin contracted and burned. Now her breath came, rapid and shallow, too fast, like her heart, suddenly galloping. She realised only a fraction of a second before he did so that he was going to kiss her.

Kiss her properly.

Kiss her on the mouth.

He turned her around and tilted her chin up. His eyes met hers again, darker gold now, intensely gold, irresistibly gold. He made the tiniest movement towards her, so subtle as to be almost undetectable, except she detected it and responded, stepping into his arms and lifting her face and slanting her lips. And he kissed her.

Cassie had been kissed before. Truth be told, men had a habit of trying to kiss her, though she gave them no encouragement as far as she was aware, and had never had any problem in actively discouraging them when necessary. But strangely, discouraging Prince Jamil simply did not occur to her.

Augustus's kisses had been worshipful and chaste rather than intimate. To be honest, Augustus's kisses had failed singularly to arouse *the rapture which dwells on the first kiss of love*, which Lord Byron had so beautifully evoked and which Cassie had been led to expect. It had been one of the things that had made her question the depth of her feelings for Augustus, for neither the *first kiss of love* nor the twentieth had roused in her anything but mild indifference. But as Prince Jamil's mouth met hers, indifference was the furthest thing from her mind, and she knew that when he finished kissing her, she would be in no doubt whatsoever that she had been kissed.

His hand cupped her head, urging her to close the space, the tiny space, between them. She did, relishing the way her curves seemed to meld into the hard planes of his muscular frame. Her breasts brushed tantalisingly against his chest and her nipples puckered in response, as they did when she was cold, except she wasn't cold, and it was quite a different sensation. His other arm curved round her waist, nestling her closer. She licked her lips, because they felt dry. His eyes widened as she did so. He made a guttural noise like a moan that made her stomach knot. Then his lips touched hers, and she knew instantly that Lord Byron had been right after all.

Rapture. A soaring, giddy feeling surged through her as Prince Jamil's mouth moulded itself to hers. He kissed as if he were tasting her, his touch plucking tingling strings of sensation buried deep in her belly. He pulled her closer, settling her against him, his fingers sinking into her hair, into the soft, yielding flesh of her waist. His mouth coaxed hers open, his lips settled on hers, harder now, making her sigh at the taste of him. She felt herself unfurling like a flower as his tongue touched hers, a shockingly sensual and intimate act. If he had not held her, if she had not clutched, with both hands, at his tunic, his arms, his shoulders, his back, she felt as if she would have fallen into an abyss. She felt wanton. She felt wild abandon. She wanted the kiss to go on for ever. She pressed herself against him, and encountered something solid and heavy pressing against her thigh.

Jamil leapt back at once. He stared at her as if she was a stranger. Cassie stared, too, her hand to her lips, which were burning, seared, marked. Shame and embarrassment washed over her. *What must he think of her?*

Jamil looked at her in horror. *What was he doing? And by the gods, why was he still thinking of doing more!* 'You see what I mean now,' he said, taking his frustration out on the cause of it, 'you are clearly not governess material.'

Cassie was too bewildered to do anything other than stare at him. She felt a strange, needy ache, as if she had been starving, had been shown a banquet and allowed just one bite before the feast was withdrawn. Her body hummed and protested and begged for more. She was mortified and confused. *Had she encouraged him? Was it her fault?*

'Well? Have you nothing to say for yourself?'

She licked her lips. They felt swollen. 'I...'

Jamil gave an exclamation of disgust, as much at his own actions as anything else. It was not like him to behave with such a lack of control. A prince must be above such emotions. 'This arrangement is clearly not going to work. It is best we acknowledge that now. I will have you returned to your sister in the morning.'

The heavy edge of his cloak brushed against her ankle as he made for the door, rousing Cassie from her stupor. 'Returned!' she gasped, as the consequences of her entirely inappropriate behaviour began to dawn on her. She was to be sent back, like an unwanted present or a misdirected missive! Why could she not just for once think before she spoke or acted? 'Please. I beg of you, Prince Jamil, to reconsider.' Cassie tugged on his cloak in an effort to halt his retreat, and succeeded in earning herself an extremely haughty stare, but desperation made her ignore it. If he left now, he would not change his mind. He would send her back, she would be disgraced for the second time, only this time it was even worse because she would be letting not only herself but Celia down, and Ramiz, too, and she could not bear that. 'Oh, please,' she said again, 'I implore you, your Highness, don't be so hasty. Just listen to me, give me a chance to prove myself, I beg of you.'

Jamil hesitated momentarily and Cassie threw herself into the breach. 'Prince Jamil. Your Highness. Sheikh al-Nazarri.' She made a low and extremely elegant curtsy, completely unaware that she was granting Jamil a tantalising glimpse of cleavage. 'You would concede that your daughter is in urgent need of a governess and I—well, to be frank, I am in urgent need of an opportunity to prove myself, so you see, we both stand to profit from making this arrangement work. I know I'm not what you were expecting, though indeed I'm still not sure what exactly you *were* expecting, but I assure you I am extremely capable of looking after a little girl like Linah. I myself lost my mother at an early age, and I have three younger sisters whose education and upbringing I've been closely involved in. I'm sure she and I will get on. I know I can get through to her, make a difference to her. Please. Don't send me back. Give me a chance. You won't regret it.'

She clasped her hands in supplication and only just resisted the urge to throw herself on her knees. Prince Jamil gave no indication of wavering, his face set in an implacable expression. Only his eyes betrayed a flicker of something else. What, she couldn't discern.

Why on earth had he kissed her like that? To teach her a lesson? And why had she let him? She wasn't attracted to him, she couldn't be, she wasn't going to allow herself to be attracted to anyone. Not ever. She'd never allowed a man such liberties before. No man had ever attempted to take such liberties before, but Prince Jamil did not seem to think his behaviour questionable. Only her own.

And he was right about that. She had behaved like a very wanton. No wonder he thought—*oh, God, she didn't want to even think about what he thought.* Cassie clasped her hands together tighter and swallowed her pride. What use was pride, after all? She had no right to it, and no use for it either, if it prevented her from using all her powers to persuade the prince that she was worthy of his trust. 'I don't know what came over me—when you—when you—when I allowed you to kiss me, I mean,' she said, blushing madly but forcing herself to continue to meet those strange golden brown eyes. 'I can only assure you that I am not in the habit of allowing—of indulging—in kissing.'

'I know,' Jamil said, surprised out of his rigid hold on his control by this naïve admission.

'You do?'

'Your kisses were hardly expert.'

Cassie wasn't sure if this was an insult or a compliment. Though she was much inclined to pursue this very interesting question, for once sense prevailed and she held her tongue. 'Anyway, whatever they were or were not, I assure you I won't subject you to them again.'

Despite his determination not to be persuaded, Jamil was intrigued. And amused. It had been so long since he had found anyone so entertaining as Lady Cassandra. Or so—confounding. Unexpected. *Interesting.* He would be quite happy to be subjected again to her kisses. More

than happy. The question was, was this a good thing or
a bad? 'My daughter…'

'Linah.'

'She is…'

'Unhappy.'

He raised a supercilious brow. 'I was going to say
difficult.'

'Yes, but that's because she's unhappy.'

'Nonsense. She has no reason to be so. She has everything any little girl could wish for.'

'Children are not born difficult, they are difficult
for a reason,' Cassie persisted, feeling herself on surer
ground. 'The trick is to work out what that reason is.
Linah is only eight years old, she has not the language
to express her feelings properly. So instead she expresses
them by…'

'Being difficult.' Jamil pondered this. All his experience told him that leniency was the root cause of Linah's
tantrums. It had not occurred to him until now that
Linah could actually be unhappy; he had assumed that
withholding the harsh physical discipline which had
been meted out to him would be enough. Could he be
wrong? The thought was discomfiting.

'You see, I do understand little girls,' Cassie continued, sensing from the look on the prince's face that
she had struck a chord. 'I want nothing more than to
help Linah. If we could forget about what happened
tonight—make a fresh start in the morning…'

Jamil raised an imperious hand. 'Enough. I admit,

you've given me food for thought, but it's late. I will sleep on it and inform you of my decision in the morning.'

'Sleep is the wisest counsel. That's what my sister Celia always says.'

Jamil smiled properly this time, showing a fleeting hint of a single dimple. 'My father used to say something similar. I will bid you goodnight, Lady Cassandra.'

Dazzled by the way his face changed, from intimidating sheikh to an extraordinarily attractive and somehow more youthful man, Cassie gazed up at him. Only his turning to go brought her to her senses. 'Goodnight, Highness,' she said, dropping another curtsy. By the time she emerged from it, he was gone.

Chapter Three

The next morning found Jamil, most unusually for him, still in two minds. It did not help that Lady Cassandra had haunted his dreams. It did not help that the memory of her lips, her skin, her nubile body, had awakened his own slumbering desires, conjuring endless teasing fantasies that made sleep impossible. He had finally quit his divan in desperation, plunging into the refreshing water of the pool before dawn had even risen, in an effort to cool his body and order his mind. He was quite unused to such carnal thoughts getting in the way of his decision-making process. The base needs of his body had never before intruded on the logical processes of his brain. Lady Cassandra confused him by blurring the neatly ordered boundaries of his mind. She was made for pleasure. She was here for a much more pragmatic purpose.

Returning to his tent to don his travelling clothes,

Jamil resorted to drawing up a mental list of the advantages and disadvantages of employing Lady Cassandra as Linah's governess, and in doing so uncovered one of the questions that had been niggling away in the back of his mind. Lady Cassandra had said she urgently needed an opportunity to prove herself. Why? he wondered. Prove herself after what?

It was the first question he put to her when she appeared before him in the makeshift throne room. She wore her travelling outfit, the blue riding habit and veil in which she had arrived yesterday, and was at pains to keep her head correctly bowed, but Jamil was in no mood to allow her to hide behind the trappings of propriety. He bade the servants draw forwards the light curtains and instructed her to put back her veil. He did not, however, bid her sit, choosing to keep her standing before him, like a supplicant. 'Explain to me, if you please, what you meant by needing an opportunity to prove yourself,' he said in clipped tones.

Cassie stared at the prince in consternation. All through the long night she had rehearsed her arguments and mustered her reasons, drilling them into a tight formation, readying them to be paraded, impeccable and indisputable, before the prince. She was ready to recite lesson plans in everything from watercolour painting to deportment, map reading to account keeping, playing upon the pianoforte—though she wasn't particularly sure that such an instrument would be available—French conversation—though she didn't know, when it came

down to it, if Linah even spoke English—botany—
though she had no idea what flowers—if any—grew in
the desert—and horse riding, the one subject on which
Cassie knew herself to be expert. All of this she had
ready at her fingertips, along with her ideas for instill-
ing strict but fair discipline, and most of all her ardent
desire to give Linah some much-needed affection.

But it seemed Prince Jamil was not interested in any
of this. Instead he wanted to know about her motives,
a subject Cassie herself was a little hazy on, just at the
moment. 'I suppose I meant that it would be good to be
of use,' she fumbled.

Prince Jamil's mouth tightened. 'Of all things, I abhor
prevarication. It leads, more often than not, to deceit.
If you are to be my daughter's governess, I must be
able to trust you implicitly. To deceive me as to your
motives…'

'Oh, no, I would never do that.'

'Then I ask you again, what precipitated this burning
desire to prove yourself?'

Blushing, Cassie shuffled from one foot to the other,
trying desperately to find a way of satisfying the prince's
curiosity without putting herself in too unflattering a
light, but a glance up at his stern countenance told her
she would do far better to give him the unvarnished
truth. He would not tolerate anything else, and she most
assuredly did not want to risk being discovered in what
he would then assume to be a lie. She clasped her hands
together and began the sorry tale of her ill-fated betrothal to Augustus, though telling it rather to her riding boot

than to Prince Jamil, not daring to look up for fear that his countenance would betray his disapproval.

'I made a mistake, a terrible lack of judgement,' she concluded. 'Had I not been so headstrong, so indulgent of my sentimental inclinations, I and my family would have perhaps been spared the humiliation of my being so publicly jilted.'

'But surely it is this man Augustus—if you can call such a desert scorpion a man—surely it is he who should feel shame?' Jamil said contemptuously. 'You are the innocent party. He, on the other hand, has behaved in a manner that shows a complete lack of honour and integrity. He deserves to be the outcast, not you.'

Cassie shook her head. 'It is not how the world sees it, nor indeed how my—my papa sees it.'

'In my world we would see such a thing quite differently.'

Cassie jutted her chin forwards determinedly, a gesture Jamil found strangely endearing. 'Well, however anybody else chooses to see it,' she said, 'I assure you, no one could be more ashamed than I, nor more determined to change. I do not intend ever to give my heart rein again.'

'A wise decision. The heart is not, in my opinion, a logical organ.'

'No. Nor a reliable one. I have my faults, but I do not need to be taught something twice.'

'He who is burned must always beware the fire, hmm?'

'Exactly.'

'So, not to put too fine a point on it, Lady Cassandra, you're telling me that you were sent out here in disgrace?'

Cassie wove and unwove her long fingers. 'No, not precisely. Papa wished me to retire to the countryside until the scandal had blown over. It was Celia's suggestion that I come out here—she knows, you see, how very taken I was with Arabia when Aunt Sophia and I came to rescue—' Jamil raised his eyebrows quizzically. 'That is to say, came to visit Celia before she was married. And I was also most eager to…to put some distance between myself and Papa's new wife, who seemed to relish adding fuel to the fire with regards to my predicament.' Cassie's breast heaved at the thought of her stepmother. 'Bella Frobisher is a grasping, selfish cuckoo in the nest and now, of course, that she's produced an heir—well! You can imagine how she crows.'

She broke off with an exclamation of dismay. 'I beg your pardon, we seem to have strayed rather from the point. The thing is, your Highness, that I'm afraid my betrothal rather confirmed Papa's opinion of me as—as a little lacking in judgement and not very dependable,' she said, blushing deeper than ever, 'and I would very much wish to prove him wrong.'

'It seems to me that your father is at fault in allowing you far too much latitude. Here in Arabia, we recognise that women are the weaker sex, and do not permit them to make life-changing decisions, such as a choice of husband, for themselves.'

Cassie's immediate reaction was to inform Prince

Jamil that here in Arabia, in her opinion, women were not so much protected as subjected, but even as the words formed she realised that they undermined her cause no end. 'My papa would heartily agree with you on that topic,' she said instead.

'Meaning?'

'Meaning, if Papa had his way, he would marry all of us off to his advantage, regardless of our wishes.'

'That is not what I meant at all. It is not my intention that Linah become a state asset, not that that is any of your business. All I want is for her to learn respect for authority, to understand that there are boundaries she must not cross.'

'Children who are unhappy are wont to misbehave in order to gain attention,' Cassie said carefully.

'Yes, so you said last night. What do you mean by that?'

'Well, Linah has been without a mother since she was a baby, hasn't she?'

'She has had any number of females to look after her and pander to her every whim. In fact, she has been over-indulged. I concede that's partly my fault. I have allowed her to be spoiled in order to compensate for the loss of her mother and as a consequence have been reluctant to discipline her.'

'It's not spoiling or discipline she really needs. Tell me, Prince Jamil, are you close to your daughter?'

'What do you mean?'

'Do you see her every day? Play with her? Talk to her? Show any sort of interest at all?'

Jamil stiffened perceptively. 'Of course I take an interest, she is my daughter.'

'How?'

'I beg your pardon?'

'How do you show an interest?'

'I am given a weekly report of her behaviour and her progress with her lessons—at least I was, until the last female I hired departed. Linah is brought to me at the end of each week to discuss this.'

Cassie bit her lip. It was exactly as she had suspected. Poor little Linah was desperate for affection, and her cold-hearted father did nothing but mete out criticism. 'So, the only time you see her is to chastise her?'

Jamil stiffened. 'I have *never* laid a hand in anger upon my daughter.'

'Good heavens, I should hope not,' Cassie said, startled by the sudden harshness in his face. His eyes glittered fiercely, and she remembered Celia's caution again. Prince Jamil was not a man to cross. 'I'm sorry, I didn't mean to suggest such a thing for a minute.

'I do not want my daughter beaten.'

'Of course not! When I said chastise, I meant tell her off.'

'Oh. I see. I misunderstood. Yes. If that is what you meant, then I do. When Linah behaves so badly, she can hardly expect—'

'She behaves badly to get your attention!' Cassie interrupted. 'For goodness' sake, can't you see that? You said last night that Linah had everything a child could wish for.'

'She does, she wants for nothing.'

'Except for the most important thing of all.'

'And what would that be?'

'Love. A father's love, your love.'

'My feelings for my daughter are—'

'Unspoken!' Cassie declared roundly. She glared at the prince, all deference forgotten in the heat of the moment. 'Well, are they not?'

Jamil got swiftly to his feet and descended the step upon which the throne stood. 'As I was saying, Lady Cassandra,' he said through gritted teeth, 'what Linah needs is discipline.'

'And as I was saying,' Cassie riposted, 'what she needs is affection.'

'Respect is what she should have for me. I see no evidence of it, and showing her affection is hardly likely to induce it. As well expose an open wound and suggest she strike there.'

Cassie stared at him, appalled. How could he talk so coldly of his own daughter? Even her own father was not so—so clinical. 'She needs love,' she said obstinately, forcing herself to continue to look straight into the prince's stormy eyes, 'I can provide that. I can teach you how to do the same.'

'How dare you! How dare you presume that you can teach me anything?' Jamil replied angrily. 'I am a royal prince, a direct descendent of generations of wise and powerful potentates, a leader of thousands. And you, a mere woman, dare to tell me how to treat my own daughter.'

'The poor girl is obviously starved of love. For good-ness' sake, you're all she has. How would you have felt if your mother had died when you were a baby? Wouldn't you have made every effort to make sure you didn't lose your father's love, too? I know when my own mother…'

The rest of what she was about to say died on Cassie's lips as she took in the prince's stark white countenance. With horror, she realised just how presumptuous her hasty words must have sounded. She had no idea, after all, about the prince's own experience. 'I'm so sorry,' she whispered, 'I didn't think—did your mother die young?'

'No, but she may as well have.' He had been five when he had been forcibly removed to the east wing. She might as well have been dead for all the contact he was allowed with her. Jamil's knuckles whitened. Realising by the way the English woman was looking at him, that his anguish was plain to see, he made a huge effort, forced the past back into its box and turned the key. 'You are impertinent, and you raise issues that are entirely irrelevant. We are talking about Linah, not me.'

Too relieved at being spared any more serious rebuke to even consider pursuing the interesting question of Prince Jamil's as-good-as-dead mother, Cassie could only nod her agreement. It was time, most definitely time, to take another tack. Time enough, when she had Linah's confidence, to return to the subject. 'Please. I didn't mean to offend you. Let me talk to you instead of what I mean to teach Linah.' Giving him no chance to interrupt, haltingly at first, then with growing confidence and enthusiasm, Cassie put forward the plans she had made for her charge. As she talked, gesticulated and talked more, Jamil watched her closely, listening even more closely, trying to focus only on what she said about Linah, not to be distracted by the way enthusiasm lent a glow to her beautiful countenance, the way her body rippled under her ridiculously inappropriate travelling dress when she made her point with extravagant hand gestures. He tried to see her as a governess. To imagine her as Linah's governess. To picture her there, in the schoolroom of the palace, and not, definitely not, as he had seen her last night, strewn invitingly over a divan, reflected lusciously in a mirror.

Her forthright attack on him rankled, and it was ridiculous nonsense, of course, but Jamil was a ruthlessly fair man. Loath though he was to admit it, Lady Cassandra talked at least some sense. And there was the point, the worrying point, she had made about Linah being unhappy. *Did all this add up to enough for him to take a chance on her?* If he did not, what were the alternatives? None, and Prince Ramiz would be offended into the bargain.

'And as to geography,' Cassie was saying, 'I have sent to England for a dissected map just exactly like the one the royal princes had. It is in French, too, which will help Linah with the language. Which puts me in mind—I assumed she spoke English, but of course that is rather arrogant of me and—'

'She is badly behaved, not stupid,' Jamil said haughtily. 'As she is a daughter of the House of al-Nazarri I would expect nothing less. She already speaks good English and a little French. I would wish her to have also Italian, the rudiments of Latin and Greek, and perhaps some German.'

'Oh. Right. Capital. I'm afraid I don't have any German, though,' Cassie admitted, looking somewhat downcast. 'But in my humble opinion that's no great loss. I've met the Prussian ambassador and frankly he was as tedious and long-winded as the language. Oh, I hope you don't have any German friends, I meant no offence.'

Jamil smiled inwardly. Despite this female's appalling lack of deference and her seeming obliviousness to all the rules of protocol, he found her amusing. On the whole—yes, on the whole, the positives of taking her on outweighed the negatives. Though of a surety both Halim and his Council would be ready to pounce on any gaffes.

'You understand,' he said, 'that your appointment would be most unusual. My country is a very traditional one—in fact, you may as well know that the majority of my Council and trusted aides will oppose your role.'

Cassie's face fell. 'You mean I will have to win their approval?'

Jamil pursed his lips. 'They may voice their opinions, but they may not dictate to me. I mean merely that it will be better not to offend them.'

Her brow furrowed. 'How might I offend them?'

'As I have already informed you, Lady Cassandra, you look as if you belong not in the schoolroom, but the boudoir.'

'Harem, actually, is what you said. I can't help how I look, your Highness. And I assure you, that I will not—last night—it was…'

'Nothing of that sort will pass between us again,' Jamil said firmly, speaking as much to himself as to Lady Cassandra. 'As Linah's governess you must be beyond reproach—is that understood?' As Linah's governess, she must now be strictly out of bounds. *Why did he feel instinctively that this would prove so difficult?* It should have been a warning, but Jamil, whose own self-discipline was so ingrained as to have become instinctive, did not heed it.

'I understand perfectly, your Highness,' Cassie said, trying hard not to feel indignant. The prince had every reason to doubt her ability to conduct herself properly after all, given what she had just told him and how she had behaved last night. There was no point in telling him it was out of character; she must let her future conduct demonstrate that.

'You will most effectively contradict any criticism by obtaining results,' Jamil said brusquely, unwittingly echoing Cassie's own thoughts.

'Can I assume then that you will visit Linah regularly to check her progress?' Cassie asked sweetly.

'I am an extremely busy man. Affairs of state keep me occupied.'

Cassie took a deep breath. 'Forgive me, your

Highness, but Linah will fare much better if I can reward her behaviour with the promise of a visit from you,' she said in a rush.

'She can be equally rewarded by the knowledge that her good behaviour pleases rather than angers me,' Jamil replied implacably.

'With respect, it's not quite the same.'

'Your persistence in this matter is becoming tedious, Lady Cassandra. If you are so sure my daughter is in need of affection, then supply it yourself. Consider it part of your duties of employment.'

Cassie's eyes widened. 'Does this mean you'll give me a chance, then? Am I indeed to be Linah's governess?'

'For one month only, subject to satisfactory progress being achieved. Then we will see.'

All else was forgotten in the relief at having achieved her objective. She was not to be sent back. Cassie let out a huge sigh. 'Thank you. Oh, thank you so much, I won't let you down, I promise.'

'I will hold you to that. I do not take kindly to those who do. We start for Daar in fifteen minutes.'

Jamil pulled back the curtains and strode out into the morning sunshine, calling for Halim. Cassie stood, gazing at the space he had occupied, her mind in a daze. She'd done it, she'd persuaded him. A smile spread over her face, and she gave a little skip of excitement. She was going to Daar. She was going to be Linah's governess. She was going to show Papa that she could do something worthwhile. She was going to show the little princess what love was, and she was going to teach the little girl's cold-hearted, autocratic, infuriating father how to love her back. Whether he wanted to or not.

This gave Cassie pause. She did not doubt that somewhere, buried very deep, was Jamil's love for his daughter, but uncovering it would take tact as well as patience. For some reason, he was very resistant to the idea. Yet cold as he was—as he liked to appear, perhaps?—he could not really be so. He cared enough about Linah to want to bring her up properly. And Cassie had her own reasons for knowing he wasn't incapable of emotion. Last night…

Stop! She wouldn't think about last night. Her own behaviour had shocked her. She just couldn't understand it. But Jamil—well, he was a man, after all. One to whom desire came easily. Cassie's skin prickled. He had seen her in a state of undress and he had wanted to…

It was her fault! He was hot-blooded. It must be the desert air, or the heat of the sun, or perhaps there was just something in the prince's culture that encouraged such behaviour. Celia had hinted at something she called sensuality, though she wouldn't explain, and to tell the truth, Cassie had been too embarrassed to ask. Whatever it was, it had to be said, there was something terribly romantic about desert princes. And Jamil was the epitome of a desert prince. A passionate sheikh with a strong sense of honour—look at the contemptuous way he had talked of Augustus! It made her feel just a bit better, to have him take her part. Sort of. Just a little.

But that didn't mean he would always be so

understanding. She would do well indeed to forget all about last night, and all about Jamil as anything other than her exacting employer. She was done with romance. Done with giving her heart any say at all in matters. She was done, quite done, with men, whether traitorous poets or desert princes, romantic or otherwise.

Cassie made the journey to the city of Daar mounted on a snowy white camel, a rare breed, though its exclusivity did not, unfortunately, make it any more of a comfortable ride than its more dowdy brethren. The high-backed saddle was more splendid than the one on which she had arrived at Jamil's camp, but it was still basically a sparsely-padded wooden seat. As Jamil made a clicking noise at the back of his throat, and the beast knelt down to allow her to mount, Cassie's muscles protested by cramping. However, she climbed on to what passed for a saddle, pleased to discover that she did so with some semblance of grace, even more pleased to see the very brief look of approval that flitted across Jamil's face. He made the clicking noise again, and the camel got back to its feet. Cassie arranged her skirts and pulled the long veil, which she had attached to her little military hat, over her face. 'I'll take the reins, thank you,' she said, holding out her gloved hand.

Jamil hesitated. It was the custom for women to be lead and the white camel was not only extremely rare but extremely sensitive, with a mouth as soft as a thoroughbred horse. What if this woman was as impetuous a rider as she was in every other way? It would just take one jerk of the reins and she would end up thrown.

'You need not worry, I won't let him bolt and I won't ruin his mouth,' Cassie said, reading his thoughts a mite too easily for Jamil's liking. He surrendered the reins reluctantly, and, mounting his own camel with practised ease, headed the caravan east.

They had journeyed all day, save for a short break at the sun's zenith, and on into the night, too, for Jamil was anxious to be home. By the time they made camp, the stars were already luminous, stitched like jewels into the blue velvet blanket of the sky. Cassie sat a little apart on a little outcrop of rocks, next to the small drinking pool, watching them set up the tents. Leaning back on her hands, she threw her head back to gaze up at the night sky, which looked so vast compared to England, the stars seeming to hover so much closer to earth than they did at home. The desert, too, in daylight, was vast, undulating and unrolling in front of them in shades of ochre and rust, of gold and tawny brown, a landscape of barren beauty, so exotic in its fierceness, and so very different from England that she felt as if she were on another planet. Celia said it had intimidated her when first she came here, but Cassie found it invigorating and beguiling. She liked its very otherness. She even liked the way it put her firmly in her place, reminding her she was one tiny scrap of insignificance in the face of nature's magnificence.

It struck her that Jamil seemed the very physical

embodiment of the desert's exotic charms. Perhaps that was why he integrated so seamlessly into the terrain. It certainly explained the ease with which he navigated the way across what looked to Cassie to be a vast expanse of nothingness. He was a product of the desert, yet not subjugated or intimidated by its harshness, seeming instead to dominate the sandy landscape.

Above her, two shooting stars streaked across the sky, one after the other. Her aches and pains forgotten, Cassie cried out with delight. *'Most glorious night! Though wert not sent for slumber!'*

'I beg your pardon?'

Cassie jumped. Jamil was standing beside her. How did he move so silently? 'It's Byron. An English poet, he—'

'You admire such a man, who has behaved so scandalously?'

'You know of him, then? I admire his poetry, regardless of his behaviour.'

'I forget, you have a weakness for poets, do you not? Or more accurately, perhaps, for poets who treat women with a callous disregard for honour. But it is much too beautiful a night for harsh words,' he added, noting her hurt expression, 'and in any event, you must be very tired, Lady Cassandra.'

'Cassie, please. My given name has too many unwarranted associations.'

'You don't see yourself as a prophetess, then?'

'Hardly.' When he smiled, as he was doing properly now, his expression softened, making him look much less austere. Cassie smiled back. 'If only I had been able to see a bit further into the future, I wouldn't have made such a fool of myself over Augustus.'

'But then you wouldn't have come here.'

'Very true.' Cassie tried to smother a yawn.

'You are tired, and no wonder, it has been a long day.'

'I am a little weary, I must confess.' Her head drooped. 'I should retire.' As she stumbled to her feet, a strong pair of hands circled her waist. 'I can manage,' she protested, but already she was falling asleep.

With an exclamation that could have been impatience, and might have been something more tender, Jamil scooped her up and carried her to her tent, where he laid her down on the divan. She was already deeply asleep. He hesitated before loosening the double row of buttons on her ridiculous little jacket, easing her carefully out of it, resisting the urge to look at the soft curves revealed under the flimsy material of her undergarment. Settling her carefully, he unlaced her boots, but left her stockings on. This much she might reasonably thank him for; any more would be a liberty.

He pulled a rug over her, tucking it securely in at the sides, for the coming dawn would be cold. She nestled her cheek into a cushion, her lips pouting into a little contented sigh. Long lashes, a darker gold than her hair, fanned on to the soft curve of her dusty cheek. Her hair was a tangle, tresses curling down her neck, little tendrils clinging to her forehead. No doubt she would be horrified by her state of dishevelment, but to Jamil the imperfections enhanced her appeal. She was no goddess now, but mortal, flesh and blood, and possibly the most disturbing flesh and blood he had ever encountered. There was something about her that made him want to cradle her and ravish her at the same time.

'Governess, governess, governess,' he muttered to himself as he made his way to his own tent, matching the words to his stride.

They rode on the next day and the next. The land began to rise as they neared the mountains, which rose starkly in front of them like a painted theatre backdrop. They passed several small communities based round the oases. The houses were ochre-coloured, built into the rocks to which they clung precariously, like small children to a mother's side. As the caravan passed, the people threw themselves to their knees. Women abandoned their laundry, men stopped their tilling of the narrow strips of cultivated land, little children rushed excitedly towards the beautiful white camels, only to be pulled back by mortified mothers. Jamil nodded his acknowledgement, but made no move to stop. Looking back over her shoulder, Cassie caught a group of women staring and pointing at her, though they immediately dropped their gaze when they saw they had been spotted.

It was the same in the next village and the next, each one larger than the last, eventually joining up into a string of settlements linked by vibrant irrigated fields, before finally the walls of the city of Daar came into view. The scent of damp soil and ripe vegetation replaced the dry dusty smells of the desert. On the steep approach to the gate where the water from the main oasis had been channelled, the dates were being harvested from the palms that grew along the banks. Huge woven baskets sat under the trees, waiting to be filled and ferried into the city by a train of mules. Cassie watched in astonishment as the pickers shimmied down the trunks of the trees at a terrifying rate, to make obeisance to their returning prince.

She had fallen behind Jamil. With every step that took them closer to the city, he became more remote, almost visibly assuming the mantle of power. Under his head dress, which was no longer pulled over his face, his expression was stern, the little frown lines apparent. His shoulders were set. He was no longer Jamil, but Prince of Daar-el-Abbah. Behind him, Cassie felt lost and a little apprehensive. Their regal entrance into Jamil's city was quite sufficient to remind her of the true nature of their relationship,

Daar was built on a plateau. The city gates were emblazoned with a golden panther rampant and some Arabic script she assumed would spell *Invincible*, which Celia had told her was Jamil's motto. They passed through the large gates into a city which looked very much like Balyrma, with a network of narrow streets running at right angles to the main thoroughfare. Each alley was crowded with tall houses, overhanging more and more as they rose so that at the top they almost seemed to touch. A series of piazzas with a fountain at the centre of each linked the main thoroughfare, which she was surprised to see was cobbled. The air was redolent with a myriad of smells. The sharp, distinctive tang from the tannery mingled with the aroma of spices and roasting meat. The citrus perfume of lemons and oranges vied with the sweet heady scent from a white blossom Cassie did not recognise. A pungent, surprisingly familiar sheep-like smell emanated from a herd of penned goats. As they picked their way through the crowds, she barely had time to track down the source of one aroma before another assailed her senses.

Everywhere was colour: the robes of the women, the blankets that were being strung out to air across the alleys, the blue and red and gold and green tiles which decorated the fountains and the minarets. And everywhere was noise, too, the braying of the animals, the excited cries and laughter of the children, the strange ululating noise that the men made as they bowed. Captivated and overwhelmed, Cassie forgot her fears and surrendered herself to the magic of the East.

Towards the end of the plateau, nearer the palace, the alleys were gradually replaced by grander houses with white-tiled walls and keyhole-shaped doors, tall turrets marking the corners. The royal palace was built on the furthest part of the plateau, surrounded on three of its sides by the city walls, which formed a second layer of protection after the palace's own. The doors of the gatehouse were of a dark wood, fronted by a heavy portcullis that was being drawn up as they approached. The golden panther was emblazoned on a crest at the apex, and emblazoned, too, on the twin turrets that were built into the corners of the high white walls. An intriguing line of little ornamental towers stretched along the top of the wall, above an intricately tiled border of red and green and gold. Fascinated, Cassie slowed her camel in order to drink in the detail, unwittingly causing a minor traffic jam as the whole caravan halted behind her. Jamil, who had already passed through the doorway, quickly sent his gatekeeper out to lead her camel in.

'I'm sorry,' Cassie whispered, once she had finally climbed out of the saddle, 'your palace is so beautiful I stopped to get a better look.'

Jamil gave no acknowledgement, shaking out his cloak and making his way across the courtyard to where Halim awaited him. Cassie stood alone in the shadow of the gatehouse, wondering what she should do. Glancing around her, at the gatekeeper, the guards who stood with their arms crossed, she was met with blank expressions and downcast eyes. She took a hesitant step into the courtyard, then another, as far as the fountain, which was its centrepiece. Neither Jamil nor Halim gave any sign of noticing her. The water, which sprinkled from a smiling fish, looked lovely and cool. She stripped off her gloves and put back her veil, holding out her hands to let it drip on to them, then dabbed her wrists to her hot forehead. Heavenly! She sat down on the fountain's rim, and trailed her fingers in the water, smiling to see the little gold and silver fish that swam in the bowl. The sound of someone clearing their throat made her look up. She encountered the impassive gaze of Halim.

'Lady Cassandra, Prince Jamil has asked me to take you to Linah.'

'But—is the prince not going to introduce me to his daughter himself?'

'The prince has more important matters to attend to.'

Cassie got to her feet. 'Will the prince be visiting Linah later?'

'I am Prince Jamil's man of business, Lady Cassandra. He does not make a point of sharing his domestic arrangements with me.'

'I see,' Cassie said. Obviously this man was not happy with her presence here. As she followed Halim's rigidly disapproving back across the courtyard and along a seemingly endless corridor to the back of the palace, Cassie's confidence ebbed. Jamil hadn't told her anything of his domestic arrangements. She had no idea what her place was in the palace hierarchy.

Halim stood back to allow her to go through a door flung open by a guard. The door clanged shut behind her. She heard the gradually retreating sound of Halim's footsteps echo on the tiled floor on the other side of the door.

The room was small, a mere ante-chamber. Two of the walls were covered in mirrored tiles that reflected the beautiful enamelled vase which sat on a gilt table in the centre of the room. She passed through another doorway, lifting aside the lace and silk curtains, and found herself in the most unusual courtyard she had ever seen. It was not square but oval, with a colonnaded terrace curving all the way round, a series of connected rooms leading off it, with a second tier of rooms above. There were two fountains playing in harmony, one with the sun as its centrepiece, the other the moon. The courtyard was decorated with intricate mosaic, which featured a gold border interlaced with blue flowers, inside which was portrayed, to Cassie's delight, what looked like Scheherazade sitting at King Shahryar's feet. A spiral staircase set in the furthest end of the oval attracted her attention. Picking up her skirts, she climbed up to the second floor, which had a covered terrace, and upwards again, to the topmost part of the turret, where the stairs ended on a flat viewing platform like a English castle's battlement. Clutching the sides, for the height was dizzying, Cassie could see that her courtyard and terrace were set into the furthest part of the plateau. Below the white walls of the palace were the ochre ones of the city. Beyond that, the lush, green terraced fields fed by the oasis stretched out, and beyond that lay the desert and the mountains.

She stood there for some time, gazing out over Jamil's kingdom, oblivious of the baking heat of the sun, until a scuffling sound distracted her. Looking down into the courtyard, she saw a small, exquisitely dressed young girl gazing up inquisitively at her. 'Hello, Linah,' Cassie called down, for it could only be she, 'my name's Cassie and I'm your new governess.'

Chapter Four

⁓⁓⁓⁓⁓

Cassie's initial enthusiasm for her new role was very quickly tempered by the reality of the challenge facing her. Linah, an astonishingly beautiful child with soulful eyes the same shade as her father's, was also an extremely accomplished tyrant, ruling her miniature kingdom through a combination of endearing smiles and extraordinary tantrums, both of which she seemed to be able to turn on and off at will.

What Jamil had referred to as the schoolroom turned out to be an entire wing of the palace, formed around what Cassie called the Scheherazade courtyard. Here, Linah and her retinue of handmaidens and servants spent their days in almost complete indolence, free from supervision since the last in the series of women who had been employed to care for her had departed somewhat hastily after her charge introduced a large snake into her sleeping chamber.

Linah, as Cassie very quickly discovered, was an extremely bright little girl. The combination, however, of bored intelligence and the complete deference in which she was held by the members of her miniature household meant she was also a little girl wholly lacking in discipline and accustomed to getting her own way. Cassie, calmly removing a series of small rodents from her shoes, her divan and even her dressing case, very quickly realised that Linah's reputation was well earned.

At first, the child was determinedly uninterested in Cassie's carefully planned lessons, drumming her fingers on the miniature desk, kicking her heels against the legs of her chair—for the room used for lessons had been kitted out, to Cassie's surprise, in a Western manner, presumably by Jamil and at great expense. There was a substantial oak desk for herself, a slate board and a large globe, all imported. When requested to desist, Linah would either roll her eyes and feign sleep, or simply throw the desk over and storm out, hiding herself within the ranks of her maidservants, a clutch of giggling, fluttery creatures who made Cassie think of a cloud of butterflies, who were only too keen to pander to Linah, soothing her with comfits, singing her to sleep in her favourite spot under the lemon tree by the fountain, so that no amount of coaxing or reasoning or even threats from Cassie could persuade her to return to the classroom. That the child was bored, Cassie could plainly see. That she had an excess of energy to fuel her regime of defiance was also obvious.

There had been some minor signs of improvement of late, but not sufficient, in Cassie's view, to yet be measured in any way as success. Linah occasionally paid attention during lessons, very occasionally she asked a question or deigned to do a few sums, but mostly she continued with her campaign of disobedience. After ten days, Cassie, having signally failed to exert her authority, was starting to wonder whether the task was beyond her.

It was evening, and she was taking refuge in her room—actually a suite of rooms, which took up the whole southern ellipse of the main courtyard, consisting of a day room that led to a sleeping chamber, a dressing room and a magnificent tiled bathing room. She'd been certain that all it would take was a little love and affection, but Linah responded to neither and Cassie, who was used to the security of her own loving little circle of sisters, was beginning to realise just how much she had taken the daily tokens of affection between them for granted—and how much they had sustained her, too, for without them she was beginning to feel as lost and unloved as poor little Linah.

Cassie sat up wearily, resolutely denying herself the solace of a good cry, and rubbed her eyes, though a few stray tears escaped. She was tired, she was a bit disillusioned and a bit homesick, that was all. With Jamil inexplicably absent, she had no one to talk her problems over with, no one to confide in, nor anyone to encourage her either. Cassie, used to the bustle of the Armstrong household where female company, whether in the shape of her beloved sisters or her formidable Aunt Sophia, was never in short supply, found herself longing even for such an unsympathetic ear as Bella's. She was lonely, and she was unsure of herself, and she was afraid of making mistakes.

Another tear trickled its solitary path down her cheek, and then another. Cassie sniffed. Crying was pointless, as was self-pity. If she was Celia—but she was not, and never would have her elder sister's calm assurance. How much she wished she was with Celia right now. Just a few moments in her company would restore her equanimity.

She sniffed again, but her tears gathered momentum. Bella was right. Aunt Sophia was right. Papa was right. She had been foolish beyond measure to think she could succeed where so many others had patently failed. Linah didn't even like her and Jamil quite obviously wasn't interested in his daughter. He'd told her as much, yet she hadn't listened, so determined had she been to hear only what she wanted to hear. Yet again.

She fumbled for her handkerchief, but the scrap of lace that her sister Caro had so carefully embroidered eluded her grasp, which made her tears flow faster still. She was useless! Linah could see that, and if an eight-year-old child could see that, it surely would not be long before her father did, too—if he ever deigned to visit them. Finally locating her kerchief, Cassie rubbed her cheeks furiously. She would not fail. She would not allow herself to fail. 'I'll show them, all of them,' she muttered, 'and in particular one uncaring man with autumn-coloured eyes who needs to be taught a lesson in love.'

Strengthened by this reviving thought, her mood lightened. The heat of the day had given way to the welcome cool of the desert night, the time she loved best. She kicked off her kid slippers, untied her garters, stripped off her stockings, and made her way out to the courtyard, wriggling her bare toes with relish on the delicious cool marble of the tiled floor. The air was lemon-scented, the moon a thin silver crescent. Making her way over to the minaret, she climbed the stairs, feeling her way with her toes in the dark. At the top of the tower, she sat, her arms clasping her knees, and gazed up at the stars, which seemed, tantalisingly, almost within reach.

Save for a fleeting visit a day after her arrival, she had not seen Jamil at all. He was away dealing with weighty matters, she had been informed by Halim, who greeted her ongoing enquires with disdain. Prince Jamil would return when Prince Jamil saw fit. It was unlikely, Halim said with a superior smile, that his first port of call would be the schoolroom. Prince Jamil was far too important, he clearly implied, to be wasting his time on English governesses and wayward daughters.

At first Cassie had been relieved not to have to face him—or at least that's what she told herself. Best not to be reminded of that kiss. Best not to be distracted by his presence. She didn't want to think of Jamil as anything other than her charge's father—though it was one thing to decide to think that way, quite another, she discovered, to do it. His absence was proving just as distracting as his presence would have been.

Throwing her head back, she looked up at the heavens. The vastness of the skies, the fierce beauty of the endless desert landscape, had an eternal quality. She could neither change nor conquer it, but what she could do was embrace it. There was nothing so pure or so perfect or so wildly exciting as nature in this raw state. It was intoxicating. The natural effervescence with which she used to embrace life began to return, and with it came a renewed determination to succeed in making Linah happy. Which meant confronting Jamil, an idea as exciting and intimidating as taking on the desert over which he alone was master. He was out there now, somewhere under the stars, perhaps surveying them just as she was. Perhaps looking at that particular one, just there. Perhaps he, too, saw the shooting star that blazed across the tip of the moon's crescent. Perhaps...

A noise in the courtyard below caught her attention. Thinking it might be Linah, who was prone to sleepwalking, Cassie got to her feet and leaned over the parapet, but the person looking up at her was most definitely not a child. A tall figure, lithe in his white robe, with eyes that glittered in the harshly beautiful planes of his autocratic face. Cassie gripped hold of the parapet, trying to ignore the absurd little flutter of excitement which rippled through her tummy. 'Your Highness—Jamil. You're back.'

'Lady Cassandra.' He made a small bow. 'Cassie. I am only just returned this past hour.'

Only an hour ago, and yet he had come here to see her! To see Linah—or at least to obtain a report on Linah, Cassie reminded herself sternly. 'I—we are flattered. I'm afraid Linah is asleep.'

'I should hope so. But you, I see, are not.'

'It's a beautiful night.'

Jamil stared up at her, what he could see of her above the parapet. The fiery tints of her hair and the pale material of her dress outlined her starkly against the night sky. He had forgotten how breathtakingly beautiful she was. She looked like a princess in a tower, awaiting rescue. 'Lovely,' he said softly.

Cassie leaned precariously over to obtain a better view. Jamil was barefoot and bare-headed, as she was. Even without the trappings of authority, his air of command was there in the way he stood, feet firmly planted, hands on his hips, head thrown back. He looked like the master of all he surveyed, she thought, then had to suppress a smile because of course he was, and there could be no mistaking the fact. Including her. Cassie shivered. It was a disturbing thought. She knew she shouldn't like it.

'If you lean over any further, you will fall,' Jamil said. 'Come down and tell me how you have been getting on with my daughter.'

His daughter. Of course, that's what he'd come to talk about. He wasn't interested in her. She had imagined the glint of smouldering desire in his expression. Reality broke into her fantasy of playing Juliet or Rapunzel, of Jamil mounting the tower—without using the stairs, of course—to come to her rescue. His daughter was his only concern. And should be *her* only concern!

Jamil watched her descend the lower, exposed staircase. He had forgotten how gracefully she carried herself, the way she seemed to glide rather than walk. He had forgotten that certain something about her which exuded sensuality, that certain something of which she seemed entirely unaware, and of which his own body was only too conscious. As she approached him across the courtyard, her progress marked by the silken rustle of her gown, his manhood stirred. He had thought absence would eliminate this inconvenient attraction, but it only seemed to have enhanced it.

Cassie curtsied. 'I trust the business that took you away from us was successfully concluded?'

'Eventually. I had not meant to be detained for so long.'

As he turned towards the cushions that lay in their habitual place scattered around the sun fountain, holding out his hand to allow her to precede him, Cassie noticed the scar, a long vicious slash running from his wrist to the inside of his elbow, angrily red, held together by some rather fearsome-looking stitches. 'Your arm! What on earth happened?'

'It's nothing. A skirmish on the border, a band of opportunistic brigands.'

'You fought them yourself? Did not your guards…?'

Jamil smiled, his real smile, the one that made her

heart turn cartwheels. 'You think me incapable of defending myself against a few cutthroats?'

'I think you capable of taking on an entire army of cutthroats if you choose,' Cassie said frankly, 'I am just surprised that your guards allowed the men to get near you.'

'I was alone. I could not sleep, and had left the caravan behind.'

'Good God, Jamil, you should have more of a care. How many were there?'

'Four.'

It was hard not be impressed—he must be as fierce a warrior as his physical attributes suggested. But to have placed himself in such danger! 'You could have been killed.'

'But as you see, I am perfectly unharmed.'

'If you can call that unharmed,' Cassie replied tartly, pointing to the wound. 'Is it painful?'

'Not really.'

'Which means it is. Sit down, let me look at it.' In her concern, Cassie had once more forgotten all about the rules of propriety. She pushed Jamil on to the cushions and knelt before him, scrutinising his arm carefully. 'It looks angry, the skin is pulling where it has been stitched, but it's not infected,' she said finally. 'I have some lavender oil, it will take away the inflammation.'

She hurried off to retrieve the bottle from her dressing case, and knelt before Jamil again, dabbing the oil carefully on the scar, frowning with concentration as she bent over him. 'There.' She sat back to admire her handiwork, holding his arm in her lap, so intent upon her task that she did not notice his expression until she looked up. 'What is it?'

'You seem very knowledgeable.'

'Only a little. Mama was interested in healing herbs and plants, and when she died, she left me her recipe book—well, actually, she didn't quite leave me it, I sort of took it,' Cassie admitted, 'as something to remember her by. I made this oil myself, it's perfectly safe.'

Male eyes the burnished colour of an English autumn met female eyes the colour of turquoise. Jamil turned his injured arm over to clasp her fingers. Her knees were pressing into his thigh through her dress. He could see the rise and fall of her breasts through the lace that covered them. The material was pale blue, embroidered with tiny white flowers. The same tiny white flowers decorated the ruffle of lace at her arm. She smelled of lavender and something else he couldn't name. Floral and heady. 'Thank you,' Jamil said again, lifting her hand to his mouth and pressing a kiss on the fragile pulse of her wrist. He felt it flutter under his lips. He heard the soft intake of her breath. Then he remembered.

Governess, governess, governess. It should not be so difficult to remember! He dropped her hand as casually as he could manage and sat back on the cushions, adjusting his position to put a little distance between them. 'Tell me about Linah.'

Cassie struggled to assemble her thoughts, which seemed to have scattered like dandelion clocks in the breeze. She tugged her skirts over her bare toes, trying to put from her mind the romantic picture they made, the two of them, sitting under the stars by the tinkling fountain, she and the desert prince.

Not the desert prince. Linah's father. Her employer. Who wanted to know about his daughter. That was all. That was absolutely all. 'Linah. Linah is—she and I are—I think we're making progress.'

She started to tell him, haltingly, of her trials and tribulations, of the breakthroughs and the setbacks, the small triumphs and the still-regular defeats. Tempting as it was to exaggerate her success, she knew better than to lie, remembering quite clearly Jamil's detestation of prevarication. 'She is learning to trust me a little, but it is early days yet. Linah is still testing the limits of her powers.'

'You mean she is still ungovernable.'

His voice contained not anger, but resignation. He thought she was failing. He had expected her to fail! Cassie clenched her fists determinedly. 'Not at all, but Linah is a very clever little girl. All her experience has taught her that such strategies as she employs—'

'Such as?'

'Well, her temper tantrums. And her refusal to co-operate. And her hiding behind those maidservants of hers. And the practical jokes, of course.'

'Practical jokes?'

'Your daughter has an affinity with wildlife.'

'You will explain, if you please?'

'Mice, snakes and a whole host of other creatures I'm afraid I don't even recognise. Linah seems to be able to tame them, or mesmerise them in some way, it's really quite amazing. Then she puts them where they should not be—you know, divans, chests, cupboards. She put a toad in the tea samovar. Really, one has to give her credit for being inventive.'

'And cruel.'

'She's not cruel—or rather, she is but doesn't realise it, and once she realised that I was not alarmed—'

'Not alarmed?'

'Truly, Jamil, it didn't bother me at all. I was brought up in the English countryside where wildlife abounds. My sisters, you see, were wont to do much the same sort of thing to Celia and me when they were being naughty. I explained to Linah that she was frightening the poor creatures more than me, and she stopped.'

'Explained?' Jamil said ominously. 'You should have punished her for her actions. By failing to demonstrate your authority, you are showing weakness. She will exploit that, one way or another, if not now, then later.'

'She is not my enemy, Jamil. It was punishment enough for her to know that she had caused distress without realising it,' Cassie explained patiently. 'And as I said, she hasn't done it since.'

'Can you be certain these unorthodox methods of yours will work?'

'Not entirely, not yet.' Cassie looked up from the intricate pattern she'd been weaving with her fingers in her lap. 'She is only eight, Jamil.'

'Old enough to understand right from wrong. Old enough to exert some control over her temper.'

'You expect too much. At her age, I am willing to bet you had a considerable temper.'

'By her age, I had already learned how to control it.'
Or to suffer the consequences.

'At eight!' Cassie exclaimed. 'I don't believe it. Why, you must be at least twenty-eight now, and I have seen you lose your temper several times.'

She was smiling, meaning only to tease, but Jamil's lips thinned. It was true, Cassie seemed to bring out extremes in him that he had not thought himself capable of, but it was not anything of which he was proud. 'It may surprise you to know that I rarely lose my temper,' he said curtly. 'In fact, the *only* time I have lost it has been in your company. And that is not a compliment.'

'I didn't take it as such. Why are you so touchy? All I meant to say was that, as a little boy, you probably had just as many tantrums as Linah, only you don't remember.'

'You are quite mistaken,' Jamil said with an air of finality.

She opened her mouth to contradict him, saw the implacable look on his face, and something darker in his eyes, which gave her pause. He had not been a happy child, that much was obvious. She decided, wisely for once, to change the subject. 'I've been thinking, it would be a good thing for Linah to have more company her own age. She's lonely, she doesn't seem to have any friends. Children need the stimulation of others.'

'That is why she has you.'

'It's not the same. Surely you are not so old that you cannot remember what it was like to play with your friends?'

'I did not have any friends,' Jamil said starkly.

Cassie's mouth dropped open. 'What? Don't be silly, you must have. At school, and—'

'I did not go to school. It is the tradition with princes of the royal blood in Daar-el-Abbah to be kept in isolation so that others may not witness their early mistakes, their growing pains. That is why our motto is *Invincible.*'

'That must be hard to live up to.'

'A prince is the ultimate role model for his people; his behaviour must be beyond reproach.'

'But you are human, for goodness' sake, you're not flawless. No one is. I would have thought your people would see a few signs of mortality as a good thing.'

'You know nothing of the matter. That is not our way.'

Cassie stared at his bleak profile in astonishment. He had not be exaggerating, then, when he said he had no friends as a child. The isolation he mentioned, it was the literal truth. Aghast at the very idea of such an upbringing, she also felt an immense pity for the lonely little boy Jamil must have been. No wonder he had no idea about how to treat his own daughter. 'Is that what you wish for Linah,' she asked, trying desperately to keep the emotion she felt from welling up into her voice, 'to be raised in isolation, to be chastised when she shows any signs of normal, everyday emotion—what you call weakness?'

Jamil stared off into the distance, giving no sign that he had heard her. 'Jamil? Is that what you want?' Cassie demanded, in her anxiety to get through to him, once again forgetting all about restraint. 'Do you want your daughter to become just like you—cold-hearted and apparently incapable of showing affection even for her own children? Well? It's not right and it's not fair, Jamil. She may be a princess, but she's also a little girl.'

At some point in her last speech, Cassie had grabbed Jamil's sleeve in an effort to make him listen. At some point in her speech, it had worked. He was no longer staring off into the distance, but right at her, and he did not look happy. She tilted her chin defiantly.

Jamil carefully detached her hand from his arm. 'Once again,' he said stiffly, 'you overstep the mark. You talk about things which you have no understanding of. *None!*'

She flinched at the vicious tone in his voice, but refused to give ground. 'Linah—'

'Linah will not endure what I did. I will not inflict such a regime on her, but—and you will listen most carefully here, Lady Cassandra, for I do not wish to have to repeat myself again—she is of the royal blood, and though as a woman she is not required to be seen as invincible, her behaviour must be superior to all others. She must learn to take control of her emotions. Do you understand me?'

'Yes, but she will learn how to do so much more

easily if the discipline is inflicted by her peers. Little girls can be quite ruthless, you know, far more so than boys. If Linah misbehaves among her friends, she will be ostracised. She will learn quickly enough that she cannot do as she pleases.' Seeing that Jamil was struck by this, Cassie pushed home her advantage. 'As a princess, she must learn not just discipline, but kindness. Surely you agree she will be a better princess for having some understanding of her subjects?'

'I don't know. It is not the custom.'

'You keep saying that, but traditions are only traditions for as long as they are maintained. You are the prince; if you wish to change something, you can do so. Set your own traditions.'

Jamil's expressions softened into one of his near smiles. 'My Council—'

'You said yourself, your Council need to be brought into the nineteenth century,' Cassie pointed out quickly. 'Or at least,' she amended conscientiously, 'I think that is what you meant.'

Jamil's smile widened. 'I see now that you are indeed Lord Henry Armstrong's daughter.'

'I will take that as a compliment,' Cassie replied with one of her irrepressible smiles. 'A compliment from you is as rare an event as a rainy day in the desert. I shall cherish it. But seriously, will you think about it, Jamil. Please? For Linah's sake? You know it—'

'What I know, Cassie, is that a wise strategist knows when to retreat as well as when to advance,' Jamil interrupted. 'Your point is well made and I will reflect on it, but you should stop now, before you lose the advantage you have gained.'

She did so most reluctantly as she had still not broached the subject of Jamil's contact with his daughter. Proud of her restraint, for it did not come at all naturally to her, Cassie nodded, fastening her lips together primly.

'I can see that you are making a significant effort on my behalf,' Jamil said, trying very hard not to laugh. Another thing he had forgotten about this beguiling creature was her more endearing qualities. She had the ability to throw him from one extreme to the other, in a way no one else could. Not that he was endeared. Just tired.

He had been away too long. The increasing demands of his kingdom were a sign of successful expansion, yet he did not feel rewarded. Halim had been appalled by the brigand attack just as much as Cassie, but for quite different reasons. Infallibility again. The shedding of blood was evidence of mortality. Halim feared for the prince, but Cassie feared for the man. No one else, it seemed to him, saw him in that way. Cared for him in that way.

'You have everything you need here?' he asked brusquely, getting to his feet.

'Yes, thank you. Linah's schoolroom is exceedingly well equipped.'

'I did not ask about Linah, I asked about you.' Jamil reached out his hand to pull Cassie up beside him. Instead of letting her go, he pulled her to him, the better to scrutinise her face. 'You look tired.' His eyes narrowed. 'Have you been crying?'

'No, I—it was nothing.'

'What have you not told me? If you are trying to protect Linah, let me tell you that—'

'No, Linah is not the cause, not really. I'm just feeling a bit sorry for myself, that's all.'

'You are unhappy here?'

'No, not unhappy but—well, being cooped up here all day, it can be a bit stifling,' Cassie replied with an apologetic look.

Jamil frowned. 'I should have thought about it before. Of course you are used to having a little more freedom. Would you like to ride?'

'Camels?'

Cassie's expression of dismay was so comical, Jamil could not restrain a bark of laughter. 'No, horses.'

He had a nice laugh, deep and infectious, extremely masculine. Cassie smiled back. Exercise, she realised, was what she needed to blow away the blue megrims, and maybe it would do Linah good, too. 'That would be wonderful. Does Linah ride?'

'It is considered improper for women here, unless they are led.'

'You are a prince—are not traditions yours to make or break as you wish?'

'Or as you wish? You tread a fine line, Lady Cassandra.'

The tone in his voice pulled her up sharply. Cassie's face fell. She dropped her eyes. 'I beg your pardon,

Highness. I would not wish to place you in a difficult position. If it would cause too much offence…'

'As you point out, I am the prince,' Jamil said sardonically. 'I will arrange it, but it must be tactfully done. You may ride, and Linah, too, but you will need an escort.'

'I'm perfectly capable of looking after Linah and myself.'

'I am not talking about your riding skills, Lady Cassandra, I'm talking about your safety. There are those who will be offended by your embracing such freedom. You must promise me never to go out without an escort.'

'Yes. Very well, but…' Catching Jamil's ominous expression, Cassie caught her words just in time. 'I promise.'

'We will begin tomorrow morning. I will accompany you personally.'

'You! I assumed you meant a guard, or a groom.'

'When I am satisfied there is no risk. For the moment, I will personally supervise these excursions.'

If she was delighted, it was for Linah's sake. If she was already looking forward to it, that was for her also. Absolutely it was. 'Thank you,' Cassie said warmly, 'Linah will be thrilled.'

His proximity was making her blush. His almost palpable maleness accentuated her awareness of her own femininity. She should say goodnight now. Drop a curtsy to release herself from his hold and say goodnight, because if she did not…

'Goodnight, Lady Cassandra.' Jamil released her and walked off across the courtyard, his feet padding soundlessly on the tiles. The huge door swung inwards. He was gone, in a flutter of white robes, before Cassie could reply, or even decide if she was relieved or not.

The prospect of a riding lesson in the company of her father sent Linah into paroxysms of excitement. She could barely be persuaded to eat, gulping down a mango sherbet and some pineapple, dancing anxiously from foot to foot while Cassie rummaged among her copious wardrobe for something suitable to wear. Terrified lest she be left behind, Linah insisted on watching while Cassie made her own *toilette*, laughing at Linah's fascinated inspection of her stays, stockings and boots.

The riding lesson went well, with Linah cowed into her best behaviour by her father's presence. Her natural affinity with animals allowed her to form an instant bond with the sprightly little pony Jamil had picked out for her. Cassie's own mount was a thoroughbred Arabian dappled grey mare, a flighty, highly strung beast that tried to throw her the minute she sat in the saddle. The mare reared up on her hind legs, and when this failed, spun round in tight circles before attempting to rear up again. Cassie, however, had had enough, and reined her in sharply, leaning over to whisper soothing words into her ear the minute she was under control. Jamil, watching with an open-mouthed Linah, was more impressed than he cared to admit. He had known her to be more than competent, and would not have seated her on the grey had he doubted her ability, but still, the grace with which she held her saddle, the way she gave her mount its head before reining it in, evidenced a horsewoman of rare ability.

'That was amazing, was it not, *Baba*?' Linah said, her admiration for her most unusual governess rousing her from her shyness.

Jamil looked at his daughter in surprise. She had not called him *Baba* since she was a small child. His own father had banned the term. *I am a father to all my people, not just you*, Jamil remembered being told pointedly. 'Amazing, but rather ostentatious,' he agreed curtly, watching the light fade from Linah's eyes, ignoring the tight feeling in his chest, telling himself it was for her own good.

They rode out through the city gates, with Linah on a leading rein, to a sandy paddock enclosed by tall cypress trees. Tethering his horse, Jamil watched while Cassie taught her the rudiments of walking and trotting. His daughter was awkward at first, glancing over each time she made a mistake. Realising that he was making her nervous, Jamil removed himself from her sight. Watching from the cover of one of the trees, he saw her grow in confidence, soon able to attempt a trot round the paddock on her own.

'Did she not do well?' Cassie said, beaming at her charge, when they rejoined him back at the stables.

'She shows some ability,' Jamil agreed stiffly. He watched Linah's face fall, saw Cassie frown at him in vexation, and told himself once more that it was for the best, but still he felt unaccountably guilty.

'Thank your father for most graciously giving up his time,' Cassie said to Linah, 'for if you do not, he will think his presence unnecessary, and will not come again.'

'Oh, no, *Baba*, I would not like you to think that. Please will you come again tomorrow?'

'Affairs of state permitting. Fakir will show you how to rub down your pony,' Jamil said, nodding at his head groom. 'You must learn to take care of your horse if you are to become a real horsewoman.' When Cassie made to dismount in order to help, however, he shook his head. 'That mare of yours is still fresh, we'll go for a gallop before the sun is too high.'

Surprised and delighted at the opportunity to put such a beautiful animal through its paces, Cassie waited only until they were back out of the city gates to release her hold. The grey mare needed no urging, flying across the sand with Jamil, mounted on a magnificent black stallion, in hot pursuit.

They rode together again the following day, after Linah's lesson, and the next and the next. Away from the confines of the palace, Jamil was a different person. Not just more at ease in the wide, untrammelled space of his desert, but more approachable, too. They found they shared a passion for the natural world, and Cassie's obvious enthusiasm for the harshly vibrant beauty of the desert, so different from the soft green landscape of

England, encouraged Jamil into increasingly ambitious expeditions in search of rare plants or obscure species. The time flew by with a speed that surprised them both. Several times Jamil had returned to the palace to find Halim in a lather of worry at his having kept some merchant or visiting dignitary waiting.

Halim did not approve of his prince taking time out from his formal schedule, not even if he did return looking refreshed. Especially, Halim did not approve of Jamil spending that time in the company of his daughter's English governess, though he was far too circumspect to give voice to such thoughts. People were talking. Such talk would end when Prince Jamil's betrothal to the Princess Adira was made public, so Halim devoted his energy to the arrangements for the ceremony. If they were watertight, this time the prince could not escape them. He would be wed and then life for Halim, and the whole of Daar-el-Abbah, would continue as it had always done.

Chapter Five

Cassie woke every morning looking forward to the coming day. Gone was her homesickness, banished were her doubts. Linah flourished under the combined regime of physical and mental exercise, her natural intelligence and surprisingly wry sense of humour were beginning to emerge. While she still shied away from any physical signs of affection, she had twice now allowed herself to be cuddled when waking from a nightmare, and once slipped her little hand into Cassie's on the journey to the stables. The tantrums had abated dramatically. The sulks were not gone, but had become rare. Her behaviour was improving, definitely improving with every passing day.

Though she was not aware of it, for she rarely bothered these days with her looking glass, Cassie, too, was improving every day. Her skin glowed with vitality, tinged with the sun, rosy with health. Her eyes sparkled, the azure of a summer sea with the sun glinting upon it. She walked with a lighter step. She hummed to herself when sitting sewing in the shade of the lemon tree. She was happy.

She was happy because she was making a difference to Linah. She was happy because she was doing something positive. She was happy because Jamil was pleased with her efforts. She was happy because in Jamil, the man she had come to know, if not yet fully understand, she felt she had found that rare thing—a true friend. The thought made her smile, for Jamil would have scorned it—had he not said that he did not want or need friends? But that made her smile all the more. Of course they were friends. What else could it be, this empathy that had grown up between them, the ease with which they talked, disputed, laughed, the way sometimes they did not even need to do that, content merely to be in each other's company?

'Friends.' She said the word aloud, as if tasting it, and again, this time more assertively. They could not be anything else. She did not wish it. He did not think of it. At least…

Sometimes, when they were alone in the desert, she caught him looking at her. Sometimes, she looked at him just like that, she suspected. Hungrily. Imagining. Trying not to imagine. Remembering. Trying not to remember. When their hands met accidentally, something akin to a shock surged through her, making her awkward, aware of something not right, something too right. She thought about that kiss in those moments. His lips on hers. His arms around her. She thought about it, then she banished it.

She banished it now, forcing her mind to focus on her one other concern. Though she and Jamil might be friends, Jamil and Linah were not. Though his attitude towards his daughter had softened, and he showed a real interest in her progress, Jamil seemed to be incapable of showing her any sign of affection. He spoke to his daughter as to an adult. He was a perfectionist, and there was nothing at all wrong with that, save that he praised so rarely and criticised so frequently. Could he not see that the child worshipped the ground he walked on? That one sign of affection would make an enormous difference to her confidence? Tough as his own upbringing must have been, from the very little he had let fall about it, surely there must have been some tender moments for him to recall?

Casting aside her sewing, a sampler she had been making for Linah, Cassie got to her feet. It was mid-afternoon, the hottest part of the day, when everyone took respite in the cool of their rooms, but she was restless. The Scheherazade courtyard was eerily quiet. Looking for a distraction, she remembered that Linah had once mentioned gardens on the eastern side of the palace, old gardens gone to ruin. The idea of a secret wilderness, a neglected and forgotten hideaway, appealed strongly to the romantic side of Cassie's nature. Opening the huge door that led to the corridor, nodding in a friendly way to the guards, she set off in search of it.

* * *

Jamil could not concentrate on the papers before him. The complicated series of commercial transactions began with the trading of Daar-el-Abbah's diamonds upon the lucrative Dutch market and ended with the import of some of the new spinning equipment from the British cotton mills. Bills of lading, interest calculations, net costs, gross costs, profit and conversions from one currency to another danced before his eyes. The end result was positive. It always was.

Jamil rolled his shoulders in an attempt to ease the tension there. This morning he and Cassie had ridden out to a nearby oasis with Linah, his daughter permitted for the first time to handle her pony without the leading string. She'd done well, sitting straight-backed and riding light-handed, in an excellent imitation of her teacher. He'd been proud of her, but though he formed the words of praise, he could not speak them. Cassie had been unable to hide her disappointment; he saw it in the downturn of her mouth, in the tiny frown instantly smoothed between her fair brows.

Jamil cursed softly under his breath. He would not let this woman's disapproval dictate his actions. He had learned the hard way just how important it was not to let anyone know what he was feeling—that he even had feelings—for feelings could be exploited. They were a weakness. For her own good, Linah should be taught the same lesson.

But, increasingly, he found it hard not to show just the sort of weakness his father had been so keen to eradicate. It had been easier, when Linah was not so often in his company. Now, with his daughter's endearing personality imprinting itself upon him every day, thanks to Cassie, it was proving difficult to maintain the barriers that had been so hard built. Sometimes he felt as if Cassie was determined to remove them brick by brick. To expose him. Sometimes he appalled himself by wanting to help her.

Abandoning his papers, Jamil got to his feet and wandered out into the courtyard. The heat was stifling. Even the ever-industrious Halim had retired for the afternoon. In search of distraction, he found himself wandering in the direction of the schoolroom, only to be informed by the guards that Cassie had left, half an hour before. It was not like her to go off unchaperoned like that. Slightly concerned, Jamil set off in search, tracing her meandering path through the endless corridors of the palace by way of the various sets of guards she had passed.

The trail went cold at the entrance to the east wing, where he paused, his frown deepening. The large oak door with its heavy iron grille was closed. There was no reason to think she would have opened it, save the fact that he knew there was no other way for her to have gone without being noticed. No guard stood at this door. No one, to Jamil's knowledge, had passed beyond the door for years. Eight years. Eight years, six months and three days to be precise. Since the day Jamil had come to the throne of Daar-el-Abbah, exactly one week after his father had died.

Just looking at the implacable door made Jamil's heart pound as if his blood were thick and heavy. There was no reason for Cassie to have entered the courtyard. No reason for him to have expressly forbidden it, either. He had locked the memories away long since. But now, looking through the grille to the dusty ante-room beyond, he knew that was exactly what she had done.

He didn't want to go in there. He really, really didn't want to. But he didn't want Cassie there, either. His palms sweating, his fingers shaking, Jamil opened the door and stepped in, back, over the threshold of his adulthood into the dark recesses of his childhood.

She'd found the door after following many false trails and dead ends. She'd known it must be the one, from the rusty look of the key. That there had been a key in the lock at all surprised her. That it turned, gratingly and reluctantly, had excited her, but then she stepped inside and the overpowering air of melancholy descended like a thick black cloak.

It was a beautiful place, a completely circular courtyard with a dried-up fountain, the marble cracked and stained, the ubiquitous lemon trees grown huge and wild, jasmine and something that looked very like clematis, but could not be, flowering with wild abandon around the courtyard's colonnaded terrace. Dried leaves covered the mosaic floor. She heard the unmistakable scuttling of small creatures as she crossed it slowly. The fountain's centrepiece, which she had at first thought to be a lion cub, she now realised must be a baby panther. She had

not seen the panther fountain in Jamil's private courtyard, but he had once described it to her, mockingly.
This must be its counterpart, which meant that this must
be the rooms of the young Crown Prince Jamil, shut up
and left to crumble into ruin, as if he had turned his back
not only on his childhood, but his past.

Cassie shuddered. The stark contrast of the dull tiles,
the weeds that grew between the cracks in the floor,
the general air of sullen neglect, with the rest of the
pristinely cared for palace, was unbearable. Sensitive
as she was to ambiance, she could almost taste the ache
of unhappiness in the air. Wandering over to another
solid-looking door, she peered through the grille and
caught a glimpse of the secret garden. Far from the
pretty wilderness she had imagined, this one was barren,
arid, with skeletal trees, the bark shed in layers like skin,
with thickets of some barbarous thorny shrub covering
the entire ground area, like a spiky, mottled carpet.

She should not be here. It was too private a place,
too redolent with intimate memories. Instinctively, she
knew that Jamil would be mortified by her presence.
Yet instinctively, too, she felt that here lay the key to his
relationship—or lack of it—with his daughter. If she
could find it—if she could understand—then surely...

Holding the hem of her gown clear of the detritus
that covered the courtyard floor, Cassie picked her way
carefully to the doorway of the apartments. Like all
the palace suites, they followed the shape of the courtyard, a series of rooms opening out, one on to the other.
The divans had been abandoned, their rich coverings

simply left to rot. Lace, velvet, silk and organdie lay in tatters. The mirrored tiles of the bathing room were blistered, the huge white bath, sunk into the floor, yellowed and cracked. She found a silver samovar with a handle in the shape of an asp, tarnished and bent. A notebook, the pages filled with a neat, tiny hand in Arabic, which stopped abruptly half-way down one page. When she picked it up, the spine cracked, the cover page separated.

Careless now of her gown, overcome with the melancholy of the place, Cassie wandered into the last room. A sleeping divan, the curtains collapsed on the bed. An intricately carved chest. On the wall above it, hanging on a hook, what looked like an ornamental riding crop. She took it down, admiring the chased-silver handle decorated with what looked like emeralds. Obviously ceremonial. How had it come to be left here?

'What in the name of all the gods do you think you're doing? Put that down immediately.'

Cassie jumped. The riding crop fell to the ground with a clatter. Jamil kicked it under the carved chest. His face looked thunderous, brows drawn in a straight line, meeting across his nose, his mouth thinned, the planes of his cheekbones standing out sharply, like the rugged contours of the desert mountains.

'Well?'

'I thought—I heard about a secret garden. I wanted to see it.'

'Well, now you have, so you can leave.'

His eyes blazed with anger, though his tone was

icy cold. She was afraid. Not of him, but of the pain she could see etched into his handsome countenance. 'Jamil…'

'You should not have come here.'

His tone was bleak, his eyes echoing his mood. She could see the tension in the set of his shoulders, in the tightness of his voice. 'They were yours, these rooms, weren't they?' Cassie asked softly.

'These are the traditional apartments of the crown prince. Mine. Before me, my father's. And before him, my grandfather's.'

'So this is one tradition you definitely intend to break with?'

'What do you mean?'

'You obviously don't intend any son of yours to stay here, or else you would not have allowed the place to fall into such decline,' Cassie said, with a sweeping gesture towards the derelict courtyard.

'If—*when*—I have a son, he will have—he will be given…' Jamil faltered, swallowing hard. 'No.' He shook his head, shading his eyes with his hands. 'No. As you say, this is one tradition that ends with me.'

'I'm glad.' Cassie laid a hand tentatively upon his arm. 'This is not a happy place, I can tell.'

'No,' Jamil replied with a grim look, 'happiness was a commodity in short supply here.' The hand he used to run his fingers through his auburn hair was trembling. 'Discipline, honour, strength—they are what matter.'

'Infallibility.'

'Invincibility. My motto. My fate.' His shoulders

slumped. He sank down on to the lid of the chest suddenly, as if his legs would no longer support him. 'Here is where I was taught it. A hard lesson, but one I have not forgotten.' He dropped his head into his hands.

Jamil was a man who had until now appeared as invulnerable as a citadel, with all the power of an invincible army. Seeing him so raw, so exposed, all Cassie yearned to do was to comfort and to heal. Careless of all else, she crouched down and cradled his head, smoothing the ruffled peaks of his hair back into a sleek cap, stroking the cords of tension in his neck, the knotted sinews of his shoulders, his spine. Jamil stilled, but did not move. She drew him closer, wrapping her arms around him, oblivious of the awkwardness of her own cramping limbs, thinking only somehow to ease the hurt, the deep-buried hurt that clung to him now like a dark aura.

She whispered soothing nothings and she held him close, closer, pressing tiny fluttering kisses of comfort on to the top of his head, enveloping his hard, tense lines with her softness. They stayed thus for a long time, until gradually she felt him relax, until he moved his head, and she realised, almost at the same time as he did, that it was nestled against her breasts. She became conscious of his body not as something to be comforted, but as something to be desired. Her own body responded alarmingly, heating, her nipples hardening. He stirred in her arms and she released him, blushing, looking away, concentrating on standing up, shaking out the leaves and twigs and dirt from her skirts.

'I must apologise,' Jamil said, rising slowly to his feet.

'There is no need,' Cassie said quickly.

'A moment of weakness. I would be obliged if you would forget you witnessed it.'

Cassie chewed on her lip, knowing that further probing might well anger him. 'Jamil, it is not weakness to admit to having been unhappy—rather the opposite.'

'What do you mean?'

'Something horrible happened here, I can sense it.' She shuddered, clasping her arms around herself. 'Don't you see that by refusing to acknowledge it, you are granting whatever it is the victory of silence?' She clutched at his sleeve to prevent him from turning away.

'You exaggerate. As usual.'

'No. No, I don't. Jamil, listen to me, please.' She gazed desperately up into his face, but the shutters were firmly back in place. 'Why can you not tell Linah how you feel about her?'

The directness of the question took him by surprise. Jamil raised a haughty eyebrow.

'I know you care for her,' Cassie continued recklessly. 'I know that you're proud of her, but you can't bring yourself to tell her. Why not?'

Jamil pulled himself free. '*Show thine enemy a heart, and you hand them the key to your kingdom.* My father taught me that lesson here in this very room with the aid of a very persuasive assistant,' he said fiercely, stooping to retrieve the riding crop from under the chest.

'He beat you! My God! I thought that thing was ceremonial.'

Jamil's laughter was like a crack from the whip he held. 'In that you are correct. The ceremony of beating the weaknesses out of the crown prince was one that took place on a regular basis.'

Cassie's face was ashen. 'But why?'

'To teach me to conquer pain. To ensure that I understood extreme emotions well enough to abandon them. To make me what Daar-el-Abbah requires, an invincible leader who relies upon no-one else.'

'There is no such thing,' Cassie said passionately. 'You are a man, not a god, no matter what your father thought, no matter what your people think. Everyone needs someone. For heaven's sake, Jamil, that is absolutely ridiculous. You are a man, and you have feelings, you can't pretend they don't exist.' Even as she spoke the words, Cassie realised that that was exactly what Jamil did. The appalling nature of his upbringing struck her afresh. Her fury at Jamil's father knew no bounds. 'What about your mother? Where was she when this was happening?'

'I was not permitted to see her, save on ceremonial occasions, once I was established here.'

'That's what you meant about losing her at an early age?'

Jamil nodded.

'What age, precisely?'

'Five.'

Cassie's mouth fell open. 'That's barbaric!'

'Unfamiliar customs often seem barbaric. We are an ancient civilisation, much older than yours.' Cassie's utter horror was written plain on her face, making Jamil deeply uncomfortable. Having locked up these rooms, he had persuaded himself he had also locked away what had happened here. Only in moments of weakness, in the dark of night, did the memories intrude, scurrying out from the crevices of his mind, like scorpions in the desert after dark, to sting him. He dealt with them as his father had taught him to deal with any weakness, by ruthlessly suppressing them. Now, seeing his childhood experiences through Cassie's eyes, he felt cornered. He had endured, but never questioned. What he had been taught here formed the foundations of his entire life. He did not want to have to scrutinise them. He did not want to even think about whether they were wrong. 'It is the way of things here,' he said, annoyed to find that his voice contained just a hint of defensiveness, even more annoyed to find himself wondering whether Cassie might have a point.

'Well, if the result of your traditions is a long line of cold, unfeeling, *invincible* rulers like you,' Cassie responded heatedly, 'then I'm glad I'm not part of it. And I'll tell you something, Jamil, I think deep in your heart, you don't want to be part of it either.'

'You know nothing about—'

'You've already admitted you won't be treating your son in the same way,' Cassie interrupted ruthlessly, desperate to find a way to get through to the man she now realised was barricaded up inside a coat of armour forged from pain and suffering. 'You told me that you wanted things to be different for Linah, too. You want a different life for your children, you're even prepared to face the wrath of your Council to provide it, but can't you see the place you need to start is with yourself? Jamil, your father was so wrong.' Her eyes were wide with unshed tears. 'To care is not a weakness, it's a strength. To stand alone, to say you don't need anyone, that's simply a lie. Everyone needs someone to love, everyone needs someone to love them, don't you see that?'

'Your love for your poet—did that strengthen you or weaken you?' Jamil asked coldly. It was a cruel remark, he knew that, but he was hurting.

Cassie flinched. 'I did not love Augustus.' Not at all, she realised suddenly. She had been in love with the idea of love only.

'You told me yourself, the first time that we met, that what you felt was humiliation as a result of this so-called love.'

He was just lashing out, she knew that. This place held such awful memories for him, it would be a miracle if he did not. And what he said was true, after all, even if it was said to divert her. To divert him. Cassie laced her fingers together, then unlaced them. Then laced them again, frowning hard. 'You're right, I did feel humiliated,' she admitted, 'but not by being in love, by being so mistaken. I was humiliated and ashamed of my stupidity, my wilfulness.'

She stared at him hopelessly. An immense pity for

the lonely boy he had been, for the solitary man he had been forced to become, washed over her. How to get through to him, she had no idea, especially since he seemed intent on preventing her. This was a pivotal moment, she felt it. If she did not make him see now, he never would. 'You are missing out on so much by denying yourself.'

'You cannot miss what you have never had,' Jamil replied curtly. 'In any case, I am not *denying* myself. I am protecting myself. And my kingdom.'

'By refusing to allow yourself to feel! To love! Do you deny your people such things?'

'Love! Why must you always bring that up? It doesn't exist, save in those pathetic poems you are forever reading.'

Seeing his determinedly set face, Cassie almost despaired. His knuckles were white around the horse whip. A horse whip, for God's sake. His father had trained him in the same way as he trained his thoroughbreds. A flash of rage gave her a surge of strength. She grabbed the riding crop from Jamil and, bending it over her knee, snapped it in two. 'There! That is what I think of your father's methods, and that is what I think of your stupid traditions,' she declared, panting with the exertion. 'Do you really want this thing to dictate your entire life?' She threw it with all her might out into the desolate garden. 'What he did to you was cruel. Disgustingly, horribly cruel, but he is dead now. You are your own man, not your father's. He was wrong, Jamil, wrong. Allow yourself to feel, allow yourself to love, and you will see for yourself how happy it can make you.'

'It did not make you happy,' Jamil retorted pointedly.

'Oh, why must you keep bringing Augustus into everything?' Cassie exclaimed. 'I'm beginning to feel as if I'll never be rid of him.' But at least Jamil was looking at her properly now. He was listening. Cassie took a deep breath. 'When you love someone, really love someone, you can feel it here…' she pressed a hand to her bosom '…or here.' She touched her stomach. 'I've never felt that, I admit it. Few people do, but when they do, they just know. That is the kind of love that makes you strong.'

'That kind of love is a myth.'

'No. No, it's not. It's just rare,' Cassie said, surprising herself now, for it turned out she did believe in love after all. 'But when you find it, as my sister Celia has, it is the greatest source of strength in the world. Far, far greater than the sword, or scimitar or whatever. It's not that you depend upon someone, it's that you have someone else to depend on. Oh, why can't you see that?'

'Perhaps I would give your little flights of fancy more credence if you spoke from a position of experience,' Jamil replied. 'But since you have already admitted that you do not…' He shrugged.

Cassie gave a rather undignified squeal of frustration. 'You don't have to have experienced something to know it exists, believe it exists! In here!' she exclaimed, pressing her hand to her breast.

Her face was flushed. Her bosom heaved with

indignation. A long tress of fiery gold hair had come undone and lay over the white skin of her shoulder, where her dress had slipped. Her eyes sparkled a blue that put turquoises to shame. The maelstrom she had stirred up was suddenly too much for Jamil to cope with. Resorting to one of the few ways he knew of to express himself, he pulled her roughly into his arms, and silenced her in the age-old way, with a passionate, angry, famished kiss.

Cassie struggled only briefly, her hands flailing against his chest in an ineffectual attempt to free herself. It was a kiss meant to punish, she knew that, knew, too, that she had pushed him to his limit. It meant nothing, she told herself, nothing more than a show of strength, but still, the touch of his lips on hers, the lean length of his body held close, but not close enough to the soft yieldingness of hers, was beginning to work its magic. Cassie stopped struggling. Her body seemed to melt into his. Her lips parted. Her skin heated. Her heart began to pound.

It was over too quickly. With a hoarse cry, Jamil pushed her away, glaring at her as if it were her fault. As it was, Cassie could see quite clearly why he would think so. For long moments they simply stared at each other, breathing, lost in a tangled jungle of emotions, unsure about which path to take to regain solid ground. It was Jamil who broke the silence, his voice harsh, edged with something less certain that gave Cassie a tiny cause to hope.

'I will not apologise for that, it was your own fault.

Once again, you dare to intrude on matters that do not concern you. You should not have entered here. I wish that you had not. This place…'

'You should reclaim it. Banish the ghosts, take it back. Until you do, it's like a dark secret, brooding away.'

'This place,' Jamil continued, ignoring her interruption, 'is none of your business. I don't want you coming here again and I certainly don't want you bringing Linah here.'

'Of course not. Jamil, you could make Linah so happy if you showed her just a little bit of affection. Loving her could make you happy.'

Jamil sighed heavily. 'You just don't give up, do you?'

Cassie took his hand and pressed it to her cheek. 'It takes courage to change the habits of a lifetime, but courage is something you have in abundance.'

Jamil's smile was twisted. 'I'm not the only one. You have the courage of your convictions.' He kissed her knuckles. 'I'll think about your suggestion.'

'That's all I ask.'

'For the moment, at least,' he said wryly. 'Come, let us leave this place.'

Turning the key in the lock of the outer door, Jamil removed it and secreted it in his robes. Cassie watched him stride down the corridor, his tunic rippling in the slight breeze caused by his rapid gait. Poor, tortured Jamil. If he could but make a start by loving Linah, then maybe some day he would be capable of real love.

Why was that thought making her uncomfortable?

She had an absurd urge to run after him, missing him more with every step he took away from her, a premonition of a time when he would be gone from her for ever. She hadn't thought about that until now. Until today. She didn't want to think about it now.

It would have been naïve to expect that Jamil would be transformed overnight, but from that day on, Cassie did detect a marked difference in him. Awkwardly at first, but with increasing confidence as Linah responded, he began to allow his feelings for his daughter to show. Cassie looked on with a pride she took care to disguise. Knowing that she had been instrumental in effecting this change was enough; she did not want his gratitude, and she most certainly did not want Linah to guess the part she had played. Besides, it was a painful enough process for Jamil to override the years of pain that had beaten his reserve into him. She did not want him worrying about her witnessing his metamorphosis.

She was watching him with Linah one day. Jamil was standing in the middle of a bathing pool, teaching his daughter to swim. He had abandoned his cloak and *igal*, but retained his tunic. The water came up to his waist. Linah, lying supported in his arms, was giggling at something he had said. He looked over at Cassie and smiled. Their eyes met and her heart did a little flip flop. His tunic, damp from Linah's splashing, clung to his body like a second skin, showing off his muscles, the width of his shoulders, the dip of his stomach. His hair was sticking up in endearing spikes. His eyes sparkled with good humour.

Father and daughter together. It was exactly the tableau Cassie had dreamt of creating, but though it was of her making, she felt excluded. Father and daughter. The obvious gap opened up before her like an abyss. They had been playing happy families, the three of them, but she was not really part of it. And yet she wanted to be, she realised. She wanted to be a lot. Because she loved Linah now, too. But mostly because she was in danger, in very real danger, of feeling something she should not feel for Linah's father. And that would be a mistake.

Cassie turned away from Jamil's beckoning smile, busying herself with packing away the lunch things. It was not too late. She had caught herself just in time. It was not too late.

'The Council await you, Highness.'

Jamil looked up from the document he'd been perusing and gazed blankly at his man of business, who was hovering in the open doorway.

'The betrothal contract,' Halim prompted anxiously. 'You rearranged the signing for today. It must be witnessed by the Council, so I took the liberty of organising the gathering. They are ready.'

'The betrothal contract.'

'Yes, Highness. You said—'

'I know what I said. This alliance is advantageous to us, it is to be welcomed.' But Jamil did not want to be married. He did not want to even have to think about marriage, about siring an heir with a female he had absolutely no interest in whatsoever. The idea of it filled him with repugnance. He was sick and tired of having to think about the endless matters of state that obtruded on his day, and sick and tired of having to spend his time resolving them, one problem after another. Sometimes it felt as if he was the only person in the whole kingdom of Daar-el-Abbah capable of making decisions. Jamil rubbed the bridge of his nose with long, elegant fingers. It had always been thus—why was it bothering him so much now?

With some caution, Halim approached the desk behind which his master sat. The prince had been behaving strangely of late, spending much time with his daughter and that English governess of hers. 'You must be heartened by the improvement in your daughter's behaviour,' he said carefully, 'the whole palace is talking about the change in her.' *And the change in Prince Jamil!* 'You will be able to hand over Princess Linah with confidence now.'

'Hand her over?' Jamil looked confused.

Halim laughed nervously. 'Well, you will hardly require the services of the English governess when you are married, Highness. Your daughter will be in the care of your new wife, as is right and proper.'

'Eventually, perhaps, when I am actually married.'

'But with the betrothal papers signed, there will be no reason to delay.'

No reason, save his own reluctance. 'I've only met Princess Adira once, remember.'

Halim beamed. 'And the next time you meet her will be on your wedding night, as is the tradition.'

Jamil thumped his fist down on the desk. 'No!' He pushed his chair back and got to his feet. 'It is time both you and the Council recognised this is the nineteenth century, not the thirteenth. I won't have my wife brought to me painted and veiled like some offering. I am not a prize stud camel, I don't perform to order. And she—Princess Adira—she's barely exchanged two words with me.'

'You are hardly marrying her for her conversational skills,' Halim said with a smirk, 'she will be first wife, not first minister.'

'First and only wife. Therefore it is, even you will admit, preferable that at the very least we do not hold one another in dislike.'

'Indeed, but the Princess Adira—'

'I am sure she has many excellent qualities, but that's not what I'm talking about.'

'What *are* you talking about, Prince Jamil?'

A beautiful face, a pair of turquoise eyes, a coral mouth curved into a welcoming smile.

'Master?'

Someone to depend upon. Someone who would share and not just take. Cassie! The beautiful creature who had created a sanctuary in Linah's apartments where he could be free from the cares of the world. Who saw him not as Prince Jamil, ruler of Daar-el-Abbah, nor as a provider, nor as a peace maker, neither as an enemy nor an ally. Who called him Jamil in that soft husky voice of hers with the quaint English accent. Who saw him as a man, not a prince. Who talked to him as a friend. Whose delicious body and delightful scent and coral-pink mouth haunted his dreams.

It would be pleasant there in the courtyard as dusk began to fall. An oasis of calm and peace, of seclusion from the world, even if it was just an illusion. He would go to her once he had, yet again, done his duty by signing away the little he had left of himself. He would go to her, and she would soothe him just by talking about the mundane details of her day. He would let her voice wash over him, and he would forget about everything else for a few precious moments.

The thought was enough of an incentive to force him into action. 'Very well, let's get this over with.' Jamil grabbed the ceremonial gold-and-emerald cloak that lay waiting on the divan under the window and fastened it around his neck with the ornate emerald pin. The sabre next, then the ring and the head dress and the golden band. He straightened his shoulders and tugged at the heavy belt holding the sabre in place. Then he nodded at Halim, who flung open the door to the prince's private apartments, and clicked his fingers to summon the honorary guard.

Six men, dressed in pristine white, formed up in the corridor behind their ruler. Halim himself picked up the trailing edge of Prince Jamil's cloak, and the party set off for the throne room at a swift pace.

The double doors of the magnificent room were already open in readiness. Two rows of Royal Guards formed a pathway to the dais, their scimitars raised, points touching. Rays from the sinking sun slanted through the high windows and glinted on the polished steel. The waiting Council of Elders made obeisance as Jamil strode by, remaining on their knees, heads bowed, eyes averted, until he ascended the steps to the throne and bowed solemnly in greeting. The contract lay before him on a low table along with a selection of quills and a bottle of ink. Jamil picked up a pen, dipped it in the ink and signed his name, waiting impatiently for Halim to heat the wax before imprinting the seal from his ring.

It was done. His duty was done. He would not think of it now. He would not allow himself to dwell on the consequences. Jamil scattered sand over the wet ink and pushed the document aside. He got to his feet so quickly that he was already halfway back down the length of the throne room before Halim and the Council realised he was going.

'Highness, the celebrations,' Halim shouted after him.

'I am sure you will enjoy them all the more for my absence,' Jamil called over his shoulder. In other circumstances, the startled look on Halim's face would have amused him. Right now, he could not have cared less. Without bothering to change out of his formal robes, Jamil took the now very familiar route to the schoolroom.

Chapter Six

As he had expected, he found Cassie sitting alone by the sun fountain. They ate early here in the schoolroom apartments and the remnants of dinner had already been cleared. Linah would be asleep upstairs, he knew, so familiar was he now with his daughter's routine. With her governess's routine.

She was sitting on the cushions with her book. Her feet were tucked out of sight, but he knew they would be bare. She relished the coolness of the tiles on her toes. He liked to see them peeping out from under the hems of her English dresses. He had not thought feet could be so sensual.

Engrossed in a volume of Mr Wordsworth's poems, Cassie had not noticed the courtyard door opening and did not look up until he was almost by her side. 'Jamil,' she said, closing the book and rising gracefully from the cushions, shaking out the folds of her gown. 'I wasn't expecting you. Linah is in bed.'

'I know.'

He looked different. Not angry but—different. His eyes were stormy. A flush stained his cheek bones. He was looking at her strangely. 'Have you eaten?' she asked. 'I could ring for some food, if you like.'

'I'm not hungry.'

She hovered uncertainly on the edge of the cushions. During the day it was just about possible for her to disguise the pleasure she took in his presence, the attraction to him that she continued to deny, but in the evening, alone with him like this, it was much more difficult. Try as she might, she could not see him as a prince, only as a man. An incredibly attractive man, who, at the moment, looked as if he carried the weight of the world on his shoulders. 'You're wearing your official cloak,' she said. 'Have you come from the Council?'

'Yes.' Jamil tugged at the emerald pin that held the heavy garment in place. He'd forgotten all about it, another heirloom passed on from his father, who had received it from his. It fell with a soft whoosh on to the tiled floor of the courtyard. The priceless emerald pin he dropped with a careless clatter on top of it.

'It will crease if you leave it there,' Cassie said, stooping to retrieve it. 'Let me—'

'Leave it.'

Startled by the harshness of his tone, which she had recently so rarely heard, Cassie did as he bid her. 'Is there something wrong?'

Jamil shrugged. 'Nothing more than usual.'

'Do you want to talk about it?'

'No.'

She could not read his mood. He had his Corsair face, impenetrable and remote. 'I was thinking—wondering— if you had considered what I was saying about Linah. About her having some friends of her own age, I mean. I think she's ready for it now, she hasn't had a tantrum in ages, and it will do her good to have someone other than you and me to talk to.'

'Is she bored with my company already?'

'Of course not, I didn't mean that.' Cassie smiled, but it was a nervous smile, her lips trembling. She sat down on the edge of the fountain and trailed her hand in the cool water, trying to regain control of herself. He looked so careworn, she wanted more than anything to comfort him, but did not know how to start when he was in such a strange mood. She stretched out her hand invitingly. 'Sit with me a while. You don't have to talk, just sit and enjoy the night. Look up, the stars are coming out, they're lovely.'

But Cassie herself made too lovely a picture for Jamil to be interested in the stars. Her dress was made of lemon-yellow silk, with some sort of complicated trimming on the ruffle at the hem. The colour brought out the fiery lights in her hair. The sleeves were shorter than she usually wore during the day, finishing just above her elbow, though a fall of cream lace covered her forearm. There was cream lace at the neckline, too, almost the same colour as her skin. An evening gown, intended to be worn in the formal drawing rooms of London and yet looking perfectly at home here, in the stark wildness of the desert. He could see the roundness of her bosom, rising and falling beneath the creamy lace. He could see one bare foot peeping out, balancing her on the edge of the fountain. He moved towards her, took the hand she was holding out, but didn't sit down. It was a delicate hand, lost in his. Easily crushed. For some reason, this made him angry. He let it go, and regretted it as soon as he had done so, and that made him even more angry.

'Perhaps it is you who are bored with my company,' he said harshly. 'Are you missing your poet, Cassie? Are you missing the simpering compliments and admiring glances of your gaggle of gallants? I warned you that life with Linah meant seclusion.'

Turquoise eyes turned on him, dark with hurt. He hadn't meant to lash out, but he couldn't seem to stop. 'My daughter is a princess of royal blood. She must learn there is a price to be paid for that privilege. And so must you.'

'Jamil, why are you being like this? It's not like you.'

'But you are wrong, Lady Cassandra, it is very like me. You don't really know me at all.'

'I don't agree. In these last few weeks, I think I have come to know you very well.'

'You see only one aspect of me. You know nothing of my life as a ruler.'

'Perhaps, but I know what you are like as—as…'

'As?'

'A man.'

'You think so?'

He took a step closer to her. The air seemed to crackle with tension. Cassie's hand lay so still in the water of the fountain that one of the little golden fish which lived there brushed against it. She couldn't understand how the conversation had taken this turn, nor why it felt so—so…precarious? Precipitous? Was that even a word? Pre-emptive? But of what?

'Tell me, then, what am I like, Cassie. As a man?'

Jamil had taken another step towards her. In fact, he was standing so close to her his knees were brushing her thigh. She could almost feel the anger pulsing from him, and something else burning there behind his tawny eyes that gave her goose bumps. 'Jamil, stop this.'

'Stop what, Cassie?' He pulled her to her feet, holding her there, almost in his embrace, with his hands lightly on her waist. 'Stop pretending that I don't find you attractive? Stop pretending that I don't think of you as I first saw you in the tent in the desert? Stop pretending that I don't remember our kiss? Stop pretending that I don't want to kiss you again? That every time I see you I see only an English governess? Why should I? Was it not you who told me I should acknowledge my feelings?'

'I didn't mean that. Please don't do this.'

'Why?' He pulled her closer. She did not resist, nor did she comply. She dropped her gaze, closed her eyes. He didn't want that. He gave her a tiny shake. 'Look at me, Cassie. Tell me honestly that you don't feel it, too. Tell me that you don't think of these things. Tell me you don't want me and I'll let you be. Only, look at me when you say the words.'

For a long moment she did not move. Then, with a small sigh that could have been resignation, but might have been something quite different, she met his gaze, and all the secret thoughts, the shameful night-time dreams that she bundled up and held securely in the back of her mind during the day, tumbled forth as if the knot that held them had been untied. He knew. He saw it in her eyes. His gaze raked over her, her eyes, her mouth, her breasts, then her mouth again.

He was going to kiss her, unless she stopped him. He was going to kiss her and she couldn't stop him. She wanted him to kiss her again, she had been wanting him to ever since that last unsatisfactory, cut-short kiss, though God knew she had tried not to.

'Cassie.' He pulled her close, his hands tight around her waist, pressing her hard against him. 'Cassie, let us have no more of this pretence.'

She closed her eyes in an effort to try to regain some sort of hold on reality, but it was already too late. Too late for calm, rational thinking. Too late to release herself from his hold. Too late to think about how wrong, how utterly wrong, this would be. It couldn't be wrong, not when it felt like this. Not when she had been wanting this, just this, for weeks now. There was no point in pretending any more that the pleasure she took in his company was for Linah's sake. No point in pretending that the urgent ache consuming her, the thing that held her fast to him, made her lips long to cling to his, was anything other than base desire. He wanted her. Her wilful heart wanted him. 'Yes,' she whispered, not really knowing what she was agreeing to, save only that she was agreeing. 'Yes.'

Jamil hesitated. Lovely, delicious, irresistible as she was, honour and duty dictated resisting. But for once, for just this moment, Jamil had had a surfeit of honour and duty. He wanted the pleasure she could give him and he wanted the oblivion such pleasure would grant him. To be, just for a while, merely a man, not to have to think, lost in the sweet delight of a woman. This woman. He tilted her chin up with his finger. Angled his mouth towards hers. And kissed her.

He kissed her softly, lingering on the soft pillow of her luscious lips, tasting her. She was so sweet. So heady. Like peaches and English strawberries, laced with fire. His kiss deepened. His manhood hardened. Pliant in his embrace, she was soft, lush and ripe for the taking. He kissed her harder.

Cassie moaned softly under the onslaught. Kisses such as she could never have imagined, dark delights such as she could never have dreamed, consumed her. Her body was on fire. His kiss demanded things from her she didn't know how to give, though she wanted to. She wanted to so much. His lips moulded hers into a response she hadn't known she could make. She opened her mouth and his tongue slid in, touching hers, sparking like a shooting star, sending echoing shivers out to the extremities of her body. Her fingers curled into his robe, her toes into the cushions on which she stood. Now she knelt as he eased her down, now she lay as he eased her further, still kissing, kissing, kissing, dark and hot and velvety.

Little kisses on her eyes now, then her throat and her neck. Her hands fluttered over the breadth of his shoulders, feeling the heat of his skin through his tunic. Daringly, she pushed his head dress back, touching his hair, then his cheeks, with their faint traces of stubble.

His lips fastened on hers again and Cassie closed her eyes. His hands traced the line of her waist through the silk of her gown, making her shiver with expecta-tion. She could feel his legs pressing against hers now. She could feel something building inside her, a knot of something that wanted to unravel. His tongue touched hers again, and she bucked under him. He pressed her back against the cushions, stroking her, her waist, the side of her breast, making her jump again, making her nipples ache in the confines of her chemise, her stays, her dress. Her clothes felt too tight, she felt too hot. His tongue touched hers again. *Should she like it so much?*

She didn't care, she did like it. His hand moulded her breast now, and she liked that, too, though her nipples strained, hard, tingling, exciting. *Should she feel that? Like that? And that?*

She didn't know. All she desired was that he do it again. Fingers brushing her breasts, lingering on the place where her nipples pressed into the fabric. More sparks. More yet as he stroked down, over her belly, her thighs, cupping the roundness of her, as if to show her how different she was, for at the same time her own fingers were boldly exploring his back, his arms, the dip of his stomach, wondering at the sheer delight of male heat and male muscle and male otherness. He was so different. So very, delightfully, different. She felt as if she was melting.

Jamil kissed the mounds of her breasts, but the lace of her dress got in the way. The fastenings were at the back. Complicated fastenings. Too complicated for now. Need, raw need was taking a hold on him. He kissed her with a new urgency. He was hard, more than ready. Still kissing, he found the hem of her dress and pushed it roughly out of the way. Toe. Ankle. Calf. Knee. The skin so soft, the shape so curvaceous. She was panting under him, her hands clutching at his robe, seeking skin. Above her knee was some sort of undergarment. He hadn't expected that. Her thigh beneath the cotton was smooth and creamy. His hand roamed higher, to the apex, and found to his surprise the undergarment was split. Curls. Damp and warm and inviting.

Through the delicious haze of her growing excitement, the words leapt unbidden into Cassie's head, delivered in that familiar clipped, censorious tone. *Remember, child, once a female has abandoned her corsets, there is no saying what else she will abandon.* Aunt Sophia's parting words to her. The effect was instantaneous; the fire of Cassie's passion was extinguished as effectively as if she had been doused in cold water. 'No! Stop!'

Jamil froze.

Cassie began to wriggle free of his intimate embrace.

He released her immediately. She pulled her dress down over her legs and sat up, her breath coming fast and shallow. 'I'm sorry—I...'

Jamil got to his feet, tugging his tunic back into place. Sitting before him on the cushions, her hair falling down in long golden tresses over her breast, Cassie looked a picture of abandon. He had never wanted anyone so much in his life, never felt such frustration.

'Jamil, I didn't mean to—I'm sorry.'

But he was in no mood to listen. He was in no mood, either, to question his own motives. 'There is no need to apologise,' he said, gathering up his cloak, his head dress, his emerald pin. 'You have my gratitude, you have spared us an experience we would both ultimately regret,' he said tersely, as he strode off.

The doors closed behind him with a snap. Cassie made no attempt to stand up. Her knees wouldn't hold her. She was appalled. Not at Jamil, but at herself. The liberties she had granted him. The liberties she still wanted to grant him. The wanton way he made her feel, as if to abandon all restraint was her heart's desire. She was mortified. She sank slowly back down on to the floor and covered her head with her hands.

'Ah, Henry, my dear fellow, how the devil are you?' Lord Torquil Fitzgerald strode over to where his old friend was seated alone in the library of Boodle's, enjoying an after-dinner snifter of brandy. 'Haven't seen you for an age.'

'I've been in Lisbon for the last three weeks, at

Castlereagh's behest. He has some notion of possible unrest in Portugal.'

'More radicals!' Lord Torquil exclaimed, his eyebrows shooting up alarmingly, making him look like a startled rabbit, and betraying the accuracy of his old Harrovian nickname.

Lord Armstrong had know Bunny Fitzgerald since their schooldays. He shrugged. 'Liverpool is reading conspiracy into everything, since Cato Street. I don't think it will come to anything. Managed to pick up a barrel or two of port while I was out there though, so it wasn't exactly a wasted journey.'

'Heard congratulations are in order, by the way. A son after all this time. You must be mightily relieved.'

'James. A fine boy.' Lord Henry smiled proudly.

'A toast to the whippersnapper, then,' Lord Torquil said, helping himself to another snifter. 'Be nice to have another man around the house, I'll wager. Quite over-run with all those daughters of yours till now. Which reminds me,' he said, thumping his forehead with his glass, 'bumped into Archie Hughes the other day, he was telling me that the fair Cassandra is rusticating.'

Lord Henry's genial expression faded. 'Cassandra is visiting her sister in Arabia. I would hardly call it rusticating.'

'A bad business, that entanglement with the poet. You must have been sick as a dog. Little beauty like that, she'd have gone off well.'

'Cassandra will still go off well enough,' Lord Henry said determinedly. 'When she returns, she will be betrothed to Francis Colchester. It is not quite the brilliant match I had intended, but it will do well enough.'

'Colchester? That the boy who was one of Wellington's protégés? A younger son, I think, but a sound choice. He's predicted to go far. Provided, of course, you can tear her away from that sheikh of hers,' Lord Torquil said with a throaty chuckle.

'Your brain's befuddled as usual, Bunny. *Prince* Ramiz of A'Qadiz is married to my eldest daughter, Celia. Had you forgotten?'

''Course not. Rich as Croesus, has that port in the Red Sea you did the deal on. No, I'm not talking about him. It's another one. Hang on a minute, it'll come to me. Jack—no—Jeremy—no—Jamil! That's it. Sheikh Jamil al-Nazarri. Principality next to A'Qadiz, I believe.'

'I have no idea what you're talking about,' Lord Henry exclaimed. 'What has this to do with Cassandra?'

'Well, I heard it from Archie, who was just back from a stint in Cairo, and he got it from old Wincie himself— though how he knew I'm not sure. But anyway, upshot is that the fair Cassandra is apparently cooped up in this sheikh's harem.'

'What!'

'For God's sake, Henry, keep your wig on, only passing on what I heard. Sorry to have dropped the cat among the pigeons, thought you knew. I'm sure it's all very innocent, though it doesn't look too good, does it?'

'I beg your pardon?'

'Well. Cassandra's a lovely girl. Stuck alone out in

the desert with a man who owns all he surveys. *Droit de seigneur*,' Lord Torquil whispered, tapping his nose.

Lord Henry drained his glass of brandy and got to his feet. 'If you value our friendship, sir, you will keep this news to yourself. My daughter is visiting her sister Celia. When she returns, she will be married to Francis Colchester. Do you understand?'

'No need to—that is, of course,' Lord Torquil blustered.

'Then I will bid you goodnight.' Accepting his hat and cane from the major-domo, Lord Henry demanded a hack and instructed the driver to take him to Grosvenor Square. It was late, but that was of no matter. His sister, Lady Sophia, was forever informing him of her inability to sleep. If anyone knew what was what, and what was to be done, it would be Sophia. Strangely, it did not for an instant occur to Lord Henry to consult Bella, his wife.

Cassie endured a restless night after Jamil stormed off, her mind circling endlessly between anger, mortification and regret as she tossed and turned endlessly on her sleeping divan. She was furious with herself for having succumbed to her own base desires, for had she not promised herself over and over again that she would not. And now she had made a complete fool of herself.

At this point mortification took the upper hand. She had more or less thrown herself at Jamil! Celia would be horrified. Aunt Sophia would—no, she could not begin to contemplate what Aunt Sophia would think—accuse her of casting off her morals with her stays, for a start. Not that she had cast off her stays, or anything else for that matter. In fact, apart from her stockings and slippers, which she had discarded earlier, she had remained fully dressed. Yet she might as well have been naked.

Oh God! Cassie's face burned at the recollection of Jamil's touch, her own uninhibited response. She was shocked, not by what she had done, but by how much she had enjoyed it, relished it. More, even, than she had imagined in those feverish dreams that had haunted her since first she had met Jamil. Dark, erotic dreams where his hand did more than rest, as it had earlier, so tantalisingly briefly on that most intimate part of her. Dreams where he kissed her more intimately, too, touched her more intimately, where his lips, his tongue, roused her to a shameless yearning for more. Dreams that made her nipples ache, which brought to life a throbbing pulse deep inside her. Dreams in which she and Jamil were naked, their bodies shockingly entwined. Dreams where Jamil—where she and Jamil…

She was a complete wanton!

She must be. Jamil obviously thought so. By kissing him in such a way she had quite obviously led him to expect—to expect more. Whatever more was. And she, she had been too caught up in the sating of her own passions to think about the fact that her behaviour could—should—be taken for encouragement.

That very first time they had met, all those weeks ago in the tent, Jamil had taken her for a woman who belonged not in the schoolroom but the harem. She had seen it for herself, in her reflection in the mirror, but had stubbornly chosen to believe that the real Cassie was Linah's responsible governess. She had been deluding herself.

She had not been fooling Jamil, though. He had known the truth all along. Cassie threw off the thin silk sheet that was her only cover and, wearing only her nightgown, padded out to the courtyard again. The sun and moon fountains tinkled at each other. A moonbeam shafted down, bathing Scheherazade's tiled image in ghostly light. The air was completely still.

The same illicit thoughts that had been keeping her awake at night had clearly been occupying Jamil's mind, too. Despite everything, Cassie found the idea exciting. The strength of his passion was so powerful, so all-consuming. He was not some weak, foppish excuse of a poet like Augustus, who expressed his emotions in sentimental doggerel, but a man of the desert, whose desires were as raw and fiery and elemental as the landscape he inhabited.

Regret came now. She would never be desired in such a way again, for she would never again meet someone like Jamil. She wished she had not stopped him. She almost wished he had ignored her protestations. But of course he had stopped, the moment she asked him to. He, who was master of all he surveyed, would not stoop to take by force. He, who could so easily have overcome her resistance, had chosen not to. The latent power in that lithe body of his was kept firmly leashed.

Cassie shivered. What would it feel like were he to

unleash it? Dear heavens, what would it be like to be
the subject of such an onslaught, helpless to do only as
he commanded? She shivered again, and felt the knot of
excitement that had not quite unravelled tense again in
her belly, felt the tinge of heat between her legs return.
Was this what Celia saw in Ramiz? Did submission
bring with it the sleepy, sated look she had observed on
her sister's unguarded countenance? No wonder Celia
preferred her desert prince to any Englishman. If Jamil
had not left the courtyard, if she had not asked him to
stop, would she, too, be feeling that way?

Oh, God! There was no point in such thoughts. The
chances were that in the morning Jamil would send her
ignominiously packing. Though really, looking back, she
remembered that he had been the one to initiate things.
Such a strange mood as he had been in. Momentarily
distracted, Cassie frowned. He had almost been intent
on picking a fight with her.

Cassie recalled her sister's warning not to become
either too involved or too attached and wished she had
paid heed to it. As ever, Celia had been right. Why could
she not be more like Celia?

Exhaustion hit her like a cold flannel. She stumbled
back to her divan and pulled the sheet up. Almost
instantly, she fell into a troubled sleep, haunted by
dreams in which she was pursued relentlessly by rav-
ening wild animals, desperate to consume her.

Jamil had stormed back to his private rooms, angrily
casting the wretched state cloak and head dress on to the

floor of his dressing room. He paced the perimeter of the courtyard around which his apartments were built. It was twice the size of any other in the palace, with four fountains and an ornate pagoda-like structure in the centre built around a fifth, much larger fountain, on top of which perched, rather incongruously, a statue of the royal panther.

Prowling dangerously in a manner very like that of the big cat, first in one direction and then in the other, Jamil swore colourfully in his native language and then, when this proved insufficient, resorted to summoning up curses in the other six languages in which he was fluent. It didn't help. His heart still pounded too fast. His fingers still curled tight into fists. His shoulders ached with tension. He flung himself down on the curved bench in the middle of the pagoda and made a conscious effort to still the emotions raging inside him.

Anger was a weapon, one which Jamil had been taught to harness. He was not a man given to losing his temper easily, yet of late it was becoming much more of an effort to control it. Everything frustrated him or irked him or felt like too much effort. His life, which had been tolerable until Cassie came along, now seemed burdened with more cares than he wished to carry.

Had he ever been content? Jamil cursed again, more viciously than before. Cassie again. Why must she question everything? Why must she force *him* to do the same, to confront things long buried? Since that day in the east wing, more and more memories of his childhood had begun to rear their ugly heads, not just in the middle of the night, but at odd times during the day. He remembered, as he had not allowed himself to do before, the overwhelming loneliness of his childhood. He remembered how much he had missed his mother. He remembered crying, alone in the panther cub court-yard, when everyone else was asleep, not for the pain his father had inflicted with his whip, but for the deeper hurt of feeling himself unloved. He remembered. He tried not to, but he did. And that was Cassie's doing.

Anger, his habitual release, helped only fleetingly. After anger came the bitterest doubt. That his suffering had a purpose had been his consolation. That it might have been unnecessary made him furious, for he had no way to revenge himself. His father was dead. The damage—if damage it was—was done. Jamil was the man his father had made him, moulded in his image. He could not change. *And why should he want to?*

He was confused, and he had no way of achieving understanding. To discuss with Cassie the turmoil she had stirred up in him was unthinkable—he had neither the words, nor could he consider the blow to his dignity such a discussion would entail. But sometimes, more and more often, that is what he longed to do. She had started it. It was up to her to help him end it. She *owed* him the succour he sought.

Jamil got to his feet again and resumed his relentless pacing. If he was honest—and Jamil prided himself on his utter honesty—it was not really Cassie's fault, save indirectly. He had not realised, until she had rejected him, just how badly he wanted her. His anger should be directed not at Cassie, but himself.

What had he been thinking! His ways were not hers. Even before he succumbed to the temptation of kissing her, he had known it would be a mistake, but he had chosen not to listen to the warning bells ringing in his mind. For once, for perhaps the first time since he was a child, he had allowed his passions to hold sway. There was no way of avoiding it. Unless he apologised to her, she would leave, and he did not want her to leave. For Linah's sake, obviously.

No, not only for Linah's sake. With a heavy sigh, Jamil retired to his divan, a huge circular bed with gilded clawed feet covered by day in green velvet edged with gold *passementerie*. The organdie curtains hung from a coronet suspended from the ceiling, forming a tent-like structure. Jamil cast aside his tunic and slippers and threw himself naked on to the soft silk sheets, but he could not sleep. Images of Cassie pliant in his arms heated him. Her untutored kisses and beguilingly naïve touch had aroused him as no other woman ever had. The combination of innocence and sensuality promised untold delights. Delights which would, for him, have to remain for ever unsavoured. He knew that, how could he not, after tonight. But still, he groaned in frustration.

Cassie was no coquette, but she was no strait-laced English rose either. Underneath the layers of buttons and lacings that guarded that delicious body of hers slumbered a soft, sensual woman with a passion crying out to be awoken. Jamil's manhood stirred into life once more. The fleeting touch of her damp sex on his hand was seared into his memory, rendering all other future pleasures pale by comparison. He must not tread that path, could not tread that path if she was to stay, and she must stay. He was not ready for her to leave. Though he was not prepared, either, to question why.

In a few hours from now the three of them would head out for their customary early morning horse ride. After his daughter's lesson, when he and Cassie were alone in the desert, he would explain, put her mind at rest. Satisfied with this, Jamil lay awake, counting the hours until dawn.

Cassie was awoken by Linah, who was already dressed, proudly sporting her new riding habit, which Cassie had made with her own clever needle. Her governess having overslept, the little girl was anxious lest they miss their riding lessons. 'Hurry, or *Baba* will think we are not coming,' she said, tugging the sheet back.

'I think it best if you go yourself today, Linah. I will ask one of the maidservants to take you to your father.'

'What is wrong? Are you ill?' The child looked at her anxiously. 'Are you missing your sisters, is that it? Do you need a hug?'

'I'm not sad,' Cassie said, smiling as the little girl put her arms around her neck of her own accord, 'but I am a little out of sorts. I don't think I can face riding today.'

A few weeks ago, the words would have sparked a

tantrum. Indeed, for a few moments Linah's lip trembled and her eyes widened, but then she straightened her shoulders and gave a little nod, a gesture that was so wholly her father's that Cassie almost laughed. 'I will stay with you, if you are ill. I will bring you sorbet and tea and I will ask cook to make your favourite pastilla, and—'

'Stop, stop. I'm getting up. Such devotion deserves a reward, Linah.'

'So you'll come riding with *Baba* and me after all?' The child clapped her hands in delight.

'Yes.' She must face Jamil some time; it might as well be now. 'Go and wait for me outside, I won't be long.'

But when they arrived at the stables, it was to be informed that Jamil would not be joining them today, and the groom was to accompany them instead. 'Did he say why?' Cassie asked, but the man only shook his head and said that the prince was otherwise engaged.

Cassie was immensely relieved to have been granted such an unexpected reprieve, but Linah was hugely disappointed and became increasingly distracted and fractious during the lesson. They were practising jumping small fences, and Linah twice lost her temper when her pony refused, the second time raising her whip angrily.

'Don't take your own incompetence out on the horse,' Cassie said sternly, staying Linah's hand before the whip made contact. 'It is spiteful to do so and a sure sign of poor horsemanship.'

'Let me go,' Linah shouted, trying to shake herself free.

'When you calm down I will do so, not before.'

'Let me go. How dare you lay a hand on me, I am a princess of the royal blood. No one may touch me. Let me go. *Now!*'

'Linah!'

'I hate you. I hate you. Go away. Go back to England, I don't want you here any more.'

'Linah, you don't mean that. Calm down, and we will…'

But it was too late. Linah kicked her heels into her pony's flank and spurred the beast forwards at a gallop. She crossed the paddock and sailed in a perfect jump over the fence before Cassie could remount. By the time Cassie arrived back at the stables, Linah had already stormed off in the direction of the schoolroom.

Satisfied that the girl was safe within the palace, Cassie decided it would be better to give her time to cool down. Though she knew Linah did not mean her hurtful words, still she was stung by them. Her spirits sank into her riding boots. Now Jamil would have no reason at all to give her another chance, for why keep a wanton, wilful governess whose only charge hated her?

Thinking only of the enticing prospect of a tempo-rary release from her cares, not for a moment consider-ing how her actions would be interpreted by a small, contrite, eight-year-old girl, never mind her autocratic prince of a father, Cassie wheeled her grey mare round and headed out of the city gates at a gallop, without so much as a backward glance.

Chapter Seven

Jamil had risen when dawn broke, to be met with a crisis of state that threw his plans into disarray, obliging him to attend emergency Council meetings for many long, tedious hours until the sun was already high in the sky. Knowing that Linah was accustomed to take a nap after the noon meal, he made his way to the school room, expecting to find Cassie in her usual position in the shade of the lemon tree by the sun fountain, quietly engrossed in one of her many books of poetry. Instead he entered the courtyard to be met by a scene of chaos and Linah, surrounded by her bevy of maidservants, sobbing as if her heart would break. The porcelain shards of a shattered jug were scattered across the mosaic of Scheherazade, the mango sorbet it had held spreading out in a sticky pool over the fairytale princess's hair. The real-life princess who ran, shrieking *Baba*, pushing aside the maidservant who would have restrained her, was in an equally dishevelled state, her hair damp and tangled, her cheeks streaked with tears.

'*Baba*, *Baba*, you must get her back,' Linah said, throwing herself at her father, hot little hands clutching insistently at his tunic.

'What in the name of the gods is going on?' Jamil demanded, taking Linah's hand, but addressing the gaggle of servants, who immediately threw themselves on to their knees, faces hidden, gazing at the tiled floor.

'It is Cassie,' Linah said, tugging at his belt in order to get his attention.

'What about her?'

'She has gone, *Baba*.'

Jamil had never felt fear, but now he felt something very like it clutch its icy fingers around his heart. 'Gone where?'

'It is my fault, *Baba*. I ordered her to go.'

Jamil picked up his clearly distraught daughter and carried her to a low stool in the shade of the terrace where she sat on his knee, racked by incoherent sobs. Eventually, after promising several times that her confession would not result in any punishment, Jamil extracted the story of the morning's dramatic events from Linah.

'I told Cassie I hated her, and I said I wanted her to go back to England, and she looked so sad, *Baba*, and I—I was pleased she looked sad because I knew that she would go back to England soon anyway and I didn't want her to leave me—and now she's left anyway.'

'When did she leave? How?'

'According to the groom, she rode off on her horse, master,' one of the women said, 'into the desert.'

Jamil got to his feet, but Linah clung to him pathetically. 'Please don't be angry, I didn't mean it. I promise I'll be good, *Baba*, if only you will bring her back.'

'Listen to me, Linah,' he said gently. 'Soon I will be taking a new wife. You will have a new mother, maybe brothers and sisters in time. Then you will not need Cassie. She must leave eventually.'

Linah's tear-stained face brightened. 'You could marry Cassie instead. That would solve everything.'

Jamil smiled wryly. 'Life is not so simple, child. My new wife—your new mother—has already been chosen.' Jamil turned to leave but before he did so, he stooped to give Linah a brief hug. 'Don't worry. I'll find Cassie. No harm will come to her, I promise.'

He found her horse first, less than ten miles out into the desert. She had been heading due east and he picked up the trail fairly easily, the distinctive marks of the horse's shoes being quite different from those of camels or mules. She'd taken the route to the Maldissi Oasis, and it was here he found the grey mare cropping in an unconcerned manner at the shrub by the edge of the main pool, but there was no sign of Cassie. The horse had not been tethered. Its sleek coat was warm, but not overheated—it had obviously been at the oasis for a while. It had been at least five hours since Cassie had left the palace and, according to his head groom, she had no water or any other form of supplies.

Securing the mare under the shade of a palm tree and quickly removing the tack, Jamil tried to ignore the knot of anxiety forming in his stomach. He needed to think rationally. Cassie was an excellent horsewoman; if she had suffered a fall, it must have been serious for her to have let go of the reins. The alternative, that she had wandered off without first tying up the mare, was unthinkable. Leading his own stallion, Jamil traced his way slowly around the perimeter of the oasis, searching the sand for hoof marks, but Cassie's mount had wandered around aimlessly, circling from one pool to another and back again, and the sand on the outer reaches was soft and churned up. The air was still, too still. Shading his eyes with his hand, Jamil squinted up at the sky, all his senses on alert. There was a sandstorm coming, not a shadow of a doubt, he could smell it.

With a new sense of urgency, he resumed his scanning of the terrain underfoot, finally tracing the path of the mare's incoming hoof prints. His own horse was frisky now, sensing, as he did, the imminent change in the weather. Keeping an iron grip on the reins, Jamil followed the tracks for two slow miles. He was heading towards the ochre plateau, which was the first of the flat-topped mountains known to his people as the Seats of the Gods. A mile further on, the clouds began to gather, still high in the sky, roiling an angry shade of red with the glow of the sun behind them. Another half-mile and the trail stopped dead.

Dismounting from his stallion, Jamil pushed his dusty head dress back from his face and, scanning his surroundings anxiously, called Cassie's name. His voice echoed round the rocky foothills, but there was no reply. He called again. No answer.

Screwing his eyes up in the fierce glare of the sun, Jamil spotted something that might be footprints veering off to his left. They were faint and intermittent, due to the wind, which had picked up and was causing the sand to ripple one way then the next, like waves breaking on the shore. His heart pounding, his desert-tuned senses horribly aware that the storm was only minutes away, Jamil followed the faint track. His cloak flapped in the breeze. He pushed the *igal* that held his head dress more firmly into place and called out again.

The stallion heard her first, his sensitive ears pricking back. Then Jamil heard her, too, her voice faint but distinctive, and he sprinted towards the sound, relief at having found her tempered by fear. He knew only too well how harsh the desert environment could be. He prayed she was unharmed.

She lay huddled in a fissure between two rocks, which offered her some meagre protection from the elements. Her face was tear-streaked, her eyes dark with fright, though she made a feeble effort to smile. It was this, such a vulnerable, wobbly little smile, which made his heart contract, made his voice harsh as he called her name, pulling her ruthlessly from her pitiful hiding place and hugging her tightly to his chest. 'Cassie, by all the gods in the heavens! Cassie, do you have any idea of the worry you have caused, running off like that? You could have perished out here.'

She trembled, clutching feebly at his arms, allowing herself to acknowledge the truth only now that he was here. She could so easily have died if he had not found her. She could have died without ever seeing him again. 'I'm sorry. I'm so sorry.' Her words were a whisper. Shaking, she clutched at him, feverishly running her hands over his arms, his back, pressing her face into his chest, drinking in the warm, musky, male scent of him, breathing it in as if it was her life's breath, terrified that if she let him go he would prove to be a mirage. 'I'm sorry,' she muttered again. 'I've been so foolish. I didn't think. I just…' Her voice became jagged as tears of remorse and relief began to flow. She trembled violently, stumbling a little, and gave a yelp of pain. She would have fallen if he had not caught her to him.

'Are you hurt?'

She bit her lip, stoically ignoring the searing pain. 'It's nothing. My ankle, I've twisted it. Such a stupid thing to happen, a snake spooked the mare and she reared. I let go of the reins and she threw me and then bolted. It's nothing,' she said again, trying bravely to test putting her weight on her ankle, but the pain was excruciating. Her face turned ashen.

'You are lucky to have escaped so lightly,' Jamil said curtly, scooping her up into his arms. Now that he had found her relatively unscathed, the full horror of what might have been was making him feel sick.

'Jamil, I'm so sorry to have put you to such trouble. If I had only thought…'

His arms tightened around her. 'But you never do, do you?' he said with a ghost of a smile. 'Stop struggling.'

'I'm—'

'Save your apologies. You are safe, that is all that matters.' He looked up at the lowering sky, frowning. 'Later, there will be time enough later for apologies and recriminations; for the moment, we have to find somewhere sheltered to sit out the storm.' Scanning the surrounding rocky outcrops, he saw a darker, deeper fissure that he fervently hoped might be a cave. Holding Cassie securely in his arms, with his horse following obediently, Jamil made his way quickly towards safety.

His instincts proved to be correct. A narrow passageway, just large enough for the horse to pass through, opened out into a deep cave. It was dark and cool inside, the direction of the entranceway fortunately at the correct angle against the prevailing wind to keep them safe from the worst of the sand, which was already beginning to blow around. 'Stay there while I see to the horse,' he commanded, lowering Cassie to the ground. She sank onto the sandy earth, easing out her cramped muscles, trying to assemble her thoughts into some explanation for her actions that sounded reasonable. Actions, she was beginning to realise, that were not only foolish, but could have been potentially fatal.

Jamil stripped his horse of its tack and retrieved from

the saddle the two goatskin water flasks he always carried with him, along with a blanket. The cave was almost
dark now, the sun's light having been almost obliterated
by the dark storm clouds. There was an air of stretched-
taut tension, which always preceded a sandstorm, but it
seemed to him there was another layer to it today. What
had she been thinking of to behave so irresponsibly? His
temper quivered on the edge of fury, like a bow strung
tight for battle, his relief at finding her safe giving way
to anger at the danger in which she had placed herself.

He made his way carefully across to where she sat,
exactly as he had left her. Draping the blanket around
her, he felt her shoulders shaking. 'You are trembling.'

Cassie nodded. 'It's the shock, I think. My own fault,'
she whispered, teeth chattering. 'Sorry.'

'Here, drink this.'

He took the lid off his goatskin flask and held it to
her mouth. Her skin was dry, dusty, heated. 'Slowly,
slowly.'

She sipped, spluttered, sipped, then coughed. 'I lost
my hat and veil in the fall. I must look a fright,' she said
with a vain attempt at humour.

In the dim interior of the cave her face was a ghostly
shadow, her hair a contrasting golden halo. The rest of
her, in her dark habit and tan gloves, now cloaked in
the blanket, blended into the background, accentuating
the fragile beauty of her face. He held the flask to her
lips again and she sipped slowly, though he was close
enough to sense the effort it took for her not to grab the
flask and gulp greedily.

'Thank you,' she said, her voice croaky.

'I'm going to examine your ankle now. It will mean taking off your boot, and it's unlikely you'll be able to put it back on again.'

'Can't it wait until we get back?'

Jamil shook his head. 'I need to make sure it's not broken.' Before she could object further, he picked up her foot and began, with great delicacy, to unlace her riding boot.

She bore his examination bravely, biting her lip as he manipulated her foot first one way and then the other, distracted by the heat of his hands as he moved them gently over the arch of her foot, her swollen ankle, her calf. His touch was expert and business-like, but she could not help remembering last night, his hands roaming over her in quite a different way, and in remembering she could feel her body flush with embarrassment and something else.

'Nothing broken, but it will have to be bound.'

'I'll do that. I can use my stocking.'

But he was already untying her garters, a breathtakingly intimate gesture in any other circumstances, first one, then the other, using both stockings to form a tight bandage, before fastening them with the pin from his cloak.

'Thank you,' Cassie said shakily. She rubbed her eyes and face in a futile attempt to wipe some of the sand away. It was stuck fast, as if baked on.

Jamil shook off his head dress and poured a little of the precious water on to a corner of the silk. 'Here, let

Get 2 books Free!
Plus, receive a FREE mystery gift

If you have enjoyed reading this Historical romance story, then why not take advantage of this **FREE** book offer and we'll send you two more titles from this series absolutely **FREE**!

Accepting your **FREE** books and **FREE** mystery gift places you under no obligation to buy anything.

As a member of the Mills & Boon Book Club™ you'll receive your favourite Series books up to 2 months ahead of the shops, plus all these exclusive benefits:

- **FREE home delivery**
- **Exclusive offers and our monthly newsletter**
- **Membership to our special rewards programme**

We hope that after receiving your free books you'll want to remain a member. But the choice is yours. So why not give us a go. You'll be glad you did!

**Visit www.millsandboon.co.uk
for the latest news and offers.**

Kasey
Michaels

Mrs/Miss/Ms/Mr .... Initials ....

BLOCK CAPITALS PLEASE

Surname ....

Address ....

....

....

.... Postcode ....

Email ....

H1FIA

MILLS & BOON

NO STAMP
NEEDED!

FREE BOOK OFFER
FREEPOST NAT 10298
RICHMOND
TW9 1BR

NO STAMP
NECESSARY
IF POSTED IN
THE U.K. OR N.I.

me.' He tilted her face towards him and gently stroked away the worst of the dirt. Then he let her drink a little more. 'Better?'

Cassie nodded. She was still shaking, but not so violently. 'Yes, though I don't deserve to be. I'm so sorry. I know I've been stupid.'

'Extremely.'

His voice was uncompromising, though his touch had been tender. She couldn't see his expression, could make out only the white shape of his robes. Was he angry? Probably. She deserved that. Whatever happened now, the inevitable result must be her return to England in disgrace. She had, by her own foolish actions, proved to be a most unreliable governess. 'I'm sorry,' she said again. 'The last thing I intended was to put you in harm's way.'

Jamil's teeth showed white. 'You did not. I know this desert like my own body. But you—you could easily have died had I not found you. What on earth possessed you? Was it Linah? She told me what she had said to you.'

'It wasn't really Linah's fault,' she said in a very small voice. 'That was just the final straw. Last night—I should not have allowed you to—encouraged you to—I should not have. I'm so ashamed. I'm sorry.'

'You are sorry! It is I who should apologise to you. I took advantage of your innocence and of your situation. It was wrong of me.'

'You didn't take advantage.'

'I would have,' Jamil said harshly, 'if you had not asked me to stop.'

'But you did stop, Jamil. Immediately. I'm such a stupid fool, I didn't realise that a kiss could lead to such—because I have never...' Cassie faltered to a halt, sensing, rather than seeing, Jamil's intense gaze upon her. She had been rehearsing her apology over and over while huddling in the shelter of the rocks, for it kept her from panicking about the possibility that no one would find her and she would perish in the desert, but what had seemed so clear was now hopelessly muddled. Jamil did not blame her, but himself. Had she not, then, behaved wantonly?

'Do you regret what happened?' She blurted the words out without thinking. The question hung in the air between them, heavy with implications. 'I should not have asked you that, you don't need to...'

'No.'

'What?'

'No, I do not regret it.' The truth, but was it wise to have spoken it? His anger had fled, sped on its way by Cassie's unexpected and wholly disarming honesty. His own honour dictated a matching of the truth with the truth, no matter that it revealed more of himself than he intended. In the dark of the cave, such revelations were, in any case, somehow easier. Jamil found her hand and clasped it between his. 'I cannot regret it, though honour decrees that I should, for you were in my care.'

She thought about this for some moments. 'You were not shocked by my behaviour?'

Jamil laughed softly. 'On the contrary. I thought it was obvious that I was excited by it. As you were by mine at first, were you not?'

The conversation had taken off into wholly unchartered territory. It was not a conversation Cassie could ever have imagined. Such intimate feelings were the domain of the great poets, but she had never encountered a poem that came close to expressing what she was experiencing at this moment. Aunt Sophia would be utterly appalled. But Aunt Sophia was thousands of miles away in England and Cassie was in the middle of a desert, quite alone with a desert prince, and what precedent was there for that situation? None. So...

'It frightened me a little,' she confessed in a whisper.

'What did?'

'The strength of feeling it evoked in me. It was as if—as if I were caught in a whirlpool and could do nothing to escape.'

'And yet you wanted it to overwhelm you?'

Cassie nodded, then realised he probably couldn't see her doing so. 'Yes,' she admitted. 'Was that wrong?'

'On the contrary, it was very right. In my country, Cassie, it is not only permissible but expected that women enjoy the sharing of passion as much as men.'

'Oh.'

'They can, you know, I promise you.'

'Can they?' A new idea. An exciting one. Illicit? In England maybe, but not here. Jamil was still holding her hand. Somehow, Cassie didn't know how, she had edged so close to him that they were sitting with their legs touching, thigh to thigh. She felt safe. Jamil had already proved himself entirely honourable. But in another sense she wasn't safe at all, because she didn't want to be.

'In my country,' Jamil continued, 'it is in fact expected that women experience pleasure. It is a man's responsibility to ensure that she does.'

This statement, so loaded with unimaginable possibilities, was also entirely contrary to the little Cassie knew about intimate relations. Aunt Sophia had quite clearly implied that such duties were unpleasant. Celia, on the other hand, seemed to enjoy hers. Pleasure was not a word that Cassie had given much thought to. She found reading pleasurable, and walking in the countryside, and dancing, but she hadn't ever associated it with love-making before. Did this mean then, that pleasure and love-making were actually quite separate things? Could one take pleasure without first giving one's heart? Was *not* giving one's heart perhaps a prerequisite? With only Augustus as an example, Cassie was forced to conclude that this might well be true. She had foresworn love, but Jamil was not talking about love and seemed to be implying that she need not foreswear pleasure. *What did he mean?*

'Can one—can a woman, then—are there different ways of taking pleasure?' she asked, shocking herself and throwing caution to the winds at the same time. If she did not ask, she would never know, and it was not likely that there would ever be anyone she could ask again, under cover of the dark, cut off from the disapproving glances of society.

Jamil smiled in the darkness. 'There are infinite ways of taking pleasure, and infinite ways of giving it.'

'Oh.' In truth, she was already beyond reason. Last night Jamil had opened a door for her. She had taken a step over the portal and what she had seen had awed her, tempted her, thrilled her, but frightened her a little with its very newness. An unknown world was not, after all, to be entered without a little trepidation. She had turned her back on it last night with one word. No. But today? Today she wanted to experience that forbidden world, for if she did not, it would not exist tomorrow.

She was under no illusions about that. Jamil would not tolerate the blurring of the two worlds if she were to return to look after Linah, nor would she wish it. Though he had not actually said he would show her, she knew from the sound of his voice, from the tension in his body, touching but not touching hers, that he would if she asked him to. He had not said so, but he did not need to. All she had to do was ask. Her throat was dry, though not from thirst. She moistened her lips. 'Jamil, would you show me…?'

Her voice did not sound like her own, it was too husky, almost croaky, but he understood her all the same. 'Do you want me to?' he asked.

'Yes. Do you want to?'

'Very much.'

Very much. It was that, his wanting her, rather than the promise of what he would show her, that swayed

Cassie. She had never been wanted in such a way. Not for her looks or for her family, but just for herself. The words, spoken in a soft growl, gave her delicious shivers. He wanted her. Just her. Though what he wanted to do to her—and what she was to do in return—she had no idea.

'You need do nothing, but enjoy,' Jamil said, as if he had read her thoughts. 'My pleasure will be in pleasuring you; I ask nothing in return. What I really want, my lovely Cassie, I cannot have. What I can have must suffice instead.' It was no lie. Though he ached to possess her, to do so would be a transitory relief compared to the guilt such dishonourable behaviour would inflict upon his soul. He would give, and she would receive, and he would therefore always be her first. That, no one could ever take from him.

'I don't understand.'

'But you will,' Jamil said confidently.

Then he kissed her, and the flames that had been subdued last night flickered immediately into life. The touch of his lips upon hers kindled a fire, the tangle of his tongue with hers stoked it, the stroking, soothing, rousing feel of his hands on her neck, her arms, her back, made a furnace of her. Cassie took no persuading to abandon all maidenly modesty. Jamil kissed her and she stepped boldly into the palace of pleasure.

He kissed her deeply, but with restraint. She sensed the leashing of his passion in the tension in his shoulders. His kisses roused and enticed, but did not savage. He set her free, with his tongue and his hands and his lips, but he did not permit himself the same liberties. The pins were tugged from her hair, his fingers running through it, fanning it out over her shoulders. He helped her shrug free of her jacket, untied the fall of lace at her throat and kissed the rise and fall of her breasts. The sensation of his mouth on her flesh made her sigh and moan as her hands roamed over the muscles of his arms, his shoulders, his chest, until he stilled them, reminding her that this was about her pleasure, entreating her to be still.

So she was. He eased her back onto the sandy floor of the cave, careful of her bandaged ankle. He kissed her neck, soft plucking kisses that raised little bumps of sensation. He kissed the valley between her breasts and the knot in her belly began to tighten. Cursing softly under his breath, he freed her from the restraints of her corset and took her nipples in his mouth, one then the other, sucking and licking, circling, causing such sweet shards of delight to pierce her that another knot, different in tension, tingling and aching, began to tighten between her legs, as Jamil suckled and sucked and she began to feel herself unravel.

He kissed her mouth again, her breasts again, and then he eased up her skirts and kissed her knees, her thighs. She tensed, uncertain, unsure, not frightened, but she had never thought—kissing there? He touched her, stroking from her knee to her thigh, her thigh to her knee, up, down, up, down, and she relaxed. He kissed the crease at the top of her thigh and she tensed in quite a different way. His fingers now, stroking into the crease,

then fluttering over a more intimate fold, and she understood then, that this was the centre of her tension, and
she wanted him to release it, needed him to ease it,
couldn't bear for him not to as his fingers stroked and
then he kissed her there again—or at least it felt like
kissing—his tongue just easing a tiny fraction into her,
making her clench her fists, arch up, making her call
out *please, please, please*, because if she didn't he might
not and then she would surely die.

'Please,' she said again as he braced her, his hands
on her thighs. 'Please,' she panted as he kissed her intimately, his mouth on her moist core and then finally,
deliciously, his tongue flicked inside, and the pleasure
was unendurable, but she endured it because she knew
that there was more to come. He licked her again, slowly,
as she arched under him until her whole body was a knot
of tension screaming for release.

It came so suddenly that she gasped and bucked and
gasped again. A violent explosion that shattered her
as if she were glass, sparkling diamond fragments of
pleasure-like crystal, flying, floating, soaring, until she
was engulfed by it, coated in it, lying panting, mindless
and oblivious on the sandy floor of a dark cave in the
middle of the desert.

Jamil held her, pulling her into his arms to cradle
her, to stroke her hair, to kiss her neck, relishing the
shivering, pulsing, shaking aftermath of her climax,
deeply satisfied on one level that he had given her this
gift, struggling on quite another with the unexpectedly
primal urge to give her more. His shaft was hard and

heavily aching. His entire body was rigid with need, pulsing with anticipation, aching with pleasure denied. Cassie, slumberous and soft and infinitely desirable, was also, in her current state, infinitely compliant. Her fingers plucked at his tunic, her body nestled closer into his. His erection pressed demandingly against her. Her mouth, her lips, were soft on his neck. He longed to feel her skin on his. He knew she wanted it, too.

But she wanted it because of what he had done. And he had promised himself, as well as her, to keep her safe. It was enough. It would have to be. Jamil tried to ease himself away, but Cassie mumbled a soft protest, snuggling agonisingly closer. He could not bring himself to make the final break, not yet. 'Sleep,' he said, hushing her, soothing her hair, 'sleep.' She mumbled his name, but, drowsy with satisfaction, made no further protest. Cassie slept. Outside the cave, the storm raged. Inside the cave, Jamil waited for a different tempest to subside. It took a long, long time to do so.

She awoke in his arms. For a few delicious moments, almost afraid to breathe lest she disturb him, Cassie allowed herself to wonder what it would be like to wake in his arms every morning. To feel safe, and wanted, and cherished. To feel this delightfully floaty, blissful, can't-tell-which-bit-is-me feeling. To have her body melded into his like this every day. What would that be like? And what would it be like if he had truly made love to her? Would she feel even more blissful?

Was it possible to feel even more blissful?

Ought she not to be feeling rather the opposite?

No. She would not regret, and she would not allow herself to feel shame. What had happened had been wonderful. More than wonderful. She would not allow its memory to be tainted, or the colours dimmed—it was too precious. It felt too right.

Right?

But it could not be right. It must be wrong, it must be—every tenet of her upbringing ought to tell her that! And if it did not yet, then surely it would soon. Very soon. Just as soon as she left this dream-like experience behind and returned to real life. As Jamil's daughter's governess, not his—his doxy!

The word made her smile, such a picture of decadence as it conjured up. But then her smile faded. She might not be a painted harlot, but that is surely how she had behaved, how the world would view it, even if she did not. If the world ever found out. Which it would, of a surety, if it happened again, and it would happen again because there was no getting away from the simple, plain fact that she found Jamil irresistible, and now that he had introduced her to the delightful world of sensuality, she would find it impossible to refuse his invitation to join him there again. And the world would know, for it would be writ large on her face, for everyone to see: Cassandra Armstrong, fallen woman.

She would be disgraced. She would have disgraced her family. And Celia, too, for she could not stay in the palace under such circumstances, with everyone thinking her Jamil's concubine. Neither could she continue to serve as Linah's governess, since the occupant of that position must, as Jamil never tired of pointing out, have a stainless reputation. But the thought of leaving here made her panic. She most certainly did not want to leave.

Not yet. Not yet. Not yet.

Which meant this intimacy must not be repeated. Ever. This was the first time. And the last time. It had to be. Determined to imprint it for ever on her mind, Cassie turned her face into Jamil's chest, rubbed her cheek on the rough hair there and drank in that tantalising scent that was him. Just him. Outside, the storm had abated. Let him not wake, not yet, she thought, but even as she did so, he stirred.

For a fleeting moment, his arms tightened around her. She felt the whisper of his kiss on the top of her head. Or she hoped she did. Then he gently put her from him and got to his feet, straightening his robe. 'The storm has passed,' he said brusquely, heading for the mouth of the cave. 'When you are ready, we will be on our way.'

Jamil did not look at her, or speak to her again, waiting outside while she righted her clothing, the short distance between them seeming, after such intimacy, more like an unconquerable gulf than a mere few yards. Despite her resolution to create just such a distance, Cassie was hurt by it. Too caught up in the novelty of her own feelings, she had not had a chance to analyse his, but now it struck her forcefully that she had no clue at all about them. His face was impassive. The shutters were closed. *Did he even care?*

Outside, the desert seemed to have shifted its contours, with new dunes formed where none had been, flat rippled sand where before there had been rolling hills. A landscape as altered as Cassie's own feelings, as alien to her as Jamil's. Sitting astride the black stallion in front of him, her back pressed close against his chest, his arm tight around her waist, she looked around her in bewilderment. 'How do you know which way to go?' she asked, relieved to be able to break the ominous silence that was growing between them. 'It looks so different.'

'A man who navigates by the shifting sands is like to be a dead man,' Jamil replied, his voice cold as he urged his horse into motion. 'I set my course by the stars.'

Night was falling, but the storm-cleared sky was lit by an almost-full moon. As they headed back towards the oasis where Cassie's horse was tethered, the silence between them became tangible. The oppressive heat had given way to more balmy conditions. Save for the soft fall of the horse's hooves on the sand, the occasional scuffle of some night creature, silence reigned. The journey should have been the very essence of romance, just the two of them on a black stallion galloping across the desert under the stars, bathed in the warm glow of sated passion, she held close in the arms of the man who was, just for the moment, her desert prince. It should have been romantic, but Cassie was aware, horribly aware, that this journey marked not a lovers' meeting, but a lovers' parting.

Not that they had been truly lovers. How she wished they had. But she must not wish that. If only she knew what *he* was thinking. Except maybe she didn't really want to know. Cassie sighed wearily.

Jamil tightened his arm around her distractedly. He had not planned what had happened. Despite the fact that, from that very first encounter in the tent, he had been unable to banish his desire for Cassie, he had until now at least succeeded in constraining it. The position she held in the royal household, coupled with a conviction that the reality of her would never live up to his imagination, had ensured he did so. Now, he had abused one and proved conclusively the falseness of the other, rousing unfamiliar emotions he had no precedent for dealing with.

He wanted her. More than ever. Giving her pleasure had given him pleasure. A strange satisfaction it had been, unsated, but satisfaction nevertheless. Jamil cursed himself for a fool. He shifted in the saddle, trying to create even a fraction of distance between himself and the distractingly soft bundle he was holding, but it was to no avail. The horse's gentle jogging brought Cassie's delightfully rounded bottom immediately back into contact with his embarrassingly persistent erection. What was it about this infuriating Englishwoman that so got under his skin? He could have any woman he desired and yet he was drawn to this one, a woman who had the ability to confuse him, rouse feelings in him he had spent a lifetime subduing. Well, he would put an end to it. It was time to re-establish order and control in his life. Enough of this mawkish dabbling in emotions. No matter how much he wanted her, the simple fact was that Cassie must remain strictly out of bounds.

They had arrived at the Maldissi Oasis. The grey mare whinnied a welcome as they approached. Jamil dismounted and helped Cassie down. She winced as she put weight on her injured ankle, but shook her head at his offer of support. 'I can manage.' The pain that shot up her leg from her injury had jolted her into reality. Jamil's silence spoke volumes. She sensed a speech coming and braced herself.

'What transpired between us must not happen again,' Jamil said.

She hung her head, lest he see the foolish tears that sprang to her eyes. That he was right, that it was just what she'd thought herself, did nothing to alleviate the stab of what felt decidedly like rejection.

'Cassie, you do see that?' Jamil said, tilting her chin up with his finger.

'I know, I know,' Cassie interrupted, jerking her face away, 'No doubt you bitterly regret it.'

Jamil hesitated, then shook his head. 'I don't, I cannot.'

She couldn't help it, her heart gave a little flutter. 'Nor can I,' Cassie said softly, just touching his arm with her hand.

He grasped her hand firmly. 'I am—relieved,' he said picking his words with care, 'but it changes nothing.

Our actions must not be repeated, you understand that, Cassie?'

She forced herself to smile, though it felt very much like a grimace. 'I understand, Jamil, completely. And I want you to know that I'm very conscious of the… the honour you do me in investing such…such trust in me—and I can assure you that I will do my very best to make sure it is not misplaced.'

Once again, her willingness to shoulder the whole burden of responsibility touched him, where recriminations, probably quite justified recriminations, would have set his back up. Jamil's smile was wry. 'I am sure you will, but I think it best if our noble intentions are fortified by some more practical considerations. There are conditions attached,' he said, thinking bitterly that his whole life seemed to have conditions attached. 'We must not be alone in each other's presence. Any contact must be in relation to Linah only. I require these terms to be strictly observed. You do see that it's for the best, don't you?'

'Of course. Absolutely. Definitely.' Stoically ignoring the ominous sinking feeling in her heart, Cassie took a deep breath and held out her hand. 'In my country, we shake hands on a treaty.'

Jamil took her hand, but instead of shaking it, pressed a kiss. On her wrist. Then on her palm. Then on each of her fingertips. 'I am not in your country, more's the pity,' he said enigmatically. 'You, on the other hand, are in mine.'

Settling herself in the saddle, trying to be pleased

by the bargain she had just struck, which had, after all, granted her exactly what she wished, Cassie cast a longing eye back at the sandy blue waters of the Maldissi Oasis. Another opportunity for a midnight dip gone. She was beginning to doubt there would be another.

Chapter Eight

For the second time in his life, Peregrine Finchley-Burke, formerly, for an embarrassingly brief period, of the East India Company, currently acting in a junior capacity within the large confines of the British Consulate in Cairo, found himself in the unenviable position of being required to assist the estimable Lord Armstrong in the recovery of one of his daughters. For it to happen once, Peregrine considered himself unlucky. For it to have happened a second time, he began to consider himself cursed.

'Why the blasted fellow had to have so many of 'em, and why he ain't able to keep them closer to home, I don't know,' muttered Lord Wincester, the Consul General, known to Lord Henry Armstrong and his other fellow Harrovians as Wincie. 'First it was the eldest getting herself kidnapped…'

'Not actually kidnapped, my lord,' Peregrine

reminded him gently, 'Lady Celia was being held for her own safety in the royal palace at Balyrma.'

'Aye, so you told me, and to be fair you were directly involved,' Lord Wincester agreed testily, 'but I'm pretty certain, despite all the hush-hush afterwards, that there was a damn sight more to it than that.'

'Lady Celia's marriage to Prince Ramiz was an excellent alliance for the crown, my lord,' Peregrine said tactfully.

It was undoubtedly true that Prince Ramiz's principality of A'Qadiz was endowed with a most convenient port on the Red Sea, a port that had already proved invaluable to Britain in opening up a faster route to India, but Peregrine was not telling, as Lord Wincester suspected, the whole truth. Even now, two years after the event, the memory of that trip to Balyrma with Lord Armstrong could still make Peregrine sweat. His journey to take up his position with the East India Company had been fatally interrupted by the affair and he had been offered a posting with the diplomatic service as a reward, Lord Armstrong had made clear, for his continued discretion. And Peregrine had in turn remained obdurately discreet. He had not spoken, not once, not even in his letters to his dear nanny, Lalla Hughes, about that scene in the royal palace harem, a fact for which Lord Wincester had not quite forgiven him.

Though Peregrine had dreamed of diplomatic glory in Cairo, operating at the hub of British relations with the crumbling Ottoman Empire, it had been mundane diplomatic graft that had sustained him over the last

years. Humble had been his beginnings in the Consulate, and humble they remained. Peregrine was Lord
Wincester's preferred dogsbody, for which role he was
rewarded by also serving as the butt of Lord Wincester's rather cumbersome wit. The kind of Old Harrovian
wit that found the placing of a pig's bladder filled with
water under Peregrine's pillow, or the replacement of
snuff with pepper, hysterically funny. Peregrine endured
such japes with unabated good humour—being an Old
Harrovian himself, he had, in fact, made a career out of
providing his school fellows with a willing victim—but
the truth was that he would take them in even better
part if only his genial suffering were complemented by
even the tiniest element of progression in his diplomatic
career.

Lord Wincester drummed his fingers on the walnut
veneer of his imposing desk, and frowned over the communiqué, sent express in the diplomatic bag, from Lord
Armstrong. 'Nothing for it, Perry, but you're going to
have to go and fetch the damned girl,' he said. 'She's in
Daar-el-Abbah, can't quite remember where that is.'

Peregrine rolled to his feet and studied the large map
of Arabia which was laid out upon one of the long side-
tables under the window. 'Here, just next to A'Qadiz,'
he said.

'Hmm. Might make sense for you to take a detour
then. Consult her sister, Lady Celia.'

'May I ask, my lord, what exactly it is I am required
to do?' Peregrine asked tentatively.

Lord Wincester's copious eyebrows shot up in

surprise, looking rather like two furry caterpillars. 'Do? Haven't I just told you, go and fetch the girl.'

'But which girl? Lord Armstrong has five daughters.'

'Lady Cassandra. You surely remember her—quite a little beauty, as I recall, even if she was prone to fits of histrionics.'

Peregrine paled. Lady Cassandra was the most beautiful woman he had ever met, and quite the most intimidating. It had been she who had persuaded him to escort her and her father and that terrifying aunt of hers across the desert. Persuaded him with those big blue eyes and those big luscious... He coloured, coughed and shuffled forwards to position himself in the shade of the map table. 'Lady Cassandra. How—what...?'

Lord Wincester chuckled. 'Locked up in Sheikh al-Nazarri's harem, or so Henry seems to think. Don't believe a word of it myself—though mind you, if I was the sheikh and she was in my palace—but there, I'm sure Henry's exaggerating. Don't need me to tell you, mind, that if he's not, the utmost discretion is needed. Henry's marked her down for one of Wellington's protégés, don't want the goods tainted. At least,' Lord Wincester added with a chuckle, 'if they're tainted, don't want any word of it getting back to Blighty. Do you understand me, Perry?'

Peregrine goggled.

'Right. Expect you'll want to be off in jig time,' the Consul General said, rubbing his hands together in a gesture that made Peregrine think ominously of

Pontius Pilate. It was a gesture of which Lord Wincester was rather fond. He slapped Peregrine's back in what he hoped was a reassuring manner, handed him Lord Armstrong's epistle and exited in search of much-needed refreshment in the form of his latest shipment of port, which had arrived with the diplomatic bag from Lisbon.

Alone in the office, Peregrine sank on to the extremely uncomfortable gilded chair that faced the great man's desk, and perused the letter with a growing sense of horror. Clutching his pomaded locks in his sweaty palms, he grasped at the only straw he could think of. 'Lady Celia,' he said fervently to himself. He sincerely hoped she would prove the answer to his prayers.

Back in Daar, both Cassie and Jamil strictly observed their new rules of engagement. Superficially at least, it seemed to work. Cassie thought of life in the royal palace of Daar as being like a Persian carpet, the surface depicting their day-to-day life, but underneath the strands were stretched and tangled with the multi-hued threads of desire. And then she would chide herself for her overheated romantic sensibilities and concentrate on the task in hand.

She continued to enjoy every day spent with Linah, whose new-found thirst for knowledge was second only to her new-found hunger for the company of her beloved pony and adored *Baba*. Linah was a rewarding pupil. She would always be highly strung, her temper would never be anything other than volatile, but with the correct balance of mental and physical exercise, the days of her tantrums were finally, truly in the past. Everyone in the palace commented on the changes in her, and while Halim was reluctant to grant Cassie any credit, preferring to attribute this to the time his master spent with his daughter, Jamil did not stint in his admiration for Cassie's talents as a governess. He had even permitted a select group of other little girls to visit the palace. Linah was finally making friends.

Cassie should be pleased, thrilled even to receive such an endorsement of support from a man whose standards in all things were of the highest. She had proved herself, exactly as she had hoped. Her own papa, Aunt Sophia, even Celia would surely be impressed. But the satisfaction such an achievement should have given her eluded her. She never saw Jamil, except in company. They were never alone. He no longer visited the Scheherazade courtyard save at times he could be sure of Linah's presence. She missed their talks and their laughter and their outings. She missed him terribly, and no matter how many times a day she reminded herself it was for the best, every day she missed him more.

Jamil had, for a few precious moments out in the desert, been her lover, and because of that, he was now a stranger to her. It wasn't fair. It wasn't right. And yet anything else would be wrong. The conflicting thoughts fought for attention in her head. She could not sleep for thinking of him, for speculating in lurid, shocking and exciting detail what exactly were the many ways of giving pleasure he had spoken of. And the many ways of receiving. But in her dreams such thoughts would have to remain. Restless and aching with unfulfilled desire, she spent many hours pacing the perimeter of the courtyard in the star-strewn hours of the night.

Jamil, too, took to pacing his own private courtyard at night. He thought of Cassie more than he had thought it possible to think of anyone. He, who had never before had any problems in denying himself, was now tossed on a stormy sea of need, frustration and unsated passion.

The same arguments that rolled and roiled around Cassie's head played havoc with his orderly mind. He caught himself staring into space in the middle of Council. When setting off for the stables or the throne room or his own courtyard, he often found himself standing outside the schoolroom doors, as if his feet had a mind of their own, as if his entire body was conspiring against him in its efforts to slake its need. He knew Halim was worried about him. He was worried about himself. He had no solution, save to stay resolute in the hope that it would pass, comforted in the belief that at least Cassie remained oblivious, but perversely not comforted by that at all. For some reason, her thinking him indifferent was unacceptable, yet her thinking him indifferent was surely the point.

He had not realised, until it was denied him, how much he had come to enjoy her company. Cassie was witty, she was endearing and, most of all, she was never predictable. She made him laugh and even made him angry sometimes, when she disagreed with him, just to see how he reacted, and that made him laugh, too.

While she was never anything but deferential upon the rare occasions they were together in the public eye, in private she was not afraid to call him to account. She would not tolerate what she had confessed to calling his Corsair behaviour. He had never had a friend, a true companion, or wanted one. As a woman, Cassie could not possibly fulfil such a role, but it was exactly in that role that he missed her. Though not only in that role. There were other parts he wished her to play. Other lines he wished her to recite. Other deeds he would have her perform. If only.

He came upon her one day, walking in the palace rose garden. Her golden hair, burnished by the sun, was arranged in a simple knot on the top of her head, long tendrils curling down over her shoulders, flaxen wisps caressing her forehead. As usual, when alone, her head was uncovered. Her dress, palest lemon with a white sash tied at the waist, showed her curves to perfection. The sun had given her pale English skin a warm glow, an endearing scatter of freckles on her turned-up little nose.

From under cover of the terrace, hidden by a colonnade, he watched her. She tripped gracefully along the little paths between the rose beds, stooping every now and then to smell a bloom. This she did, as she ate, with relish, closing her eyes, her coral-pink mouth pouted into a delicious smile, completely unaware that she was being watched. She moved with the sensuous grace of a dancer. She looked so delectable that he could not be anything else but aroused by her as she flitted between the flowers, overshadowing their beauty, no English rose but something far more exotic. Jamil's manhood stirred, stiffened.

A statue of Ra, the Egyptian Sun God, stood at the centre of a riot of pink and peach, a gift to his mother from one of her relatives. Here, Cassie stopped and consulted what looked like a sheaf of papers. To his surprise, she threw her head back to look into the eyes of the marble god, casting an arm dramatically wide as if she were on the stage. She was clearly in what she had once told him, laughingly, her sister Celia referred to as her 'full Cassandra mode'. Intrigued, Jamil made his way around the terrace until he was behind her, then padded closer, the better to hear her performance.

'For Cassandra, upon the occasion of her accepting my hand,' Cassie intoned. Momentarily abandoning her pose, she addressed the statue in her normal voice. 'Would that I had not, for then in his misery perhaps Augustus would have been inspired to write something a little more accomplished.' She cleared her throat and began again.

Delectable gaoler, thou doth guard my faint heart,
In that most tempting of prisons, from where love doth start.
The bars that contain me from gossamer are made,
Manacles of beauty on my ankles are laid.

Cassie giggled. 'Poor Augustus, it really is quite dreadful,' she said to Ra. 'I'm not surprised you're looking so pained. I'm afraid there's more, though.

Trapped in my cell by thy loving embrace,
The key to my freedom is in thy sweet face.
A lifetime sentence will be mine 'ere long,
When I make you my bride, Cassandra Armstrong.

She finished with a deep curtsy. Standing only a few feet away, Jamil struggled to contain his laughter, resisting the urge to applaud only because he wished to see what she was going to do next—for he realised this was not just a performance, but a rite.

Cassie emerged from her curtsy with a regal nod at the sun god. 'I was going to read them all, but you know, I don't think I can bear it, and I see no reason why you should have to endure it either,' she told the statue. She shuffled the sheaf of paper, upon which, Jamil could now see, were numerous poems, all written in the same rather untidy scrawl.

Cassie took the first, and began to tear it into strips, then into scraps. 'Cast yourself upon the winds and fly,' she declaimed. 'Begone, ghost, begone.' With one extravagant gesture, she threw the shredded pieces of poetry into the air, twirling round as she did so, and coming face to face with Jamil. 'Oh! What a fright you gave me.' Colour flooded her face. 'How long have you been there?'

'Long enough to work out that your Augustus was not only a despicable man, but a truly mediocre poet.'

'Do you know, Jamil, I am positively glad now that he did abandon me. Only think, if he had not I may have had to listen to such doggerel every morning over the breakfast cups.'

'That would indeed have been tragic, though I would have thought that such a romantically inclined person as yourself would have been happy to listen to poetry at any time of the day.'

She slanted a look up at him from under her lashes. If she did not know him better, she would have said he was flirting with her. She could not resist being charmed, so beguilingly handsome was he, and so delightfully romantic the setting. 'True, but it depends upon the quality of the poetry.'

'I hope you find this to your taste,' Jamil said sweeping her theatrically into his arms. '"Shall I compare thee to a summer's day? Thou art more lovely, and more temperate." Your Mr Shakespeare's lines, but they could have been written for you, most lovely Cassandra.'

He kissed her then, what was meant to be a courtly kiss, a stage kiss, but the touch of her lips, warm and soft and yielding, lit a fire in him. Pulling her upright and close into his arms, he kissed her passionately and, with a soft moan of long pent-up need, she twined her arms around his neck and kissed him back with equal fervour. The heady scent of the roses wafting up as their clothes brushed the petals, the arid heat of the desert sun brightly blazing down upon them, the bitter-sweetness of the forbidden, gave to their kisses a romantic, never-to-be-repeated edge. Their lips drank deep, for they knew they would not drink again. They kissed, and kissed again, and again, until finally Jamil drew away. He was breathing heavily. His face was flushed, his eyes burning dark and golden.

'To quote another of your poets,' he said huskily, '"Since there's no help, come let us kiss and part."'

'"Nay, I have done,"' Cassie finished, with a sad little smile, '"you get no more of me."'

Picking up her skirts, she made her way swiftly out of the garden. The heavy door into the palace swung shut behind her. Jamil stood among the roses, as still and impassive as the statue of Ra. On the ground, unnoticed in the heat of passion, the torn remains of Augustus's poems swirled aimlessly in the breeze.

It was the time of the annual ceremony of Petitions, the traditional handing out of alms to the nomadic tribes. The week in the desert amongst his people, resolving disputes and acting as mediator in marriage negotiations, was usually one of Jamil's favourites, but this time he found himself unable to concentrate, wishing himself back at the palace. He missed Linah. He missed Cassie more—much, much more than was good for his peace of mind. He wondered if she missed him, too, and chastised himself for such mawkish thoughts, but could not banish them. Her face hovered before him each night as he drifted off into a troubled sleep. His body ached with unfulfilled longings. In the midst of a crowded tent filled with grateful tribesmen, in the middle of a celebration around a camp fire, surrounded by his loyal and adoring people, Jamil felt lonely. He was tired of being a prince, weary of being the all-seeing, all-knowing ruler. Cassie, only Cassie, saw him as a man. A man with flaws.

He was not invincible, and he was beginning to wonder why he had ever aspired to be so. Feelings, vague longings, long-suppressed emotions he hadn't even realised were there, seemed to be uncurling themselves, as if they had been hibernating and were now emerging blinking into the light, seeking a voice. But it was a voice only she could hear, and so it remained unspoken. And the silence hurt him. He missed her. It gradually dawned on him that only she could ease him. Whatever it was that ailed him.

Returning to Daar in the cool of the evening, his first impulse was to seek her out, but, knowing his daughter would be sleeping, and therefore unable to perform her role as unwitting chaperon, Jamil resisted the urge with immense difficulty. This self-imposed treaty of theirs was proving to be an agonising burden. Truthfully, he knew it would take very little temptation to break it. Very truthfully, what he wished was for something or someone to put temptation in his way.

Wearily, wishing he were headed in quite the opposite direction, Jamil made for the hammam. A long relaxing steam bath was just what he needed. At least, if it was not what he needed, it was what he could have.

Though each of the main palace courtyards had their

own bathing chambers, the hammam was housed in a separate building. It consisted of a series of interconnected rooms, each with a domed roof. Only the first, the changing room, had windows set high into the walls; the rest were completely enclosed. Impatiently dismissing the servants who would normally oversee the bathing ritual, Jamil stripped off his tunic, head dress and slippers and headed naked into the hot room. The plunge pool, a tiled bath of cold water constantly refreshed from a spring located deep underground, was octagonal in shape and formed the room's centrepiece. Ignoring the steps, Jamil launched into the icy depths, relishing the shock as the cold water enveloped his body, taking his breath away.

Emerging shivering, he threw himself down on one of the full-length marble tables which were arranged around the hot room, interspersed with little basins with gold taps which were built into niches in the round walls. Lying on his stomach, he closed his eyes, allowing the steam to envelop him, willing the heat to lull him into a much-needed torpor. Eventually, it did.

It had been Linah's suggestion that her governess make herself some looser-fitting clothes more appropriate to the desert climate. Cassie, who was heartily sick of the way her English garments, and in particular her English undergarments, clung to her skin, eagerly made the expedition to the souk for materials, accompanied by one of Linah's handmaidens. She did not know if Jamil would approve, but Jamil was not here to ask. His week-long absence attending the Petitions ceremony should have been a relief, a period for sensible reflection and acceptance of the boundaries that constrained their relationship, but though she tried—*how she tried*—it just wasn't working.

The more she tried not to think of him, the more she did. The more she told herself, sternly, that to think of *such* things was wrong, the more they crept, with startling, arousing clarity, into her dreams. Invoking Aunt Sophia made no difference. Telling herself the sacrifice was worth it for Linah's sake made no difference either, Cassie was ashamed to admit. What had happened in the cave had changed her for ever. She could not now un-know. She could not help wanting to know more. She could not—would not—have it undone. And she was pretty certain that Jamil felt the same.

That was the difficult part. She caught him watching her, time after time, when he thought himself unobserved. She saw the look of naked desire on his face and it made her own flare and flame. She recognised it from her mirror, that desire. It was not only she who was denying herself. She *could* deny herself, but how she wanted. Ached. Yearned. Pined, wickedly wished for the fates to throw them together, alone, just once more. She would not resist the fates. She was pretty certain Jamil would not either. But the fates, unfortunately for Cassandra, seemed quite oblivious of her wishes.

As usual, everyone save her was asleep. As usual, Cassie was restless. Deciding to take a walk around the palace grounds, she donned one of her new outfits for the first time. A pair of loose pantaloons, which Linah told her were called sarwal or harem pants, pleated at the waist, billowing out over her legs, then gathered in at her ankles with a beautifully worked piece of braid studded with little pearls, they were made of dark blue gauzy material, which rustled alluringly when she walked. Over these rather daring items, she wore a long silk caftan in her favourite cerulean blue, slit almost to the top of her legs to allow ease of movement, with long, loose sleeves, finished with the same braiding that ornamented her sarwal pants and fastened down the front with a long row of tiny pearl buttons. Little slippers, also pearl-studded, of the softest leather she'd ever come across, covered her feet. Aside from a tiny scrap of silk like a sleeveless shirt, she wore nothing else. No stays, no chemise, no petticoats, no stockings. Her hair was combed down, held back from her face with a tortoise-shell clip, a gift from Linah.

Looking at herself in the mirrored tiles of her bathing chamber, Cassie was confronted by an exotic creature, the curves of her body quite clearly defined through the softly draped clothes, though in fact there was little actual flesh on show, and the neckline of her caftan was much higher than her day dresses. Despite this, she knew Aunt Sophia would be shocked, not just at her lack of English corsetry, but by the way such a lack allowed her body to move freely, and for the movements to be quite apparent as she walked.

Was she verging on the indecent? Aunt Sophia would say so, but Celia would not—Celia herself dressed all the time in just such garments. And Linah's servants, too, though their clothes were plainer, wore no more than these three items of clothing and slippers. When in Rome, and all that. In any case, no one would see her, not at this time of night. It was just a question of becoming accustomed to unfamiliar garments, and she could not do that if these lovely new clothes lay unworn in the chest in her sleeping chamber.

Reassured, Cassie opened the door of the courtyard. The guards were too well trained to display any reaction, and, as she had hoped, she met no one else. With the rose garden strictly out of bounds in her mind, Cassie wandered off to the opposite end of the palace, where a strangely shaped building stood surrounded by shady palms. Intrigued by the series of little domed-roof rooms, assuming from the lack of guards that it was some sort of summer house or perhaps even a plant house, Cassie opened the large door and stepped inside.

The walls of the changing room were not marble, but tiled, Roman-style, with intricate mosaic pictures of various gods, some of whom she recognised, some not. The images were what Aunt Sophia would most decidedly have called *warm*. Men and women entwined in any number of embraces. Cassie, examining them more closely, found herself blushing. And wondering. These images were designed to stimulate, and they did, providing her with some astonishingly arousing images of herself and Jamil doing those very same things.

Captivated, entranced by now being able to give some form to her own already fevered imagination, Cassie followed the mosaics round the room, growing more and more heated as she tried to picture Jamil doing *this*, or herself doing *that*. By the time she came to a break, formed by the door opposite the one by which she had entered, she was flushed, and not particularly from the heat of the room. Realising now that she must be in the Roman-style baths the locals called a hammam, she hesitated with her hand on the handle, but no one would be taking a steam bath at this time of night. Besides, there had been no sign of the attendants, and she wanted to see more of these mosaics. She suspected that in the next room they would have progressed to even more compromising positions, the kind of compromising positions Jamil called pleasure. If she could not experience, at least she could understand.

The door opened silently. Closing it behind her, Cassie's vision was momentarily obscured by the cloud of steam that rose up to meet the cooler air. The room was fiercely hot, the air damp and extremely humid, lit by oil lamps built into the walls. Her silk tunic began to mould itself to her skin.

She didn't notice him at first. The plunge pool attracted her attention. Stopping down, she dipped her fingers in the icy water, dabbing some of it on to her temples. Standing up again, slightly giddy with the cloying heat, she saw that someone was lying flat on a marble bed. A man. A naked man. With an exclamation of dismay, she was about to head quickly out of the room, when he looked up. Autumn eyes. Even through the haze there was no mistaking them, or their owner.

'Jamil!'

He had been dreaming of her, and now here she was, clad most alluringly in silk and organdie, the damp material clinging deliciously to her curves. She stood rooted to the spot, her eyes wide, fixed upon him. He remembered he was naked, save for the small strip of towel upon which he lay. His robe was in the changing room. The larger bathing towels were kept in the warm room. There was no way to avoid her seeing him. Part of him relished the prospect.

This thought startled him, for though many women had admired his body, Jamil was very far from being a vain man. Cassie looked delectable, with her skin flushed and her hair clustering in damp tendrils on her brow. The caftan suited her. The sarwal pants showed her shapely legs to perfection. 'Cassie.' Desire gripped him. She was here, just as if the gods had gifted her to him, dressed as if they had done so for his pleasure. This time, he would not—*could not*—resist.

'Jamil. I didn't know anyone was here.'

'You look delectable.'

A blush stole over her already heated skin. She stared at him, as if mesmerised. Had she not been wishing, only a few moments ago, for just this? Had the fates finally thrown her an opportunity? If so, would it be wrong to ignore it? 'I should go,' she said uncertainly.

'*No!* Don't go. No one will disturb us here. Stay.' Jamil held out his hand towards her.

She didn't seem able to move, in any case. Her feet in their seed-pearl slippers seemed to have taken root on the tiled floor. Her eyes were riveted on his body. She could not force them to look away. She had seen naked statues and she had seen paintings of naked gods, but nothing had prepared her for the reality of this man. He was quite beautiful, and so very, very different from her. The breadth of his shoulders tapered down to a trim waist. His back was muscled, his buttocks taut, his legs long, rough with hair. His skin was the same golden colour all over. All around him, on the walls, the gods sported together, coupling intimately. The steam was making her light-headed. She was hot, her clothes were damp and clinging. She couldn't seem to breathe properly.

She wanted to touch him. She wanted to run her fingers down the long line from his neck down his spine to the slope of his buttocks. 'I really ought to go,' she said breathlessly, but still made no move.

'No,' Jamil said softly. 'This was meant. You see that, don't you?'

She nodded, and with her nod cast farewell to the last of her reservations. It was meant. It was inevitable and they both knew it.

'Come here, Cassandra,' he commanded.

She did. As if in a trance, she skirted the pool and stood beside him, looking down at him. Her eyes were wide, her pupils dark. Her lips were plump and ripe. Beneath her caftan, her nipples peaked against the silk.

He did not want to frighten her, but he could not lie here for ever. Jamil sat up swiftly, deftly wrapping the towel around his waist, covering up the all-too-obvious evidence of his arousal. It was enough, barely.

'I was looking at the pictures on the walls,' Cassie said, still gazing at the far more beguiling picture in front of her.

'Touching is much more sensual than merely looking,' Jamil said, taking her hands and placing them on his shoulders.

She ran her fingers down his arms, to where the soft downy hair began, back up to his shoulders, following the contours of his muscles, down to the swell of his chest. There she stopped, unsure, shocked, aroused. 'I can't,' she whispered, all the time thinking, *can I*?

He took her hand between his, pulling her closer so that she was standing between his legs. Slowly, he undid her caftan, making a play of each button, giving her time to move, to leave, holding his breath lest she did. The final button ceded to him. The tunic fell in a crumpled heap on to the floor. She stood before him, blushing wildly, but holding his gaze, her excitement mirroring his in the rapidity of her breathing, in the swelling of her nipples, clearly visible now through the thin layer of silk that covered them.

Jamil bent his head to envelop one hard bud with his mouth, breathing through the silk on to her skin. She moaned, and slumped forwards, supporting herself on his shoulders. He did the same to the other nipple and was rewarded with another soft little moan. 'Touch me, Cassie,' he whispered huskily, taking her hand and placing it on his chest, untying the silk top at the same time to release her breasts to his ministrations. 'Make me feel what you are feeling.'

Jamil stroked the creamy skin of her breasts, cupping their weight in his hands, suckling with his mouth, tugging and licking and caressing. Heat that had nothing to do with the steam room flushed her skin as her body remembered and rejoiced and then began to clamour for more. More of his touch. More of hers. She ran her hands over his chest, smoothing them against the hard wall of muscle, dipping down, to the concave of his stomach under his rib cage. His skin felt so different. His touch made her shiver and heat and shiver. The yearning she'd felt since the last time he'd touched her, which she thought sometimes she'd been feeling since she'd first set eyes on him, made it impossible to do anything other than comply with his wishes. For they were her wishes, too.

He kissed her passionately, his tongue tangling with hers, his hands on her waist, pulling her closer, crushing her breasts against his chest. His hands skimmed her hips, loosening the sarwal pants. Eager to please, eager to learn, eager for his touch, she kicked off her slippers and stepped out of the pantaloons. She was completely naked. She was hardly ever naked, save in the privacy of her own bath. She should have been embarrassed, but the sharp intake of breath, the blaze of something primitive in Jamil's eyes, told her that she pleased him.

Shyly, she stood while he freed her hair from the clip that held it, smoothing it out over her shoulders, each touch, each look, telling her how much he liked what he saw, giving her confidence, feeding the fire in her belly, making her quiver with what she now realised was desire. Byron's *effusions that spring from the heart*, which truly did *throb with delight*.

'Beautiful,' Jamil whispered into her ear, and then words in his own language she could not understand, though she did not have to, for they curled round her like wisps of smoke. He stood and the cloth that covered him dropped to the floor between them. Automatically, Cassie looked down, flushed fiery red at what she saw and looked away.

'Don't be frightened,' Jamil said.

'I'm—I'm not.' She wanted to look again, she wanted to look at him as he looked at her, but it was shameful, surely? The statues she had seen had been either discreetly draped or—or—or not at all like Jamil.

He tipped her chin up with his finger, forcing her to meet his gaze, a smouldering blaze of gold. 'We have five senses, Cassie. We can touch.' His thumb grazed the tip of her nipple. 'We can smell.' He nuzzled her neck. 'We can hear,' he whispered, licking the shell of her ear. 'We can taste,' he said, licking into her mouth, 'and we can see. Each adds to the pleasure of the others. Don't you want to look?'

He took a step back from her, and Cassie looked. From his handsome countenance, her eyes travelled down, his shoulders, his chest, his belly, faltered at the thin line of hair arrowing down, then followed it, to the scimitar arc of his erection. Such strength. She could not imagine how—but already, thanks to the mosaics, she was imagining.

He pulled them both onto the tiles so that they sat facing each other, legs entwined, close enough to touch, and to kiss. Smothering kisses. Flesh on flesh. Damp skin on damp skin. Hot steam, hotter passion. His hands were on her thighs now, on her flank, then on the soft skin on the inside, stroking into the source of heat nestled between them. She could feel the same mounting, clutching tension as before, only this time it was not frightening. This time she embraced it, welcomed it, sought it. His fingers slipped inside her, and softly caressed the hardening source of it all.

When Jamil spoke his voice was ragged, as if, like she, he was having difficulty breathing. 'Do you like this, Cassie?'

'Yes.'

'And this?'

'Yes.' His touch, stroking and circling and thrusting, was taking her to the precipice over which she longed to jump, but this time she wanted more. She wanted to take him with her. She wanted him to fall into the dark abyss of pleasure, too. 'Jamil, can I—will you let me…?'

'Yes. Yes, touch me, Cassie.' He placed her hands on his manhood. Unexpectedly smooth, silky smooth and hard. 'Like this,' Jamil said, showing her how to stroke him, his breath coming faster, showing her that she pleased him. A small groan escaped him. She stroked again, and he groaned again, and then he resumed his stroking, too, and almost immediately it started, the slow build, the faster climb, the pause, the excruciatingly exciting pause at the top as he held her there, touching but not enough, and her own inexpert touch on his shaft became more confident, and she felt him tighten and swell, echoing a swelling and tightening in her, and she stroked again and heard his low guttural cry of release mingle with her own soft, wild cries, his hot seed spilling onto her hand, and then she fell, fell, fell, and floated like before, only more because this time she was not alone. She had pleasured and was pleasured in return. Here in the steam room surrounded by images of pleasure, she had opened another new door.

'Byron was right,' she murmured rather incoherently into Jamil's shoulder, lying damp and sated, clasped tight.

Chapter Nine

Jamil did not want to move. Once his needs were slaked, he usually desired to be alone, for a melancholy stole over him that he never wished to share. This time, however, the familiar ennui failed to appear. The pulsing pleasure of his climax held him headily high, then floated him gently back to earth as if on a magic carpet. His body felt heavy, his limbs reluctant to move. Limp and damp and warm in his arms, Cassie felt every bit as delightful as he had imagined. His release had come with more force than he had ever experienced before, but, amazingly, his manhood was stirring again.

'Hot,' Cassie murmured, opening her eyes, gazing up at him with the unmistakable look of a sated woman.

Jamil's erection hardened. Instead of sadness, he felt a sudden, unexpected surge of joy. 'How hot?'

Cassie stirred, easing herself away with some

difficulty, for their skin was slippery with sweat. 'Too hot.'

Jamil got lithely to his feet, pulling her with her. 'So you want to cool down?'

Confused by the laughter in his eyes, by the smile she could see trembling on his kiss-frayed lips, Cassie eyed him uncertainly. 'What do you mean?' Catching the direction of his glance, she saw the plunge pool and remembered its icy feel. 'No,' she squealed, but it was too late. Before she could stop him, he picked her up and jumped in, holding her close, laughing as she screamed when the water hit her, kissing her protesting mouth into submission as they emerged, standing shivering in the waist-high pool, Cassie still clasped tight to his chest, kissing until desire took them once more, and Jamil carried her up the shallow steps and through the next door into the warm room. The place the Romans called the *tepidarium* was designed for cleansing, and was amply supplied with scented oils and fragrant soaps. It was also equipped with an ingenious device that sprinkled warm water over the body. Designed like a fountain, the water shot out from the mouths of a shoal of little golden fishes built into a niche in the wall, controlled by a tap in the form of a conch shell.

Cassie jumped when the first jets of water sprinkled her body, and then, as the warm water drenched her, smiled with delight at its soothing touch. Picking up an enormous sponge and lathering it with jasmine-scented soap, Jamil stepped into the jets with her and began another long, slow onslaught of her body. He might not be able to take her in the way he most wanted, but he could ensure that she never forgot him. The sponge swept over the delightful curves of her, down her spine, the slope of her bottom, up to her breasts, where the nipples peaked rosily, begging for his attention. The sponge fell to the floor as Jamil fell upon her hungrily.

She couldn't believe it could happen again so quickly. Kissing, touching, wanting, starting slowly before becoming more urgent. She could feel Jamil's erection pressing into her thigh. She could not help wondering how it would feel pressing inside her. He was kissing her mouth again now, his lips ravaging her, devouring her, as their bodies twined closer and closer, and all the time the warm soothing water cascaded over them. She was leaning against the tiled wall of the fountain, clutching on to one of the golden jets for support when Jamil knelt to kiss her thighs, her sex, and she came suddenly and violently, crying out his name. He held her until the storm of her orgasm passed, before standing up, his erection standing proud, nudging insistently into her thigh.

What he made her feel, surely he should feel, too? What he had given, surely she could return? Without giving herself time to think, filled with a desire only to please as he had pleased, Cassie slid down on to her knees, just as Jamil had done. She kissed his thighs, just as he had done.

'Cassie.'

The rough edge of his voice told her she was right. The solid, curving heft of his manhood confirmed her

thoughts. She touched it, marvelling at the silken hard-
ness of it. Jamil groaned. A surge of desire, a different
kind of desire, heated her. She wanted to please him.
She hoped this would provide pleasure for both of them.
Gently she cupped him before taking him in her mouth.
The result was beyond her wildest hopes.

Later, they lay entwined on one of the wooden beds
used for massages, allowing the gentle warmth of the
air to dry them, too sated to speak. It was Cassie who
moved first, aware that it must be nearly time for the
palace household to be stirring. 'I must go. If I am seen
leaving…'

'You are worried about what people will say of
you?'

'No, I'm worried about what they'll say of you,' Cassie
retorted. 'You're the one who has been at immense pains
to tell me how important it is that I behave with discretion, remember? The Council…'

'The Council are my subjects, just like everyone else.
I won't tolerate gossip!'

Cassie could not but smile at this. 'You may be a
prince, but you can't actually stop people talking.' Her
smile faded as reality began to creep in. 'They will say
I am your concubine.'

For some reason, the truth of this enraged him.
Jamil's eyes darkened. 'Any man who implies any such
thing…'

'But they will, and it is the truth and…' Then the
truth, the real truth, hit Cassie with a shock that made

the icy plunge into the pool earlier feel like a hot bath. She was in love with him.

'Cassie?'

She was in love with Jamil, Prince of Daar-el-Abbah.

'Cassandra?'

Of course she was in love with him. Why else would she have behaved like a strumpet? *Her foolish, foolish heart had done it again, only this time she knew it was profoundly different!* True, undying, eternal love. The kind of love she had always dreamed of, just as she had described to Jamil that day in the secret garden. A love that made her feelings for Augustus seem absurdly trivial. She was in love with Jamil, Sheikh al-Nazarri. In love, in love, in love.

'Cassie! What in the name of the gods is wrong with you? Why are you looking at me like that?'

'Jamil.' She took a step towards him, holding out her hands as if in supplication.

'I will ensure your reputation is protected, if that is what you are worried about.'

'It's not that. I don't care about that.'

Despite the heat, the colour from her cheeks had faded. Despite what she said, she clearly did regret their lovemaking, Jamil realised. Her regret pained him, as did the need for secrecy, for it placed the last few hours in a sordid light that made him uneasy. What had happened was not sordid. It was nothing to be ashamed of. In fact, quite the opposite. He *wanted* the world to know. That she did not, that she was right not to wish such a thing, only served to make him rail all the more at the situation. Why did it all have to be so complicated? Why could she not have kept her feelings to herself? She had pierced the bubble of their interlude, forcing him to step back into reality, out of the oasis of wonder they had temporarily created. 'You are ashamed,' he said harshly, 'I should have known.'

'*No!* Jamil, don't.' Cassie dashed a hand over her eyes. The euphoria that had enveloped her, clouding reality in a rosy pink hue, had vanished. 'Please don't think I wish we hadn't—please don't. You don't understand.'

'Then explain to me!'

'I can't.' She wrenched herself from his grasp and ran for the steam room. Grabbing her sodden clothes, she scrabbled into them and, wrapping one of the dry towels from the changing room around her like a cloak, made it somehow back to her own rooms undetected.

Stripping off her damp clothes, Cassie lay shivering under the thin silk sheet and finally gave way to tears. She was in love, and it should feel like the best feeling in the world, and it did. But it also felt like the worst. She buried her head beneath a heap of satin cushions and prayed in vain for sleep to take her.

Back in the hammam, Jamil jumped into the plunge pool, but the icy water did nothing to cool his ire. How did she do that so effortlessly, turn his emotions upside down? He, who had been taught at such an early age to exercise iron control? And why, despite having experienced the two most amazing climaxes of his life, was he still burning with desire for her?

Cassie was obviously not a woman easily tired of. In fact, right now, Jamil could not imagine tiring of her at all. Despite her English reserve, she was in spirit a true wild flower of the desert. He could teach her not to be ashamed. He could show her real passion, real fulfilment, in the joining of their bodies. He could teach her that there were some feelings he knew more about than she.

But he could not have her, honour forbade it. There were some boundaries he could not cross. Unless…

Unless honour was first satisfied.

Something Linah had said the day Cassie had gone missing in the desert popped into his mind. He smiled. Out of the mouths of babes and innocents. It was ridiculous, of course. The barriers he would have to demolish. The diplomatic hoops that would have to be jumped through. And there was the not insignificant obstacle of the already signed agreement. Jamil frowned heavily as he towelled himself dry and donned his tunic.

But as Cassie had pointed out, he was a prince. If he could not do as he wished, who could? Had he not, for some time, been fretting at the ties that bound him to duty, the burdens of state that were becoming so onerous? Could not this really rather enticing solution provide him with renewed enthusiasm for serving his kingdom? In fact, were the advantages of such an alliance, bringing as it did such excellent connections, not actually something for which his people should be thankful?

It would take some thought, and a great deal of negotiation, but he had Halim, that master of tact, and he had precedent, too, in the shape of Lady Celia. And, most of all, it was what he wanted. For the first time in his life, he would be taking what was right for him. Jamil nodded emphatically to himself as he strode across the gardens from the hammam to the palace. He would think it over tonight. And then, in the clear light of day, he would act.

Time after time, when some minor catastrophe struck, Celia's best advice to her sisters was to sleep on it. 'Things always look better in the morning,' she would say, 'then we will know what to do.'

Usually she was right. Solutions to problems that had seemed insurmountable would be resolved with a clear head and a fresh day. But as she made her *toilette* the morning after running away from Jamil in the hammam, back in her corsets and one of her muslin dresses, Cassie frowned. This particular problem would not be so easily resolved. Pinning up her hair into a tight chignon on top of her head, bereft of any of her usual defiant curls, she bit her lip hard to stop the tears from falling.

This time, the advice had failed her. She had woken with no idea of what to do. No, she did not for a moment regret coming here, how could she, for otherwise she would never have met Jamil. She loved him. She would have realised it sooner or later, even had she not surrendered to the passion he roused in her. She loved him, would always love him, would never have truly loved had she not met him. Fate, something in which Cassandra had always been inclined to believe, a tendency for which she was indeed most aptly named, had brought them together. She would not have had it any other way. She was made to love him.

Despite the dilemma that hung, like the desert storm clouds, lowering and ominous, over her, Cassie smiled. She loved him so much. She loved the proud hauteur that kept him apart from other mortals, but what she loved most about him was the man beneath the princely cloak. The man only she knew. The man no one else would ever know—for despite the advances he had made with his daughter, Jamil had not changed at all, when it came to the most important thing in the world. Love. He did not believe in it, and who could blame him, given his upbringing? Even if he did allow himself to come out from behind that armour of invincibility long enough to allow it to happen, would he even know how?

The idea of Jamil in love with anyone else was too awful to contemplate. The idea of him finding another confidante to replace her was awful, too. Except if he didn't, he'd be lonely again, and she didn't want that either. What she wanted was for him to be happy.

She could make him happy. 'I could, I really could,' she told her reflection. But she couldn't.

Could she?

Celia had done it. Celia was happy. Very happy. The happiest person Cassie knew, in fact. But the difference was, Ramiz loved Celia. Jamil only desired Cassie, and that was not enough. 'Because desire can fade without love to sustain it,' Cassie said sadly to the mirror, 'and I could not bear that.'

It seemed the night had, after all, brought wise council. All her instincts told her that she should leave. To stay would be to destroy something, for she would not be able to resist Jamil, and he would surely tire of her eventually. Unless…

At this point, the vicious circle of Cassie's rather illogical reasoning was interrupted by an unusual summons. Prince Jamil wished to have an audience with her. The formality of the request set her heart beating wildly in her breast. This was the end. The decision had been made for her. Perhaps his Council had spoken.

Telling herself it was for the best—was it not exactly the conclusion she had reached herself?—Cassie finished her *toilette*. The white muslin dress with its close-fitted sleeves and lace-covered neckline was plain and sombre, eminently suitable for the occasion. She picked out a white Brussels lace scarf, a birthday present from her sisters, and fixed it on her hair with more pearl-headed pins, pulling it down to veil her face. It would serve the dual purpose of disguising her reactions and covering the distress that would inevitably result from her dismissal. She did not wish Jamil to see how upset she was. She would not cry. She would not!

The walk to the state rooms felt like it would never end. Balling her hands into fists in an effort to stop them trembling, Cassie followed the male servant along

long marble corridors to a small ante-room tiled in the royal emerald. The double doors were flung open. A seemingly endless narrow green carpet led towards a dais. The chamber—it must be the throne room—was sparkling with light, the sun bouncing off the immense crystal chandeliers which put even those at the Brighton Pavilion to shade. The doors swung shut behind her. Her escort, along with the two guards, remained on the other side. The room was empty, save for one person seated on a strange and rather hideous golden throne set upon the dais. Jamil.

Cassie began the journey towards him. Part of her, the Cassandra part of her, rather relished the dramatic scene: the ornate room, the waiting prince, the green carpet, herself all in white, making her steady way to her fate. But Cassandra could not compete with Cassie. Cassie was terrified and horribly nervous, and on top of it all, seeing him again, knowing just how much she loved him, she had to fight the urge to run all the way to the dais, cast herself at his feet and beg him to love her in return.

Or maybe that was Cassandra, too? Then she got to the first of the shallow steps of the dais and looked up at Jamil, and Cassandra melted silently into the wings. Cassie it was who took centre stage, shaking like an actress with first-night nerves.

He was dressed in formal robes, much more ornate than any she had seen him wear before. A head dress of gold silk edged with emerald, the *igal* that fastened it made of gold thread. His tunic was of the same green, the heavy gold belt buckle decorated with an enormous emerald surrounded by yellow diamonds, the like of which she had seen only once before, in the dazzling crown jewels that Ramiz had worn on his wedding day. A golden cloak, heavily braided and jewelled, pooled at Jamil's feet and trailed down the steps of the dais. It would take at least four pages to bear. It was fastened with another fantastically ornate piece of jewellery, the panther emblem in gold, a yellow diamond for his glinting, impassive eye.

Cassie curtsied low, taking advantage of her veil to survey Jamil's expression. He was not frowning, but not smiling either. Inscrutable. His Corsair look. *Why did he have to be so very handsome?*

'Your Highness.'

'Lady Cassandra.'

'You desired an audience with me, your Highness?' She was relieved to hear her voice sounded almost normal. Almost.

Jamil nodded. 'I have some important news to impart to you.'

Cassie's knees began to shake. The moment she'd been dreading had arrived.

'I have decided,' Jamil continued, 'that it would be in the best interests of my kingdom for you to become my wife.'

Once, years ago, a friend of her father's who had been to the South Seas had brought back a huge pink conch shell. 'Listen, and you can hear the sea,' he'd said to Cassie. She had, and had heard not the familiar sound of the sea, but a rushing, whistling kind of sound. She heard the same thing now, and her mouth went dry. The green carpet beneath her, Jamil's golden cloak on the steps, began to shimmer in front of her eyes, as if in a heat haze. 'Your wife?' she said, her voice trembling on the edge of hysteria.

'I have decided we are to be married,' Jamil said, frowning. 'Obviously, there will be obstacles to be overcome.'

'Obstacles?' Cassie repeated blankly.

Why was she not smiling her joyful acceptance? They were alone, he had broken with tradition to ensure that they would be. *Why was she not embracing him?* 'Nothing that cannot be overcome, I assure you. The advantages of this match over the one that my Council has arranged—'

'What?'

'Obviously, that contract will have to be nullified before we can marry.'

Cassie hastily put back her veil. 'What are you talking about, Jamil? What contract? Are you saying that you are already betrothed?'

Save for a bright slash of colour across her cheekbones, and the luminous blue of her eyes, her face was as alabaster white as the dress she wore. 'It is nothing,' he said dismissively, 'a prior commitment arranged by my Council.'

'Nothing! You call the fact that you are formally betrothed nothing! Why did you not tell me before?'

'Why on earth should I? It was none of your concern.'

'Good grief! Of course it concerns me. It concerns me very much that you were engaged to be married when you were—when you and I were...'

'What you and I were doing had nothing to do with the Princess Adira.'

'Princess Adira! So you at least know her name.'

'I know her name, I know her family, I know what the alliance will bring in tangible terms of gold, silver and diamonds,' Jamil said angrily, 'and I also know what breaking it will cost me in terms of ill will from my Council and from Princess Adira's kinfolk, but I am prepared to endure all that in order to take you as my bride.'

They were words that Cassie had not dared hope to hear, not even in her wildest dreams, and yet they rang hollow. He had not said the most important words of all. *I love you.* 'Why?'

'I beg your pardon?'

'Why do you want to marry me?'

'There are all sorts of sound reasons. For a start, your own strategic connections to the British Empire far outweigh any offered by Princess Adira's family, and though your dowry will be negligible compared to hers, it will not matter, for my own personal wealth is more than sufficient.'

Cassie stared at him, open-mouthed. 'You talk about marriage as if it were some sort of commercial contract or diplomatic treaty. In fact, you sound *exactly* like my father.'

Jamil made a little bow. 'Thank you.'

'I did not mean it as a compliment.' She dashed a hand across her eyes. The man she loved had asked her to marry him. It should be the happiest moment of her life. It was turning into the worst. 'I can't believe this is happening,' she said, a stray tear trembling on the end of her eyelash.

Jamil, who had been about to clasp her in his arms, paused. Somehow he knew these were not tears of joy. 'It is not just a matter of your valuable connections,' he said, 'it is the fact that your English heritage brings with it modern ideas. You will be an ideal role model for the women of Daar-el-Abbah. Much admired and copied.' He smiled encouragingly. 'Then there is Linah. You have been an excellent influence on her. I would wish that to continue; anyway, I know you have grown very fond of each other. This way the bond need not be broken.'

'All sound practical reasons, I grant you,' Cassie sniffed, 'but what about the most important one of all?' It was a faint hope, but she had to know.

Jamil smiled. 'You mean my need for an heir. Naturally, that is of prime importance. After yesterday, I have no doubt that we will both find the execution of that particular duty a delightful and continued pleasure.'

Now she knew! 'Execution of duty! That is what you call it! I can't believe what I'm hearing.'

'Come, Cassie, our countries may be thousands of miles apart, but the customs are not so dissimilar. People of our class and rank marry for two reasons—mutual benefit, and the continuance of the line—you know that as well as I do. Are you not the great Lord Armstrong's daughter? Has he not approved just such an alliance for your sister? It is serendipitous that another such alliance will bring you and me great enjoyment.'

'You may think so, Jamil, and no doubt so, too, may my father, but I am sorry to inform you that I do not.' Just for a moment she had allowed herself to hope. Just for a moment she had allowed herself to dream. Yesterday, she had been making love to Jamil while Jamil had merely been taking pleasure. That is all he would ever do. The realisation was like a kick in the stomach from a mule. Disappointment made her reckless. She felt as if he had taken her most cherished romantic dream and trampled on it. 'I'm sorry, Jamil, but I can't marry you. You do not want a wife, you want a brood mare.'

She had gone too far. She knew that, in the way his face set, his eyes narrowed, in the way he withdrew, mentally and physically, retreating up the stairs of the dais to stand over her, every inch of his rigidly held stature emanating cold fury. 'I had thought you had outgrown such intemperate remarks,' Jamil said. 'I had given you credit for having acquired, in your time here in Daar, a little of the sound judgement you told me at the outset you lacked. Obviously I was wrong.'

'Obviously!' Cassie threw at him. She didn't care now. She had nothing left to lose.

'I see now that you are quite undeserving of the honour I was willing to bestow on you,' Jamil said, bowing stiffly. 'I will make the preparations for your departure. In the meantime, you will consider yourself confined to your quarters.'

He strode down the steps of the dais. Maybe there was something to be said for abiding by tradition after all. A lesson learned. As well for him that it had been one taught in private. Cassie was staring at him, her eyes wide with unshed tears. Something told him he was missing something vital, but his pride, which had ruled him from such an early age, was in no mood to explore what it was. His father was right after all! To expose a need is to expose a weakness. One alone is better than many. Or even two. Jamil walked quickly up the length of the room. The extravagantly long state cloak stretched out behind him. With an exclamation of annoyance, he undid the clasp and let it fall.

The doors slammed shut behind him. The huge room was eerily silent. Cassie's knees finally gave way. She sank down on to the lowest step of the dais and dropped her head into her hands. Tears trickled in a steady flow down her pale cheeks. She sat there, a solitary ghostly white figure, for more than an hour. When she finally rose, cramped and shivering despite the heat of the day, she was resolved. Her heart was broken, but her spirit was not. She must leave this place before that, too, succumbed and was shattered into a thousand pieces.

Jamil's fury knew no bounds as he made his way to his own apartments. That she had dared turn him down! And in such a way!

He could not believe it.

He could not understand it.

He would not accept it!

And still he wanted her. Having decided to make Cassie his wife, no other would now do. He did not know why that was the case, but it was. The fates had sent her to him for a reason. Not that he believed in the fates, but in this instance—in this instance, it felt *right*. Cassie was meant for him. He would not be denied her.

Jamil changed hurriedly out of his formal state clothes, cursing in any number of languages, none of them bringing him any relief at all. That he, Sheikh al-Nazarri, Prince of Daar-el-Abbah, should have been refused by a mere woman! The same woman, moreover, who had betrothed herself to a penniless poet in the teeth of her family's opposition.

He paused in the act of pulling one of his favoured simple white tunics over his head. Perhaps that was where he had gone wrong, not proposing through the correct channels? Hastily fastening the collar of a plain *thoub* of white cotton round his neck and ramming his head dress in place, he made his way out of his apartments to the stables, deep in thought. Having incurred her father's wrath as a result of her incomprehensible misalliance with the poet, Cassie was not likely to defy him a second time, he realised, springing into the saddle and spurring his horse into motion.

But she would not need to. She must surely know, as he himself did, that Lord Armstrong would welcome this alliance with open arms. Her sister's marriage to Prince

Ramiz had been a great diplomatic success. Cassie's marriage into the royal family of Daar-el-Abbah would consolidate Britain's position of influence in Arabia, protecting the vital fast-trade route to India. Lord Armstrong would do everything in his power to bring that about, were it proposed. Including bringing his daughter to heel.

But for some reason, this made Jamil uncomfortable. He did not want Cassie to be brought to heel. He wanted her to come to him of her own accord. More than that, he wanted her to come to him willingly. Yesterday, in the hammam, she had shown herself more than willing. Why then had she refused him?

Riding out at a gallop over his beloved desert, past the Maldissi Oasis in the direction of the cave in which he and Cassie had taken shelter from the storm, Jamil's anger dissipated as he pondered this most perplexing of questions. Cassie was wilful, he knew that. Truth be told, it was one of the things he liked about her, for it was part of her passionate nature. She spoke without thinking. If she was ordered to do one thing, the chances were she would choose to do the opposite, not because she was contrary, but because it was in her nature to resist having her will subverted to another. A little like him. Jamil smiled wryly. A lot like him. He had handled her badly, he could see that now. He should have allowed her the pretence of considering instead of presenting her with a *fait accompli*.

There was more to it than that, though. What was it she had said? The most important thing.

The most important thing to him was her. Startled by this thought, Jamil reined in his horse and took a long swig of water from his goatskin flask. The best interests of his kingdom, which had until now always been his primary consideration, no longer felt quite so important. He had never felt like this before and it was all Cassie's fault, Cassie who had awoken these feelings, Cassie who had made him see that such feelings were not wrong.

The most important thing to Cassie, Jamil realised hot on the heels of this revelation, was romance. Hearts and flowers and pretty speeches. What she called love. True love, such as she had described so fervently to him that day in the ruined east wing. Jamil's lip curled. Love. Upon that subject she had not changed his mind. Love of that kind was a myth dreamed up by those damned poets she favoured to explain away passion, nothing more. Poor, deluded Cassie—could she not see that the desire that flamed between them was far more tangible and even more long-lasting? Past experience should have taught her that much.

Jamil's fists clenched. No matter how shallow were her feelings for the man to whom she had been betrothed, he did not like to think of her feeling anything for anyone but him. A simple, primal possessiveness gripped him. She must be made to see that what they had together was something much more tangible. It was not love that made the heart beat faster, but desire. If he could make her see that, if he could show her how real could be a body's fulfilment, she would have no need for empty declarations. If he could show her that, she would see that what they had between them was more than most had. He would prove it to her. He was already looking forward to proving it.

As soon as he got back, he would talk to Halim about the cancelling of his current betrothal. It had been a mistake from the start. He should have known, from his own uncharacteristic prevarication, that it was wrong. It would be messy, and would cost him dearly, but he cared naught for that. He would not marry Princess Adira. Cassie or no, he doubted he would ever have married the Princess Adira. Thank the gods for Cassie.

Turning his horse for home, Jamil smiled to himself. For once his own desires and those of his kingdom were in harmony. He could hardly wait to claim her. Blood rushed to his groin at the thought of finally thrusting into Cassie's warm, yielding flesh. To spend himself inside her. To feel her velvet heat sheathing him. To plant his seed in her garden of delights. Such rapture, he was certain they would experience such untold rapture. His erection curved hard against his belly. Soon she would be his, and no one else's.

Spurring his horse into a gallop, Jamil headed back to Daar, his head full of delightful plans for Cassie's deflowering.

Chapter Ten

Peregrine Finchley-Burke's journey by dhow down the Red Sea to A'Qadiz had provided blessed relief from the claustrophobic heat and dust of Cairo. He had enjoyed his time on board immensely. Watching the pretty coral reefs and the local boys diving for pretty coloured fish took his mind off the tribulations of his diplomatic career, which was also pretty. Pretty disastrous, that is. Lying in the back of the little craft under the shade of the canopy, idly trailing his hands in the water, with his neckcloth loosened and his waistcoat unbuttoned, Peregrine imagined himself as a pharaoh of ancient Egypt, waited upon by sultry-eyed slaves, who would bow and scrape at his feet and pander to his every whim. It was a beguiling fantasy, one with which he happily whiled away the hours as the dhow made its meandering way south, allowing him to forget all about the travails which undoubtedly lay ahead.

Until, that is, they joined the swarm of river traffic that made negotiating their way into the ever-expanding port of A'Qadiz a most hazardous affair. Peregrine kept his eyes tight shut amid the chaotic bustle until a gentle prod from the boatman indicated that they were safely berthed. He stepped gingerly ashore into the fray of braying mules and bleating camels and gesticulating, sweaty stevedores and clawing, insistent hawkers offering him everything from a new camel to a new wife, most of which, fortunately, he did not understand. A tiny sand-cat kitten, its ringed tail twitching in terror, was placed into his hands. A small child held determinedly on to his cutaway coat, tugging at one of the decorative silver buttons in a most alarming way. Attempting to brush the child away, Peregrine dropped the kitten, which landed, claws out, on the left leg of his dove-coloured pantaloons. Peregrine shrieked. The kitten hissed. The small child laughed. A man selling incense took advantage of the pause in the procession to douse Peregrine liberally with something that smelled distinctively of old dog, and waited, hand extended expectantly, for payment.

With a sigh of resignation, Peregrine reached into his pocket for the inexhaustible supply of pennies he had learned, in Cairo, to keep there for just such occasions. His dream of himself as King Akhenaton vanished in the puff of noxious smoke emanating from the incense bowl. 'Balyrma,' he announced, to no one in particular, followed by the very few words of the language he could command. *Camel. Tent. Guide.* Few words, but sufficient, for within an hour, after some haggling, entered into with gusto on the part of the would-be guide, with resignation by his customer, Peregrine was seated uncomfortably upon a camel headed east.

Three hot dusty days later, he arrived at Balyrma to be greeted with some surprise by Prince Ramiz and his wife, Lady Celia, formerly Armstrong, now Princess al-Muhanna.

'Mr Finchley-Burke,' Celia said, handing him a glass of iced tea, 'what an unexpected pleasure, I hope you are well.'

Although he was used to the Eastern habit of sitting on the floor, it was not a position in which Peregrine was ever comfortable. The not-insubstantial bulk of his stomach made it difficult for him to do anything more dignified than loll, and he was—correctly, as it happened—rather horribly afraid that he looked more like a grounded walrus than a man of fashion. 'Oh, tolerably well, thank you,' he said, wriggling his ample buttocks on to a large—but not quite large enough— satin cushion. 'Can't complain, you know.'

'And you are enjoying your new career at the Consulate?' Lady Celia continued politely, trying not to catch her husband's eye.

'Absolutely,' Peregrine said, smiling bravely.

'I'm sure you must have made yourself quite indispensible to Lord Wincester by now.'

Peregrine blushed. Despite having over a year of sound British diplomatic training under his belt, lying did not come naturally to him. 'Well, as to that—well.' He took a sip of tea.

'You are too modest,' Celia said with a smile. 'Why else would Lord Wincester send you here to us on what I am sure must be most important business?'

'Yes, just what exactly is this mission of yours?' Ramiz asked pointedly. 'I was not informed of your impending visit.'

'Ah.' Peregrine took another sip of tea. 'Thing is, not actually an affair of state. At least, not strictly…'

Intrigued, Celia set down her own glass and cast her husband an enquiring look. 'You have come here, perhaps, on business of your own?'

'No, no. Lord, no. Don't get me wrong,' Peregrine said, flustered, 'I mean lovely to be here and all, lovely to see you both again, but—no. Fact is,' he blurted out, diplomacy forgotten, 'it's about your sister.'

'My sister!' Celia paled, and sought her husband's hand. 'Which one? Has there been an illness at home? Why has not my aunt, or my father—? Peregrine, please tell me you are not here to inform me that there has been a tragedy.'

'No, no. Nothing like that. Not involving one of *those* sisters any road. I'm talking about the one here in Arabia. Lady Cassandra.'

'Cassie! What has happened to Cassie?'

'I beg you to be calm, Lady Celia. Didn't mean to alarm you.'

'Then you will tell us, if you please, exactly what it is you have come here to discuss, and you will tell us quickly without further prevarication,' Ramiz said in clipped tones, all amusement gone as he pulled his wife protectively towards him. 'Don't worry,' he said to Celia, 'if Cassandra had come to any harm, we would have heard it direct from Prince Jamil before now. I am sure of it.'

'Of course. Of course,' Celia said. 'Silly of me.' She turned her attention once more to Peregrine. 'Please explain, Mr Finchley-Burke, you have my full attention.'

But when Peregrine finished his halting and somewhat expurgated explanation, Celia was more confused than enlightened. 'But I don't understand—why is my father is so keen to have Cassie return to England forthwith?' she asked.

Peregrine shrugged embarrassedly. 'Mine is not to reason why. I suspect he is concerned for her—ahem—safety.'

'But that doesn't make any sense. I wrote to Papa when Cassie left for Daar to inform him that she was taking up the role of governess there with my full approval, but he must have sent his communiqué to Cairo before that. How, then, did he know of Cassie's presence there? And more to the point, *what* precisely does he think she is doing there?'

'Ah,' Peregrine said, shuffling uncomfortably on his cushions.

'Ah?'

'Suspect he thinks it's a little less above board than—

you know how these rumours fly at the Foreign Office, Lady Celia.'

'I do indeed, Mr Finchley-Burke,' Celia replied acerbically. 'Let me assure you, my sister and I have been in regular correspondence since she went to Daar, and she is not only perfectly happy there, she is very well thought of, and is making an excellent fist of her role as governess. Prince Jamil is her employer, nothing more.'

'I'm sure, I'm sure. But regardless of that, I'm still under strict instructions to facilitate her immediate return to England,' Peregrine said despondently, 'whether the young lady wishes it or not. It is not a task I relish, I can tell you, but there you have it, needs must. I will rest here tonight, with your permission, then set off for Daar tomorrow.'

Celia turned to her husband. 'Perhaps it is for the best if I accompany him, dearest? I am overdue a visit to see Cassie, and Bashirah is weaned now. I'm sure there is nothing at all wrong, but I would rather see that for myself, just to make sure.'

Ramiz nodded. 'It would make sense.'

'Then it is settled. I will accompany you to Daar, Mr Finchley-Burke, if you have no objection.'

'Objection? My dear Lady Celia,' Peregrine said with enormous relief, 'that is a most capital idea, a most capital idea indeed. Your assistance in this matter would be most gratefully received.'

Clearly buoyed, Peregrine left for 'a bit of a wash and a brush up' as he put it, and Celia turned to her husband.

'I just need to make sure this ridiculous man doesn't upset Cassie unduly, that's all. She is still recuperating emotionally from this Augustus business. I don't want a combination of Papa and Mr Finchley-Burke setting her back. I'll only be gone a few days.'

'One day is too many,' he replied, kissing her deeply. 'I will have the caravan readied for the morning. Hurry back, my beloved.'

'Don't worry, I won't be away from you a day more than I have to,' Celia replied, melting into his arms. 'Anyway, I am already looking forward to you welcoming my return.'

Upon his return to the palace later that same morning, Jamil wasted no time in summoning Halim and informing him briskly of his decision to terminate his betrothal to the Princess Adira. 'I want you to work out suitable terms,' he said, glancing through the stack of papers that Halim had left for him to sign. 'Be generous, I don't want her father to bear us any ill will.'

'Not bear us any—but, Highness,' Halim exclaimed, aghast, 'you cannot have considered the consequences of such a rash course of action.'

'Of course I have,' Jamil replied impatiently. 'It will be a tricky challenge, but one I am sure you are more than capable of meeting. I have every faith that you will be able to redraw the marriage agreement in the form of an alliance treaty, and...'

Under any other circumstances, Halim would have blossomed under the rays of such warm praise, but these were not any other circumstances. Never before, to his knowledge, had a betrothal been broken without a war resulting. 'Prince Jamil, I beg you to reconsider…'

'I have considered. I'm sick of considering. I have never, as you perfectly well know, wanted to marry Princess Adira, and I have decided now that I shall not do so. Come, my friend, you underestimate your powers of negotiation.'

Jamil smiled, one of his rare smiles, but Halim was too distraught to respond, rocking back and forwards on the balls of his feet. 'Yes, yes, I am flattered you have such faith in me—but no amount of negotiating on my part can produce an heir for Daar-el-Abbah, Highness.'

'An heir. Yes, I know how much you are worried about my heir, but there's no need to.'

Halim stilled. 'You have another bride in mind?'

'I do.'

'Another from the Council list?' It was said hopefully, but Halim was experiencing a rather horrible sensation. He felt as if his stomach was creeping slowly towards his knees.

'No. It is Lady Cassandra.'

Halim crumpled to the floor and began to beat his breast. 'No, Jamil—Prince Jamil, I beg of you.'

'Get up. For the sake of the gods, Halim, get up and stop sobbing like a woman. I know you don't approve of Cassie, but—'

'Don't approve! She has no royal blood, she brings with her no lands. She is not even one of us.'

Jamil had taken Halim's understanding for granted, just as he had taken for granted his support. Now he realised that his man of business was in his own way just as blinkered as the Council. So, mustering his patience, he explained at some length just why it was that his marriage to Lady Cassandra would be even more advantageous for Daar-el-Abbah than his marriage to Princess Adira or any other of the Arabian princesses on the Council's list.

Halim remained deeply skeptical, but neither his rational counter-arguments, nor his pointing out that tradition decreed the prince's marriage to be subject always and completely to the Council's approval, made any difference. The prince merely reiterated his own point of view again with renewed force. Nothing he said would persuade him to change his mind. Prince Jamil, Halim realised with sudden clarity, though he did not know it, had completely fallen under the spell of a pair of blue eyes. This was not about breaking tradition or advantageous alliances, this was about a young English governess. Halim sighed. He did not like to see his prince brought low by a mere woman like this, but the only course of action open to him now was damage limitation. 'If you were to visit the Princess Adira's family yourself, Highness, inform them in person of the change in your plans, it would be less of an insult,' he suggested tentatively.

'There is no insult to the Princess Adira. You yourself told me that I was one of five men being considered for her. She did not choose me, any more than I chose her.'

Jamil ran his fingers through his hair, dislodging his head dress. *Why was nothing simple in his life?*

'You would not wish Daar-el-Abbah to go to war over a mere woman,' Halim said, playing his last card.

Jamil gave a growl of exasperation. 'Summon the Council now. I want this over, and I want it over now. But be assured, I will not permit Princess Adira to be the cause of us going to war.'

'She is not the woman I was referring to,' Halim muttered to himself as he bowed and slowly backed out of the room.

Cassie endured a horrid night. No matter that she returned to the schoolroom apartment determined to leave just as soon as arrangements could be made, no matter that her head told her quite unequivocally that to do so was the one and only sensible course open to her, her heart refused to listen.

The idea of being married to Jamil, of being his wife, of sharing his bed, if not his heart—oh, it was so very tempting. She loved him. Of course she wanted to marry him. To bear his children. To share his life.

But he did not love her. Perhaps if she loved him enough, then surely he would come to love her, too? But it did not work that way, even the poets agreed on that topic. He would not come to love her and when his passion for her faded—what then?

No, love for her had to be not just unequivocal, but utterly reciprocal. And love was an integral part of marriage. So in the end, it was simple. She could not marry

Jamil, no matter how tempting the compensations. And since she loved him and only him, it meant she would never marry anyone and was doomed to remain childless.

A spinster.

A virgin.

She would never experience true love-making with him. And could not, with anyone else.

When dawn broke, Cassie rose wearily from her divan, dressed in one of her English muslin gowns, and dejectedly began to pack. If she could be ready to leave as soon as arrangements were made, it would all be for the best. A clean break from Linah. From Jamil. From her heart. It was for the best.

But the day passed, with Linah subdued, sensing something was wrong and obviously afraid to ask, and still no word came from Jamil or any of his officials. The Council were in session, one of Linah's handmaidens informed her, and Cassie assumed that state business had taken precedence—as it always would. Nevertheless, she resented being ignored. Obviously she was being taught a lesson as to her irrelevance in the grand scheme of things. So it was, when the summons came for her to join his Highness in his private courtyard, Cassie was inclined to reject it.

But of course she did not. Instead, she donned one of her most elegant of evening gowns, a cream crepe slip worn under an overdress of gold spider-gauze. It had a low décolleté, too low for her to have worn it in public here in Arabia for it showed rather a generous amount of Cassie's creamy bosom, but if this was the last time she was going to see Jamil she wanted to look her best. Between the tiny puff sleeves and the long, elegant cream kid gloves was just a hint of dimpled flesh. She wore her locks up, braided into an elaborate coronet on top of her head, and affixed her diamond earrings, a coming-of-age gift from Aunt Sophia, to her ears. Her neck she left unadorned. Cream silk stockings with gold clocks, which she'd never before worn, cream kid slippers and a matching shawl of gold spider-gauze, completed the ensemble. A quick glance in the mirrored tiles of her bathing chamber satisfied her. Despite the sleepless night, she looked passable.

The servant attending her hurried her along the corridors. She was late. Belatedly, Cassie realised that while she considered the time well spent, there was a chance Jamil might not agree with her. Still, at least he intended to communicate the arrangements for her departure in person, rather than have some lackey do it. That, at least, was something.

Heart pounding, head held high, determinedly ignoring the fluttering in her stomach and the trembling in her knees and the flush that she just knew stained her cheeks, Cassie stepped into Jamil's private courtyard. He was standing by the fountain, dressed in a plain caftan in emerald silk. His feet were bare, his head uncovered, an endearing lick of auburn hair standing up over his brow. Without his robes of state, he was not the Corsair, but simply the most handsome man she had ever seen. Or would ever see.

Cassie could not help it, her eyes positively ravished him, the fierce little frown between his brows, the sharp cheekbones, the almost-tilt of his lips, the burnish of his autumn eyes. He was watching her impassively, but she could feel the hunger in his gaze. Her nipples tightened in response. She thanked heaven that she had her corsets and her chemise and her underdress on to disguise this blatant physical response. He must not see. She must not falter.

But already she was faltering. Imagining the touch of his fingers on her skin. Her own on his. The soft folds of his caftan showed off his perfect physique. She wondered if he wore anything beneath it. She wished she hadn't wondered. Then she couldn't help but wonder. Then she remembered how angry he had been yesterday, and though there was no trace of it now, she would do well to be cautious. 'Your Highness,' she said stiffly.

'Jamil.'

'You wanted to see me?' Her voice sounded all wrong. She compensated for its breathiness by glaring.

Jamil spread his hands. He smiled at her, partly to reassure her, for she looked like she was walking on broken glass, and partly because he was simply glad to see her. More than glad. 'You are looking quite ravishing tonight, Cassie,' he said, taking her hand and pressing a kiss on her palm. 'Do you know, you are quite the most beautiful woman I've ever known? And the most desirable.'

Why was he speaking to her like this? He never spoke to her like this! *Why was he making it so difficult for her?* 'Please don't say such things.'

Jamil caught her in his arms. 'Why not, when they are true?'

'Because I—because we—just because. Let me go, Jamil.' But her body was already yielding, melting into the hard planes of his.

He pulled her closer, effortlessly stilling her attempt to free herself, and tilted her chin up. 'I don't intend to let you go, Cassie.'

His voice was husky. His eyes glowed fiercely as they rested on her face, on her heaving breast. Her heart was pounding, slow and heavy, thump, thump, thump. She was afraid to ask what he meant. Afraid she would be wrong. Men like Jamil did not change overnight. But she so much wanted to be right. *Oh God, she was weak.* 'Jamil…'

'Cassie, about yesterday. When I asked you to marry me, I did not make the nature of my feelings clear.'

She felt faint. Were it not for his embrace she would surely slip to the floor. 'Feelings?'

Jamil smiled wryly. 'Don't look so surprised. You were right, I do have some.'

Hope began to tap its way out of the shell in which she had encased it, like the frantic pecking of a baby bird. 'What—what feelings?'

'I have never desired anyone more than you.' He would not make her pretty speeches, but he could speak the truth of what he felt; she had taught him the value of that. Though he had never before made any such admission, curiously it felt liberating rather than destructive. The truth of how he felt. Surely not something she could resist? 'I have cancelled my betrothal to the Princess Adira. I cannot marry her. I cannot marry anyone but you.'

The egg shell cracked. The fledgling that was hope peeped through.

'Yesterday,' Jamil continued, 'I spoke of practical reasons, advantages. Those remain valid, but they are not the most important thing. The most important thing is what we have together, the special emotion we feel for each other.'

Cassie waited, scarce able to breathe.

'Passion,' Jamil said firmly.

The fledgling paused in the act of spreading its wings. 'Passion?' Cassie repeated.

'What you call love, Cassie, does not exist, save on the pages of a book or in a poem. Pretty words and sentimental nonsense, they mean nothing. Hearts do not speak, but bodies do,' Jamil said, too caught up in the unexpected relief of finally speaking his mind aloud to notice that he was making what, to all intents and purposes, was a pretty speech. 'What we feel for each other is real. More than most can aspire to. More than I have ever experienced, or ever hoped to have. We can share that, surely that is enough?'

She wanted to believe him. She wanted to be persuaded. If he could speak as he just had, if he could admit to so much that he had never before admitted to, and speak of it, too—she wanted so much to hope that *this* would lead to *that*. She knew she should resist, but that was the one thing she did not want to do. She was in danger of being swept away. Oh, lord, how much she wanted to surrender to the surging tide of her love for him. 'I—Jamil, I...'

'Cassie. Cassie, Cassie, Cassie. I want you so much. Let me show you how much,' he said urgently, pulling her close, moulding her body into his, smoothing his hands over her back, down her spine to the delightful little curve where it ended at her bottom. 'Let me prove to you that passion is enough, more than enough, to base a marriage on. Let me show you that *this* is what really matters.' He nuzzled the tender skin behind her ear lobe, licking into the crease there.

She wanted to be persuaded. She wanted to give him every chance. She wanted, wanted, wanted. His hands were trailing heat. His mouth was plucking desire from deep within her, raising it to the surface so that her skin burned with it. How could she resist?

'Cassie?'

She could not deny him. She could not deny herself. He was sure he was right? But how could she prove to him that she was right? 'Make love to me, Jamil.' She kissed his neck, the hollow of his throat, relishing the tangy, masculine scent of him. 'Make love to me.' *Please, please, let me be right. Let it be love.*

She tilted her head back so that he could kiss her throat. His lips trailed heat down to where her breasts rose and fell from her décolleté.

'I have waited so long for this moment,' Jamil murmured huskily.

He placed little fluttering kisses on the pulse at her collar bone, up to her ear, round to her mouth, making her thirsty for his, making her moan and clutch at him, until finally, finally, he kissed her, and she was lost. She had never tasted such kisses, could not ever imagined having enough of such kisses, thought she would die if she did not have more.

He kissed her and, somehow, she did not know how, he had loosened her dress, and now he was kissing her breasts, sucking hungrily at her nipples, tugging kisses, first one, then the other, and then the first one again, so that she could not think, could not think of anything save the aching pull that connected Jamil's mouth, his hands, her breasts, the throbbing, swelling pulse between her legs.

She was lying on a divan now, though she had no memory of getting there. Her dress was loose. Her slippers were gone. Her skirts were rucked up. Jamil's kisses were hard, demanding, his fingers stroking at the heat between her legs, making her buck under him, making her body clamour for satisfaction, for gratification, for him. 'Please,' she said, 'please.' *Please love me. Please don't ever leave me. Please.* She clung to him and her climax neared, neared, neared, came, making her cry out.

Barely had she floated back to earth than she became conscious of him naked beside her, his erection proud and curved and frighteningly large. He was arranging her on the divan, placing pillows under her, murmuring soothing phrases, promising her it would not hurt. *What would not hurt?*

He looked at her, barely able to believe it was finally about to happen. He ached with need, was heavy with the seed he was desperate to spend inside her. And she was so ready for him, so wet and pink, still pulsing from her climax. He angled himself carefully over her. Not his favourite position, but the one least likely to hurt her. And he wanted to see her face. His manhood nudged at her entrance. By the gods, let him be able to control himself. He kissed her deeply, slowly, and slowly began to nudge inside her, almost crying out aloud at the delight of it.

He pushed gently, deeper, testing for the point where her maidenhood would end, meeting it, readying himself to thrust, so taut with the strain of controlling his own urge to pound into her that he could barely breathe. 'I will try my best not to hurt you, trust me,' he said, and thrust.

A sharp pain, like the tearing of cloth. Cassie tensed, but it was gone almost as quickly as it happened, submerged in the waves of something much more piercing. He was inside her. She could feel him, shaped into her, the most wonderful, unbelievable, indescribable feeling, as if he were made for her. Who would have thought? She opened her eyes, a hazy smile on her bruised lips, to tell him, and saw the strain of his control etched on his beautiful face. Instinct took over.

Cassie arched her back the tiniest bit to encourage him. 'Please,' she whispered, this time in no doubt of what she wanted. Jamil tilted her towards him. He kissed her, tongue pushing into the heat of her mouth, and his manhood pushing into the heat of her sex. Like petals unfolding, like leaves unfurling, she felt herself give and give as he moved ever deeper into her, so slowly she felt every tiny fraction of him easing his way until he was sheathed. Ripples of sensation made her cling to him. She felt him pulsing as she clung, and clung all the more fiercely to him.

Ecstasy. She was ecstatic with sensation. Jamil withdrew and then pushed back inside her, like an ebb and a flow, more decisive now, as if the tide were turning as she tightened around him. She arched her back and he plunged ever deeper. She could hear his little grunts of effort, heard her own strange mewling response, felt his shaft swell and thicken, felt herself tensing again, and, as he cried out his gratification as he surrendered suddenly to the intensity of his own climax, she felt her own surge and swirl around her again and again, catching her up and casting her adrift, lost in a world that was only she and he and the one that they had become. Who would have believed it? Cassie thought, clinging and clinging to him, holding him to her, inside her, feeling the last ripples of his orgasm send responding echoes of her own shivering through her, until she thought she would die of pleasure.

Jamil rolled over on to his back, pulling her with

him, reluctant to disconnect from her, already wanting more. It was all he had dreamed. All he had fantasised. More. He had never felt so—satisfied? Not just that. Sated? Not yet. Whatever it was, he wanted more. And he could have it now. Any time. Every day. Cassie was his. With a lazy smile of satisfaction, he twisted a long golden curl of her hair, which had escaped its elaborate braid, around his finger. Jamil was not a possessive man, but there was something primal about his feelings for this wilful, beautiful Englishwoman that made him want to mark her as his own. His woman. His wife.

Cassie opened her eyes to find Jamil gazing down at her, his eyes glowing with satisfaction and intent. 'A penny for them,' she said, smiling up at him.

He looked quizzically at her. 'An English saying,' she explained. 'It means tell me what you are thinking.'

Jamil's laugh was a low growl of intent. 'I'm thinking that, having made my point so eloquently, I would like to make it again. Right now.'

She could feel his stiffening manhood nudging against the small of her back. He was indeed more than ready to take his pleasure. To give her pleasure. To make love? A crushing weight of disappointment hovered like a cloud, waiting to envelop her in its gloom. He had not said it. The words, which she was having to almost physically swallow, were never going to touch his tongue. She had poured her love over him, on to him, into him, in the hope that it would rouse the same feelings in him, but it had not. It had not. *Had it?*

She had to know. 'Jamil, don't you feel any different, now that we have…?'

He nuzzled her neck. 'Feelings, always feelings with you, Cassie. You know how I feel.' He took her hand and placed it on his manhood. 'This is what I feel for you.'

Passion. Desire. Not love. It would never be love. She had her answer. *What a fool she had been! What a complete and utter fool!* She felt the little fledgling of hope drop broken-winged to the ground. Jamil did not love her. Jamil would never love her. Worse! He'd made it clear, perfectly, abundantly, unequivocally clear, that he did not want her love. He wanted her body. It was all he'd ever want from her. She'd hoped he'd wanted her, Cassie, the person inside, not the packaging. She felt sick. And angry. And cheated. The pain enveloped her, a dense black mass of despair. She had to get out of here, away from him, before he saw, because that would be the ultimate humiliation. Pushing herself free from his embrace, Cassie sat up. 'No!'

Jamil tried to pull her back down again. 'Did I hurt you? Next time, I promise it will not…'

She struggled frantically to release herself, terrified lest her love, her poor wounded love, would clutch at the crumbs he offered, pleading that they would be enough, knowing they were not. She had to get away. 'Leave me alone. Get off me.' She struggled to her feet, breathing harshly.

'Cassie, I didn't mean to hurt you.'

'You didn't hurt me. And there won't be a next time.'

'If you mean you wish to wait until after we are married, then I would respect your wishes,' Jamil said reluctantly. It would be a compromise. A severe compromise, but the rites could be arranged quickly. Well, relatively quickly. Six weeks. The very notion of waiting six weeks filled him with horror.

'We're not getting married.'

Her words had a finality to them that cut into him like a dagger. For a few moments Jamil could only stare at her in stupefaction as Cassie began to right her clothing. 'You are being ridiculous,' he finally managed. 'I thought you understood. Tonight—'

'I do understand. I wish I didn't, but I understand. You've made it perfectly clear.' She was trembling. Her fingers could not manage her buttons. She could not tie her lacings. Hastily clutching her dress together anyhow, she clenched her fingers into little fists and folded her arms across her chest, partly to steady herself, partly to hide her anguish from Jamil. If only he would not look at her so. If only...

She steeled herself. *If only* belonged in the world of fairytales and poetry. This was the real world. 'I'm sorry,' she said, her voice cracking, 'I can't marry you.' He looked so thunderstruck that she could not resist touching him, putting her little clenched fist to his arm, but Jamil shook her off angrily.

'You still insist on love, Cassie? You are deluded, for

you are looking for something that does not exist. You will not find it. Here or anywhere else.'

Cassie flinched. *I have found it, I have*. But it was no use. 'I'm sorry,' she said again, for there was nothing more to be said.

He felt as if the world was coming crashing down around him. All his certainties. All his plans. Gone, in an instant. Suddenly, it was too much. 'Get out!' he roared. 'Get out of here, and never let me set eyes on you again.'

She had the distinct impression that her heart was breaking, something that turned out to be no poetic licence. Not just her heart. Her world. She was on the brink of a precipice. The urge to hang on with her fingers was so strong she almost followed it. To have just a little was surely better than to have nothing?

Cassie wavered. To be his wife, to be desired, if not loved—surely that was still worth having? But one look at Jamil's face told her that option was no longer open to her. And anyway, in her heart, that poor, wounded heart of hers, she knew it would be wrong. She loved him absolutely. Nothing else would suffice.

Jamil's skin was pale, his lips two thin lines. Almost, Cassie did not recognise him. 'I'll bid you goodbye then.' Her voice wobbled. She waited, but Jamil made no reply, staring resolutely over her head, as if she did not exist. Cassie turned, with a heavy heart, and made for the courtyard door.

After it closed behind her, Jamil retrieved his scimitar from the ceremonial case in which it lay glittering wickedly. Returning to the courtyard, with a fierce intake of breath, he lifted it high over his head and brought it down in a series of smooth, vicious arcs, neatly slicing through a row of ornamental bay trees, leaving the tops of the bushes lying like the heads of decapitated soldiers on a battlefield.

Chapter Eleven

Jamil left Daar-el-Abbah early the next morning. Cassie had dealt a bitter blow to his pride, but the knowledge, lurking in the dark recesses of his mind, that it was not sufficient to quell his overwhelming need to make her his, was what made it necessary for him to leave the royal palace. Knowing she was there, within its walls, was too much of a temptation. He would not beg, he would not demean himself by showing such weakness, but Cassie had the ability to scramble his senses so effectively he decided not to take the risk. Taking decisive action would help restore his shattered equilibrium. He decided to act on Halim's advice and deliver the news of the broken betrothal to Princess Adira's family in person.

He rode out on his white camel at the head of a small caravan. At least, it was what Halim called a small caravan, for it consisted of ten guards, about the same number of servants, and twenty mules carrying, in addition to the tents and hangings, a number of valuable gifts for the princess and her family. Jamil did not wish to be accused of a lack of generosity. Most certainly he did not want to risk offence. Though no one, he thought cynically, could possibly be offended by such an excessive hoard of gold and precious jewels.

He had no real reason to break the betrothal now, but he was more convinced then ever that he could not take the Princess Adira or the Princess Anyone as his wife. In fact, the very notion of a wife at all filled him with repugnance. With one exception. But *that* he would not think about.

Yet later, unable to sleep, padding silent as a panther beyond the perimeter of the camp, Cassie was all Jamil could think about. That he still wanted her with an unabated passion, he could not understand. She had rejected him not once but twice. That fact alone should be enough to tear her from his thoughts, to rip all desire for her from his body, but it was not. He could not fathom it, any more than he could understand Cassie's refusal. Her passion for him was as strong as his for her, there was no mistaking that. She had given herself with an abandon that fired his loins, had relished their union every bit as much as he. She would have given herself again with very little persuasion, he was sure of that, yet she would not take him as a husband. It was ironic—not that he was in the mood for irony—that all he believed of Englishwomen previously was proving quite untrue. They had a reputation for being keen to snare a husband, but less than enthusiastic about activity in the marital bed afterwards. Cassie, unfortunately, was proving to be the exception.

Jamil sat down on a large boulder at the furthest edge of the oasis and watched morosely as two scorpions carried out an elaborate mating dance on the sand. Ritual and instinct. The dance. The copulation. The production of young. Not so very different from the way he had been raised to think of his own marriage. The wedding contract and formal rites. The mating. The production of heirs. The separation of the harem, of women and children from men. As in the world of the scorpions, so in the world of the royal palace. He had his role. His wife had hers. So it had always been.

Not any more. He did not want it. He would not have it. Traditions had often irked him, but until recently he had not been inclined to challenge them. It was Cassie who had questioned, Cassie who had given him pause, Cassie who had, without him noticing, subtly altered his whole way of thinking. And Cassie who had made him realise how lonely life as a prince could be. She had taken away that loneliness, too.

Everyone needs someone! A curse upon her! If she had not challenged and provoked and forced him to see his life through her eyes, then he could have carried on as he was. As he had always been. If not happy, then content.

But that was a lie. He had not been content; she was right about that, too. His past had always haunted him. He realised with a start that it no longer did. The dreams, the memories that had tortured him, had gone since that day she had broken his father's whip over her knee. Cassie had performed some sort of exorcism.

She did not deserve his curses, she deserved his admiration for the way she had adapted to a foreign land, one with a fierce climate and an alien tongue. Had thrown herself with gusto into the fray, transforming his daughter in the process, demonstrating a love of the desert and Daar-el-Abbah's history that rivalled his own. She had even begun to master the rudiments of the language. Underneath that beautiful and desirable exterior lay a quite remarkable person, Jamil could now see.

He smiled, thinking of the many occasions upon which she had blurted out her thoughts, the way she would cover her mouth with her hand as if to push the words back, the endearing combination of guilt and defiance in her big blue eyes. The memories triggered others. The fearless way she rode, the endless patience she displayed with Linah, the care she put into the smallest of tasks, the way she smiled and the way she laughed and the way she frowned, chewing on her lower lip when she was thinking something over. The way she clasped her hands when she was nervous. The tender way she talked about her sisters. The hurt she tried to hide when talking of her father. She never lied, or even prevaricated. She said what she thought, often— too often, maybe—regardless of the consequences. She would not be ordered, but she would be guided. And she listened. She really listened, in a way that no one else did. She wore her feelings plainly on her beautiful face.

The scorpions had gone. The oasis was perfectly still. Above him, a crescent moon shone weakly through an unusual covering of light cloud. Jamil picked up a handful of sand and let it sift through his fingers. He had made no arrangements for her departure, but he had given no commands to prevent it, either. That note of finality in her voice could not be ignored. She would go, might even be gone by the time he returned. He should be pleased. Temptation would be removed. But as he watched the sand trickle from his palm, Jamil felt a piercing sadness. Closing his fingers, he tried to catch the last few grains, but it was too late. His hand was empty. Beyond the oasis, the vast plain of the desert stretched. His desert. His kingdom. His life. Empty.

There was a time for enduring alone, a time for nursing one's feelings back to health without anyone ever knowing they had been hurt, a time for trying to prove that one could rise above one's reputation as the flighty, irresponsible one of the Armstrong girls. And then there was a time to seek solace with the person who had been her chief comforter and solid supporter since Mama died. Cassie's first action the morning after making love to Jamil was to write to Celia, urging her to send someone to fetch her as quickly as possible. She must get away, and until she did, she must stay clear of Jamil. After last night, she was under no illusions about her strength of will. She would surrender herself to him whenever he asked. Her body was his—and he knew it. Her heart, too, though that, he did not know and must not. And her soul. That, she must keep safe, for both their sakes.

It would take ten days, she calculated, for the letter to reach Celia and for her requested escort to arrive. When Linah informed her that Papa was gone, and would be away for at least three nights, she should have been relieved, but was contrarily first offended that he had left without taking his leave of her, then simply hurt and very lonely. She missed him as if he had become part of her. His absence was like a permanent ache that served to emphasise the need to leave this place, for the more she had to endure his presence, the harder would their parting be. But part they must. And she must find the strength to get herself through the next ten days without betraying herself.

Tears, which had come so easily to her in the past, now refused to flow. Her grief was too great for such gratuitous expression; the devastation she was enduring at the destruction of her world was too fundamental a pain to articulate with extravagant gestures. The dramatic and flamboyant Cassie of old would not recognise this quiet, withdrawn and unutterably sad creature.

She endured. For Linah's sake, she even managed to put on a brave face. Though her smile felt rigid, and every movement was an effort, she managed it—or thought she did. She smiled and shook her head dismissively when Linah asked what was wrong. Then she claimed a headache. Then Linah stopped asking, and took to staring at her in a disconcertingly worried way, holding her hand tightly. She did not like to let Cassie out of her sight.

That, too, Cassie endured. At times she felt as if she were watching herself in a play. She wanted to scream at the fates for the unfairness of it all. Why could not Jamil love her? Why not? Why not? Tears would have been a relief then, but still they did not come. She felt as if she were hewn from stone.

What did arrive, unexpectedly, was Celia. While Cassie was sitting in the courtyard staring absently into space, the heavy door was flung open to reveal the familiar figure of her beloved sister.

'Celia! Oh, Celia, I can't tell you how good it is to see you,' Cassie said, throwing herself with relief into her sister's arms. 'But how do you come to be here so quickly? I only despatched my note the other day. And Mr Finchley-Burke,' she exclaimed, catching a glimpse of Peregrine, hovering uneasily in the background. 'Quite a delegation!'

Peregrine stepped forwards and made an elegant bow. 'Lady Cassandra. Pleasure to see you again.'

'Are you here in some official capacity? Is something wrong? Have you a message from home? One of my sisters? Oh goodness, is it Papa?'

'No, no, do not be alarmed,' Celia said, 'it is nothing like that.'

'Then what—oh, I beg your pardon, I am being most

remiss, you will be wanting tea after your journey. Won't you come and sit down?'

With resignation, Peregrine followed the two sisters over to the ubiquitous heaps of cushions, lowering himself down carefully. While Cassie poured tea, and Celia took covert note of the dark shadows under her sister's eyes, Peregrine prayed for guidance. Warring tribes and broken treaties were one thing, but affairs of the heart and young lady's delicate sensibilities were quite another. A specialised field, in his experience. A field he had become bogged down in before. He need not have worried, as it turned out. His plea for divine intervention seemed to have been answered.

'I am so glad you have come, Celia,' Cassie said, ignoring her own tea, 'I wish to leave here as soon as possible.'

'Leave!' Celia exclaimed in surprise. 'But I thought you were so happy here?'

'Leave!' Peregrine exclaimed in relief, 'Excellent news. Capital!' He was suddenly aware of two pairs of Armstrong eyes viewing him with disapproval. 'Obviously hope there's nothing wrong. Didn't mean to imply—simply meant I'd be delighted to help in any way. Get you home, that is.'

Cassie addressed her sister. 'I was happy. Very happy.' Her voice trembled, but she took a quick breath, and straightened her shoulders. 'I just—things have become complicated—I just need to leave.'

Peregrine clapped his hands together. 'Righty-ho. What say we just turn the caravan around immediately?

Camels will barely be in the stables. If I just pop round now,' he said, creaking to his feet, 'we can be on our way in jig-time.'

'No, wait. I can't go today.'

'Nonsense. Best not to put it off,' Peregrine said with an encouraging smile.

'I can't. I have to say goodbye to Linah properly. Tomorrow, maybe, or...' *The next day. When Jamil might be back.*

'Tomorrow's not looking so good,' Peregrine said, dismayed by the sudden indecision in Lady Cassandra's voice. 'Storms forecast apparently,' he said, quite untruthfully. 'Best to go now.'

Seeing that her sister was in the grip of strong emotion, Celia put an arm around her. 'Tomorrow will be soon enough,' she said firmly to Peregrine, 'but there is nothing stopping you leaving today and returning to Cairo. After all, your mission would appear to be successfully completed without any need for your intervention.'

Cassie gave herself a little shake and freed herself from Celia's embrace. 'Mission? Precisely why are you here, Mr Finchley-Burke?' she asked.

Faced with piercing eyes every bit as blue as he remembered, and a figure every bit as luscious and distracting, too, Peregrine felt his eloquence desert him. 'I—your father, that is—worried about your safety, you know,' he spluttered. 'Thought you'd be keen to get back to England—enough of the heat and the flies and what not,' he added, shuffling his feet.

'As it happens, I do want to leave Arabia,' Cassie told him with a wobbly smile, 'though how my father…'

'Oh, you know Lord Armstrong,' Peregrine told her bracingly, 'always one step ahead, always knows what's best.'

'Cassie? Are you sure you really want to go back to England?' Celia said.

Cassie nodded. 'I must.'

Peregrine rubbed his hands together and began to shuffle backwards towards the courtyard door. 'So, in that case I'll be off then, back to Cairo. Secure you a place on a ship. Or I could stay and escort you, if you wish.'

'No. Really, Mr Finchley-Burke,' Celia interposed, 'my husband will wish to make those arrangements personally.'

Peregrine had reached the doorway now and made a bow from the safety of the other side. 'As you wish, happy to oblige. Lovely to see you again, Lady Cassandra. Your humble servant, Lady Celia. If I can't be of any further service then? No. Right. Well. I'll bid you adieu.' With a final flourish of his hat, Peregrine Finchley-Burke concluded his visit to Daar. An hour later, anxious to be off before either Armstrong sister could dream up another commission for him, he was seen heading out into the desert with only a guide, a mule and a camel for company.

'How very strange that Papa should have sent for me at this time,' Cassie said to her sister, back in the Scheherazade courtyard. 'I suppose I should not be surprised; he never wanted me to out come here in the first place.'

'And I thought you did not want to leave,' Celia said. 'Your letters have been so full of Linah this and Linah that. Where is she, anyway?'

'Visiting friends. She is permitted to do so once a week now.' In the excitement of Celia's unexpected arrival, and the need to preserve face in front of Mr Finchley-Burke, Cassie's woes had retreated to the back of her mind, but now they returned to her with full force. 'I sent you a note,' she said, slumping back down on to the cushions by the fountain. 'You obviously haven't got it yet. I'm so glad you're here, anyway.'

'No.' Now that they were alone, Celia took the opportunity to look more closely at her sister. It was not just the dark shadows, but the lack of animation in her beloved sister's face that worried her. Cassie's eyes were dull, her attention seemed to be turned inward. When she smiled, as she was trying to do now, it looked more like a grimace. Something had hurt her; her misery was obvious in the tense way she was holding herself. But to hold a tight rein on her emotions—that wasn't like Cassie. Nor was the distinct lack of tears. Her sister was being most un-Cassandra-like, Celia noted with growing alarm. 'What is it, dearest? Tell me what on earth has been going on. And no shilly-shallying, if you please, I want the truth.'

Under her sister's concerned gaze, Cassie's throat clogged. She shook her head, avoiding eye contact. 'I can't. You will think I'm so foolish. And you're right, Celia, I *am*.'

'Please, Cassie, tell me what's wrong. I can't bear to see you like this. You look as if someone has died.'

Cassie's chin wobbled. 'Not someone, but something. Crushed to death. I love him so much, Celia.'

'Love him? Who?'

'Jamil. Prince Jamil. I am in love with him.' Her confession came out in a rush.

'Oh, dear.'

Her fingers plucked feverishly at the embroidery on one of the satin cushions. It was almost a relief to say it. 'I know. I know. I know. And he wants to marry me, and he's so angry that I said no, and now he's gone away and he hates me. He hates me, Celia, and I love him so much.'

'Marry you!'

'It was the most awful thing. He sounded like Papa, and he said it would be a pleasant duty for him to pro- duce an heir, and he said that his betrothal to the Prin- cess Adira didn't matter, and…'

'He is already betrothed!'

'Not any more. He's off breaking the news to her family at the moment. And now he won't have anyone to give him an heir. And I don't want anyone else to give him an heir. Except I don't want him to be alone either.' Cassie gave a hysterical little laugh. 'Oh, Celia, it's hopeless, all of it. I must get away from here, you see that, don't you? I can't see him again, but I can't bear the thought of never seeing him again. I can't. I just can't. Please, please, please, just take me away.'

At this point, Cassandra would normally have thrown herself on to her sister's shoulder and sobbed, but she did not. Cassie simply resumed her frantic plucking, unravelling a beautiful fringe of emerald-and-gold *passementerie*, winding the strands around and around her fingers, rocking back and forth, staring off into space with an expression of misery on her face that Celia had not seen since their mother died. Then, Cassie had not cried either. With a sense of foreboding, Celia began patiently to extract the story. From the things Cassie left out, together with her own experience of just how very seductive the desert and its princes could be, she surmised with some accuracy the full extent of Cassie's indiscretions. She could not blame her, having been just as indiscreet herself when first she met Ramiz, but nor could she see a way out of the tangle. Nothing Cassie said gave her the slightest hope that Prince Jamil loved her. And on this matter the sisters were in complete accord. Without love, Cassie could not—should not—marry.

'So you'll take me away from here?' Cassie said, looking at the carnage she had wreaked on the cushion with some surprise. 'Tomorrow. Only I must stay to see Linah first. She will be so upset; we have become very close. My only consolation is that I have done some good there. Jamil—Jamil—he loves his daughter, and she loves him.'

'Then you have indeed done some good, and should

be proud of yourself,' Celia said bracingly. 'Tomorrow, then, we'll start back to Balyrma. If you're sure.'

White-faced but determined, Cassie nodded.

But Linah took the news very badly indeed, and Cassie's self-control was tested to the limit. The child was distraught, blaming herself, pleading with her governess to stay, promising never to misbehave again. Touched to the core by this evidence of her affection, Cassie was overwhelmed with guilt.

Broken-hearted, Linah begged for one final outing on horseback together. Desperate to make amends, Cassie agreed. But when they arrived at the stables the next morning as dawn was breaking, they discovered that Jamil's groom, who always accompanied them when he was not able to do so himself, was smitten by a fever. Linah's disappointment knew no bounds. Cassie was powerless against her frantic pleas. Though she knew it was forbidden, she decided just this once to take Linah out alone.

They set out at a slow trot through the city, out of the gates and into the desert, taking the familiar route to the Maldissi Oasis, where they stopped for a refreshing drink of water. The sun was rising in the azure-blue sky. They sat in the shade of a cluster of palm trees and sipped from a goatskin flask, dangling their bare feet in the shallows of the pool.

Anxious not to be away too long from the palace, Cassie put her stockings and boots back on, and helped Linah into the saddle, but the little girl wasn't ready for her treat to end and begged that they go on just a little bit, that they have a race. Cassie agreed, unwilling to deny Linah on this their last ever day together. They set off, Cassie giving Linah a head start.

Spurring her pony into a gallop, the little girl headed due east, directly into the sun. Cassie's stirrup had come loose. She took some time to adjust it, and by the time she was back in the saddle, Linah was lost in the dazzle of the sunlight. A knot formed in Cassie's stomach. She should not have let her out of her sight. Pulling on the reins, she set off towards the speck in the distance that must be her charge. How had the child got so far so quickly? Urging her grey mare into a gallop, Cassie called her name, but Linah either ignored her, or her voice was lost in the wind. She called again, and saw the speck slow. Relieved, she began to do the same.

She was only two hundred yards from Linah when three men on camels appeared from behind an outcrop of ochre rock directly into their path. The child pulled her pony up so quickly she tumbled off, and Cassie gave a cry of dismay. Leaping down from the mare almost before she came to a halt, she gathered Linah to her, relieved to find her dazed and bruised, but with no broken bones.

'Thank you,' she said to the nearest man, who had a hold of the pony's reins, but when she made to take them from him, he growled and snatched them back, spitting an oath. The pony shuffled nervously in the sand. Linah shrank against her side. Cassie looked from one man to the other, noting the ragged clothing, the straggling beards, the hungry look in their eyes beneath their red-and-white chequered head dresses. Brigands.

Fear ran like an icy river down her spine, but she knew better than to show it. Cassie cast the man holding the reins a haughty look. He had a vicious scar running from his ear down to his neck. 'Thank you for your kind help,' she said again, holding out her hand imperiously. 'I will take these now.'

The man growled something incomprehensible. Linah whimpered and huddled into Cassie's skirts. Cassie's mare was some fifty yards away now, for she had let her go in her rush to get to Linah. She surveyed the motley group. The other two men were watching the one with the scar, obviously taking their cue from him. Each man wore an unsheathed scimitar tied around his waist. She had no weapon but surprise.

Without giving herself time to think, Cassie made to snatch the pony's reins. The scarred man leapt from his camel, pulled a dagger from behind his back and grabbed her. She did not know whether they meant to rob or murder her; her only thought was to get Linah to safety. As the thin point of the blade made contact with her neck, Cassie dealt him a vicious kick on the shins. He yelped and dropped the reins.

'Run, Linah, run,' Cassie screamed, pushing the little girl towards her pony, grabbing the man's belt and digging her heels in to prevent him from giving chase, at the same time sinking her teeth into the hand that held the knife. The scarred man howled, his two henchmen dismounting in order to come to his aid, were already on the sand when Linah scrabbled into her saddle and spurred her pony into a wild gallop. As Cassie kicked and bit and threw sand indiscriminately at each of the men, she caught a glimpse of Linah's terrified face looking over her shoulder. 'Ride!' she screamed. Then a vicious blow to her temple from the hilt of a scimitar knocked her unconscious to the sand.

She awoke to darkness and agony. Her mouth was dry; it felt as if it had been washed out with sand. Her head was a ball of fire, centred on her right temple. She tried to sit up. White light blazed, a searing pain, and she lost consciousness. Some time later, she came to again and this time lay completely still, trying to assess the situation The ache was now a dull throb. Her mouth was almost glued shut with thirst. She was lying on her back in the sand, in what appeared to be a cave. She wriggled her toes, then tried to move her feet, only to find them bound. Her arms, too, were tied at the wrists and bound to a stake in the ground. She had only a groggy memory of how she had come to be here.

'Linah?' Her voice was the merest croak, echoing eerily into the darkness. No reply. 'Linah,' Cassie said again. Nothing. Good, she had escaped. Or else she was being held separately. Or else—*no, no, don't think that*.

Time passed. She had no idea how long. She lay fitfully between sleeping and waking, waiting, trying not to wonder, for to wonder was to panic. Linah had escaped. She would fetch Jamil. No, Jamil was not there.

She would fetch Halim. Not there either, he was with Jamil. The guards then. Or—or Peregrine Finchley-Burke. Light-headed with dehydration, Cassie giggled as she tried to picture apple-shaped Peregrine riding to her rescue. He would not get even as far as the Maldissi Oasis. And even if he did, how would he know where to look next? He did not know the desert. Besides, he was probably halfway to Cairo by now. Only Jamil knew this desert well enough. And Jamil probably didn't care. And even if he did, he wasn't there. And…

Tears rolled down Cassie's cheek. She could taste them, salty and hot on her tongue. They made her even thirstier. What would she rather die of—thirst or whatever the brigands had planned for her? A thousand cuts? Were they going to stake her out in the heat of the sun and leave her to the predators? Or maybe they would first ravish her. Maybe they intended not death, but life as some sort of slave. She recalled the hungry look in their eyes and shivered so hard her bonds dug into her wrists. If only she had not read all of those tales in *One Thousand and One Nights*. To think that she used to believe them romantic, even the most bloodthirsty. She did not want to die like a heroine. She had a sneaking suspicion that she was not going to make any real sort of heroine anyway. A real one would surely have found some way of freeing herself by now.

Cassie strained, but the ropes merely cut deeper into her wrists and her ankles. They must have taken her boots. How dare they take her boots! And her stockings, too—her feet were bare. Somehow, this minor violation was the one which offended her most, and fed her courage. Cassie took a deep breath and screamed at the top of her voice.

'Help! Help! Help!' Her screams resounded and echoed. 'Help! Help! Help!' She was giving herself a headache. She tugged frantically at her bonds, wriggling and squirming in the sand in an effort to pull the stakes free, but to no avail. Exhausted, her head pounding like a smithy's anvil, Cassie lay panting and attempted to reason. If they wanted her dead, they would not have staked her out like this. Therefore they wanted her alive. Therefore they would be back, soon maybe. She must conserve her energy. She must try to reason with them. If not reason, she must fight. She did not want to die, but she *would* not submit.

At first, they could make no sense of what Linah said, for the child, having mustered all her strength and courage to get back to the royal palace, collapsed in a state of shock, muttering Cassie's name over and over. It was Celia who finally coaxed the story from her, and Celia who dispatched two servants hot foot, one in the direction of Prince Jamil, the other to her husband.

Even allowing for a child's natural tendency to exaggerate, what Linah told her of the kidnap was terrifying. Sick with dread, she resisted, with extreme difficulty, the completely useless but wholly natural impulse to rush out into the desert and search for Cassie herself. Instead, she interrogated Prince Jamil's head groom and with his help organised a search party consisting of palace guards. They were out all day, and into the night, but though they found the spot at which the kidnap had taken place, there was no sign of tracks leading from it, and no one in all of Daar seemed to have any knowledge of where the brigands came from, what tribe they might belong to.

Celia spent the night pacing the floor, trying not to imagine what fate Cassie had met. That they had not murdered her on the instant was her only consolation, and it was a poor one, augmented only by the lack of a body, alive or—but, no, Celia refused to think of that.

Linah had woken several times in the night, hysterical with fear. Morning brought neither a ransom demand nor any sign of Prince Jamil. In despair, Celia consulted with the groom over another search party. Then she set about pacing the floor, wringing her hands and telling herself not to panic.

Meanwhile, Jamil had concluded the better part of the treaty negotiations. The Princess Adira had graciously accepted his apologies for the inconvenience and, with even more alacrity, accepted his gifts of jewels and precious stones. The concessions that Jamil had prepared in advance with Halim, he allowed her father to barter hard over. Honour was finally satisfied. The old man's sensibilities were further oiled by the gift of an unusual rose-coloured diamond. The celebratory feast was an elaborate affair. Tables groaned with food and drink, musicians played in the background. The festivities were in full flow when the messenger bearing the letter summoning Jamil home arrived. Reading it with numb disbelief, Jamil felt as if his own senses had been kidnapped. Abandoning his caravan and his host summarily, and leaving Halim to smooth things over, he selected the best of his guards and set out in the dark. Stopping only for water, he rode the whole long night and morning before reaching Daar.

Let her be alive.

Let her be safe.

Cassie. Cassie. Cassie. He muttered her name to himself like a talisman as he urged his camel to a speed that even his pedigree beast found difficult to sustain. He prayed. He bartered with the gods. He prayed again. He offered himself in her stead. He would have offered his kingdom. That was when he realised. He would have given anything to have her back and safe. She was more important to him than life itself.

He loved her.

This need for her. This passion. This urge to keep her only to himself. The desire always to be by her side. The way he wanted always to talk to her, to ask her opinion. The way her face was etched in his mind. The feeling he had, that part of him was missing when she was not there. He loved her.

Not in a flowery, sentimental way either, but in a profound, deep-rooted way. What he felt for her, he felt in his bones. In his soul. In his heart. Truly, in his heart, just as Cassie had described it. That aspect of what the poets said was true. He thought of her and his heart ached.

He loved her. He was in love with her. In love. The realisation brought with it an elation and an enormous sense of relief, as if he were breaking free from a prison, the prison of his tormented past. He was not alone. He did not have to stand alone any longer. With Cassie by his side he was strong enough to conquer the world.

By his side. If she died—if she died so, too, would he. He loved her so much. He would not let her die. *Cassie. Cassie. Cassie.* On and on Jamil rode, the beating of his camel's hooves pounding out her name, his love, her name, his love, over the miles of desert that separated him from Daar.

He would not believe she was dead. He would know. He would feel it. Here, in his heart, he would feel it. He would know. He told himself that as the grey light of dawn broke and despair began to rise with the sun. He would know. Of a certainty he would know.

That they had parted in anger he could not bear to think about. That they had parted without him telling her how he felt, he could not abide.

He loved her. And she loved him. *How could he have been so blind?*

That was why she would not marry him. Not because she didn't love him, but because she did. Believing him to be indifferent, she knew only unhappiness could result. He would change all that. He would make her happy. He would make her happiness his life's work. By the gods, let her be alive. Let him have the chance to put things right.

'I love you.' He said it under his breath. The words

sounded strange, but pleasing. 'I love you,' he said, looking up at the fading sky. Altair, the eagle star, one of the
brightest, could just be made out. Jamil closed his eyes
and wished on it, just as he had as a child, mindless of
how nonsensical it was. 'Be safe, Cassie,' he wished. 'I
love you.'

As he spurred his flagging camel towards the Seats
of the Gods mountain range that marked the home strait,
Jamil, Sheikh al-Nazarri, Prince of Daar-el-Abbah, felt a
tightening in his chest. *I love you.* The words, in Cassie's
breathy voice, were so clear he had to check over his
shoulder to make sure they hadn't been carried to him
by the wind.

She was alive. He would find her if he had to rake
the desert inch by inch with his bare hands.

He reached the royal palace mid-morning and
headed straight for the schoolroom courtyard where he
found Celia pacing the oval perimeter and muttering to
herself.

'Thank God,' she exclaimed, all formalities abandoned as she rushed towards the prince with whom she
was barely acquainted. 'Oh, thank heavens you have
come. My sister…' Celia stopped, her voice weighted
with tears. She blinked rapidly, taking several deep
breaths. 'I'm sorry. I just—I have been so worried. But
then so must you. Linah. Your daughter, she's all right.
Cuts and bruises, nothing more. She's still very upset,
not surprisingly. But she was very brave, she rode all

the way back on that little pony of hers, you must be so proud of her. You'll want to see her, of course.'

He was pale, coated from head to foot in dust, his mouth a thin, set line. His eyes—such striking eyes, she had forgotten—were fixed piercingly on her. 'In a moment. First, tell me exactly what happened,' he said curtly.

She did, as succinctly as possible, gathering all the salient facts and placing them before him in a logical, orderly manner, from the kidnap to the various searches she had organised. Later, her handling of the situation would earn his admiration, but at present, he was impatient for her to be finished.

'You say they have found no trace?'

'Nothing. No trail, nothing. No one knows who they might be, nor does anyone claim to have seen them before. Have you any enemies, someone who bears you a grudge?' she asked.

Jamil shook his head. 'None that would dare encroach upon my territory. The culprits are more likely to be opportunistic brigands. They probably don't even know Linah and Cassie belong to the royal household or else they would not have dared attack them.'

'Perhaps when they realise the error of their ways they will release her,' Celia said hopefully.

'Perhaps, but I do not intend to leave that to chance. In saving Linah, Cassie has placed her life in danger. I warned her—more than once, I warned her not to go out without an escort.' Jamil ran his fingers through his hair and sank on to the wall of the sun fountain. 'I should not have left. We argued.'

'She told me,' Celia said gently, perching beside him.

'What did she tell you?'

'Enough.'

'I see. You must think me an arrogant fool.'

Celia smiled. 'You will forgive my presumption in the circumstances, but I think you no fool, merely a man in love.'

Jamil rubbed his knuckles in his eyes. 'Cassie always said you were the clever one. It seems you knew before I did.'

'The main thing is you know now. Now go and find my sister, Prince Jamil. Bring her back safe and well, I beg of you, for both our sakes.'

He grasped her hands between his. 'By all that is sacred, I promise that I will.'

He left immediately, pausing only to hug his daughter fiercely to his chest, to tell her she was as brave as a panther, to promise her, to fervently promise her, that he would bring Cassie back.

Chapter Twelve

The brigands brought her water. She remembered, just in time, Jamil's warning not to drink too thirstily and forced herself to sip it slowly. They untied her and watched impassively as she struggled to her feet, her ankles throbbing painfully as the blood returned to them. To her utter relief, they allowed her to remain upright, though she was still hobbled like a camel. The air in the dank cave was fetid.

'What do you want of me?' she asked in her faltering Arabic.

The man with the scar, clearly the leader, leered and rubbed his thumb and fingers together. 'Money. Someone will pay a fine price for a pretty filly such as you.'

'It is you who will pay the price when Prince Jamil hears of this.'

'What has the prince to do with it?' the scarred man snarled.

'You don't know what you've done, do you?' Cassie replied triumphantly. 'The little girl with me? She was Princess Linah. I am her governess. Prince Jamil will have you hunted down and killed like dogs if any harm comes to me.'

'Numair,' one of the other men said, his voice tinged with fear, 'I want no part of this. Let her go now or Prince Jamil's wrath will descend on all our heads.'

'Silence, you spineless cur,' Numair said. 'I need time to think.' They left Cassie alone in the cave.

Later, she woke from a light-headed doze to hear raised voices outside. Creeping cautiously towards the cave's entrance, which seemed rather strangely to be uphill, she listened hard.

One of the others seemed to be arguing for her release. 'Gold is no use to a dead man,' she heard quite distinctly. 'He will show us no mercy. We have offended his household. I say let her go.'

But the man called Numair shook his head vehemently. 'No. We have hooked a bigger fish than we intended, that is true. But if we keep our heads then the price of our catch will be higher, too.'

Something alerted them to her presence. Numair stood up and grabbed her, holding his knife to her throat. Cassie felt it graze the skin. 'You were spying on us,' he said. 'Maybe it would be better to kill you, cut our losses.'

'I won't say anything,' Cassie said, her voice a mere thread. 'Please, just let me go and I promise I won't say anything.'

Numair simply snarled and pulled her clear of the cave's entrance, which turned out to be no more than a hole in the ground, forcing her to her knees in front of him. 'Move another muscle, and I will make sure you never speak again. Maybe I should sample this fine catch of ours first, make sure it is of the requisite quality.'

With a swift movement, he cut the front of her riding habit open with his knife. Cassie screamed, piercingly loud. She was released so suddenly she fell to her knees. Numair laughed contemptuously. 'Not yet, not yet, perhaps. But soon, you have my word on it.'

Jamil patted the glittering scimitar which he wore unsheathed in his belt. Not the ornamental weapon of state, but a working sword, with a chased silver hilt and a steel blade freshly sharpened that morning. His dagger, he wore in the classic position for war, strapped between his shoulders, and tucked into his boot was another, smaller dagger with an ivory handle.

He rode out on a fresh camel, the royal colours of emerald green and gold flying like a flag from the saddle covers, his emerald cloak and head dress a challenge in themselves. He was the Prince of Daar-el-Abbah and he wished the scum who had kidnapped Cassie to know who they were dealing with.

The search parties had tried all the obvious places, but no one knew this desert—*his desert*—like he did. Putting himself in the minds of the brigands, it came to him. The Belly of the Vulture, an hour beyond the Maldissi, where there were a set of underground caves formed by a long dried-up oasis. An obvious place, if you knew about it. Few did.

As he neared the desolate location, Jamil's hands tightened on the reins of his camel, slowing the beast down to a walk, anxiously scanning the barren remnants of the well. Hoof prints. Feet. Three sets. He saw them, cowering behind a rock, near the entrance to the cave. *Bastards.*

Raising his scimitar, he drew his camel to a halt a few yards in front of them. Already, two were shuffling backwards, fear in their eyes. They would cause him no problems. The other one, the one with the scar, looked like more of a challenge. A heavy-set man, but muscled. Jamil's blood lust rose. *Bastards.*

He addressed himself directly to the leader. 'Where is she?' His voice was cool, steady as a rock. Show the enemy no fear.

'Safe enough where she is,' the man replied, spitting contemptuously on the ground.

'Bring her out.'

'For a price. One might even say a princely sum.' He smiled, showing yellow, uneven teeth.

'I do not pay scum like you,' Jamil snarled. 'Bring her out,' he said to the other two, *'now!'*

They did as he bid them, ignoring their leader's protests, too overcome with awe and fear to do otherwise. Bowing and scraping, they disappeared into the depths of the cave, emerging almost immediately with a bedraggled figure, bound at the ankles and wrists.

'Cassie.' In an instant Jamil dismounted from his

camel and strode over to her, scimitar drawn, though
it was not needed, for the men made a final obeisance
before taking advantage of his distraction to turn on
their cowardly tails. Gathering her close, keeping one
eye on the scarred leader, Jamil looked anxiously at
Cassie. 'Are you harmed?'

She gazed up at him in stupefaction. Three days
without food, only a minimum of water, and her hold
on reality was extremely loose. 'Jamil?'

'Cassie, have they harmed you?'

She must be dreaming. Only in her dreams did he
look at her so tenderly. Only in her dreams did he gaze
at her in just this way, as if she were the sun and moon
and stars to him. As he was to her. She must be dreaming. 'Jamil.' She clutched at his arm. It felt real. 'You
came.'

Her voice was no more than a whisper. There was
dried blood on her neck. A huge purple bruise on her
temple. Her skin was hot and dry, her eyes glazed. A
cold fury such as he had never known possessed him.
Gently, he laid her down by the cave's entrance, hastily
cutting her bonds, handing her his flask before turning
his full attention on her captor.

The scarred man, realising he had been abandoned,
was himself trying to back away, frightened now,
alarmed by the murderous look on his prince's face.
'She took no harm, Highness,' he said, raising his hands
as if in surrender.

A thirst for vengeance swelled within Jamil, granting him the power of a hundred men. He seemed to

visibly grow with it. 'No harm! You call that no harm,' he growled, releasing the catch on his cloak, testing the weight of his scimitar, slicing it over his head.

'Highness,' the scarred man said, 'forgive me.' He made as if to throw himself on the ground, but in the same movement drew his own sword. He had nothing to lose now. With a guttural cry, Numair launched himself at his prince.

Cassie couldn't understand what was happening. She wasn't in the cave any longer. She had been dreaming that Jamil came to her rescue. Jamil, in an emerald cloak, looking so fierce and so angry. Because she had disobeyed him by taking Linah out alone. Because he had been put to the effort of rescuing her. *I'm sorry*, she wanted to tell him. *I love you*, she longed to say.

But it was a dream. And now he wasn't there and she was sitting outside in the sun, leaning against a rock. Her head was buzzing. She raised a hand to rub her brow and realised she was no longer bound. Dazedly, she looked down at her ankles. Free.

Just in front of her, there was a flurry of movement. Two men. Fighting with scimitars. She couldn't focus. She could hear the hiss as the blades arced through the air, she could hear heavy breathing, and the scuffling noise of feet in the sand. She got shakily to her feet. The scarred man. Numair. And Jamil.

She almost called his name. Luckily it stuck in her throat. She almost ran towards him. Luckily she stumbled. Luckily, for just then the scarred man raised his sword and were Jamil's attention not completely focused he would have been slain there and then.

Cassie watched, scarcely able to breathe as the battle raged. The men were well matched, but Jamil fought with the skill and determination of a man possessed. It felt like for ever, but it was over in minutes. A feint. A side step. A movement of the arm that was almost balletic, and Jamil's scimitar sliced through Numair's shoulder, neatly disabling the arm. Blood spurted, crimsoning on the sand. Numair fell to his knees, screaming in agony, his own scimitar dropping useless to the ground.

Cassie tottered towards Jamil, calling his name. He turned towards her. She was almost beside him, her arms held out, thinking only that it really was him, it really was, thinking of nothing else, when the glint of steel caught the corner of her eye. Numair had drawn a knife, was holding it in his left hand, was aiming it high, into the middle of Jamil's back.

Cassie screamed and threw herself between them with all her remaining feeble force. The cold kiss of steel pierced her as easily as a needle through silk. Blood blossomed on her dusty habit. She looked at it in astonishment, for she felt no pain. In slow motion, she saw Jamil, his face rigid with horror, pull a small vicious dagger from the strap around his ankle. He sank the dagger deep into Numair's chest. The brigand fell back on to the sand. Blood trickled from his mouth. Jamil turned to her. He was saying something. It sounded like her name. It sounded like 'I love you'. So this was a dream after all, then. It was a dream and now she was very, very tired. She had to sleep. 'I love you,' she said to Jamil before she sank into the blissful, black-velvet oblivion of unconsciousness. 'I love you.'

He feared for her life. The blood loss, combined with her weakened state from lack of sustenance, would make it a close-run thing. Though he bound it as best he could, and made the journey back across the desert to Daar at a painstakingly slow pace in order to prevent any jolting causing the wound to open again, by the time Jamil handed Cassie over into the care of her sister, she looked so lifeless that he could not help thinking the worst.

He paced nervously up and down all through the long night. He prayed as he had never prayed before. He watched, feeling completely helpless, as Celia changed the blood-soaked bandages, changed the sweat-drenched sheets in which Cassie writhed. He listened terrified to Cassie's feverish ramblings. He knelt by her divan, clasping her hot, dry hands in his, willing some of his own life-force to transfer itself to her, offering it all if only she would live.

Still Cassie's fever raged. Not even Prince Ramiz's arrival, along with her infant daughter, could lift Celia's mood.

On the fifth night, Jamil rode out alone into the desert, to the sanctuary of the ancients. The ritual was described in one of the oldest texts and kept under lock and key in the vaults of the palace, for its profane practices contravened all the sacred laws. But Jamil was desperate.

The moon was full, a good omen. He took the ring, the great seal of Daar-el-Abbah, from his finger, a symbol of what had been most precious to him. His kingdom. He offered it up as a sacrifice for something more precious still. Cassie.

He laid the ring on the stone boulder that had been used for centuries as an altar. He tore open the front of his tunic to reveal his bare chest. Then he took his dagger and made a cut over his heart, murmuring the ancient words. Blood dripped down his torso on to the altar. Throwing his arms wide, Jamil looked up at the moon and made his fervent wish. For love to heal.

Dizziness caught him unawares. A rushing in his ears. A blackness, like a thick blanket. He tumbled forward on to his knees. Blood dripped from the cut over his heart, crimson drops on to the silver sand. He fell. As he lost consciousness, a white owl, the traditional messenger of the ancients, hovered overhead, watching.

In the royal palace of Daar, Cassie stirred and opened her eyes.

He arrived back at dawn to find the palace in an uproar. Such an uproar he thought at first that Cassie had died, until he saw that Celia, rushing to meet him, was crying from happiness, and that she was smiling. 'The fever broke in the night,' she said, clutching at his sleeve in a most un-Celia-like manner. 'She's sleeping now, a proper, restful sleep. Oh, Jamil, I think she's going to live.'

He watched from the curtained doorway of Cassie's chamber, too afraid to wake her, so shaken with love and tenderness that he could not, in any case, trust himself with more for the present. Beside him Linah tucked her little hand into his. 'She's going to get better, *Baba*,' she whispered. 'Now you don't have to be sad any more.'

Jamil stooped down to give his daughter a hug, holding her fiercely close. 'No, now none of us need be sad any more,' he said gruffly.

He watched for hours. He had no comprehension of time. Cassie slept. Jamil stood guard. He was almost asleep on his feet when she spoke.

'Jamil.'

Her voice was so faint he barely heard it. Instantly, he was at her side, gazing anxiously into her beloved face, so pale and wan. Her eyes though, her beautiful turquoise eyes, no longer had the opaque glaze of fever.

Cassie blinked. She was so tired. How could she be so tired, when she felt as if she had been sleeping for ever? 'Jamil. What are you doing here? What happened? Why can't I move my arm?'

'The brigand stabbed you. You saved my life.'

She remembered. Vague pictures, becoming clearer. 'You killed him.'

'Yes,' Jamil said tersely.

'I'm glad. He was going to kill you. I couldn't bear that. Is Linah…?'

'She's all right. You can see her later.'

'I had the strangest dream about a white owl. When I woke up I found this in my hand.'

She handed him his ring. The ring of Daar-el-Abbah, with the seal. The ring he had left on the altar of the ancients. Jamil stared at it in astonishment.

'In my dream, your heart was bleeding,' Cassie told him. 'You'll think that's silly. Hearts don't bleed, you'll say.'

'No. I was wrong. I know now they can and they do.'

He had not intended to declare himself like this. Though Cassie was still weak, he found he could wait no longer. Kneeling down on the floor, he took her hand in his. 'My heart was bleeding for you. I love you, Cassie. I was wrong. It exists. True love. Real love. One love. I love you with all my heart.'

'Jamil!' A single tear trickled down her pale cheek. 'Don't say it unless you really mean it. Please, I don't want you to say it just because you think it's what I want to hear. Or out of honour or duty because you think I saved your life. Or because you feel sorry for me. Or because—'

'Darling Cassie,' Jamil said with a smile, 'I am saying it only because it is true. You will forgive me for not saying it earlier, but I didn't realise I was in love with you. Halim did. And Celia did, too. I was too blind, too stupid to see it, but now I do.'

'Please tell me this isn't a dream.'

'It is no dream. Or if it is, it is the most wonderful one, one we will never wake up from.'

'Jamil,' Cassie said softly, 'I love you, too.'

'My darling.' He kissed her. Gently, a whisper of his mouth on her cracked lips. He held her tenderly against his heart, felt the faint flutter of her own against his chest, and felt a settling take place inside him as if something was finally resolved, concluded. As if something had taken root. Happiness.

He held her until she fell asleep, her head nestled into the crook of his arm. He held her while she slept, and he was still holding her when she woke again, ready to reassure her, to tell her how much he loved her, how much he would always love her, how he already loved her more than when he had first told her and how he would love her more again the next time she asked.

Ten days later, Cassie's strength was fully returned. She and Celia were sitting by the sun fountain. Linah was taking an afternoon nap. With baby Bashirah asleep in her basket in the same room, the sisters were free to talk confidentially.

'We thought we were going to lose you,' Celia confessed. 'I even wrote to Papa, to prepare him for the worst.'

'Lord Armstrong will have had a surfeit of mail from Arabia then, because I, too, wrote to him,' a strong male voice said.

'Jamil,' Cassie said, jumping to her feet.

'Cassie. You look well.'

'I am well. I'm very well. I've never been healthier,' she said fervently. 'In fact, I am completely recovered, am I not, Celia?'

Celia, too, got to her feet, shaking out her caftan. 'Completely,' she said with a smile.

'No small thanks to you, Lady Celia. You have my eternal gratitude. But your work here is done and you must be anxious to be reunited with your husband.'

'I confess I am.'

'As you should be,' Jamil said with a smile. 'I have taken the liberty of readying your caravan. Your maid-servants have just finished your packing. My guards will escort you to the border, where your husband will be waiting to meet you. He will be as pleased to see you both as you are to see him, no doubt.'

'He is a good husband and a fine father. I am blessed,' Celia replied.

'He is to be envied,' Jamil said.

'I am sure one day soon you, too, will make an admirable husband and father,' Celia said, with a side-long glance at Cassie.

'Jamil,' Cassie said quickly, embarrassed by her sister's blatant probing, 'You mentioned writing to my father. What about?'

'We will discuss it later,' he said with an enigmatic smile. 'First you must say your farewells to your sister. If you will excuse me, I have some things to take care of.' He raised her hand to his mouth, and planted a kiss on her palm.

Cassie stared after him in consternation. 'What…?'

Celia chuckled. 'What do you think? He wants to be alone with you. Now come and help me change into my travelling clothes.'

Celia left just an hour later with Bashirah strapped, Bedouin-style, across her chest. The caravan disappeared out of the palace gates, leaving Jamil and Cassie alone. She was nervous. So, too, it seemed, was he, though she could not understand why.

'I have a surprise for you,' he said, taking her by the hand and leading her to the eastern wing of the palace. She had been there just once before, but she had never forgotten it. The door to the courtyard had been newly painted. It stood ajar. She looked up at Jamil questioningly, but he said nothing, only urging her forwards, into the ante-room.

White tiles, with a mosaic pattern of emerald-and-turquoise. The sweetest smell of orange blossom and something more familiar. Lavender, that was it.

Cassie took a tentative step through and into the courtyard. It had been transformed. Gone was the panther-cub fountain. In its place, a new fountain tinkled, with a mermaid as its centre piece. Outside, the garden had been replanted. Bay trees and lemons, oranges and figs. Gone was the air of desolation. Gone were all traces of Jamil's boyhood quarters. The place had been transformed into a riot of colour and light.

A little stream meandered into a pool where water lilies floated and silver fish darted in the green depths. A delightful little pavilion was tucked into another corner, jasmine and honeysuckle mingling on its trellis. The jasmine flowers were closed with the rising heat, allowing the sweet scent of the honeysuckle dominance. Delighted, Cassie smiled up at Jamil. 'The hedgerows in England are a riot of honeysuckle in the early summer. How did you know I loved its scent—oh, Celia, I suppose. There's a lane going down to the mill pond at home, I used to sneak out of the house before any of my sisters were awake, to walk there—and sometimes if there was no one around I would bathe. Jamil, this is beautiful. It's wonderful. How did you manage to do all this without my knowing?'

They wandered arm in arm through each of the rooms, Cassie's fingers trailing over delicate hangings, her slippered feet curling into rich carpets. The bathing chamber had the most enormous bath she had ever seen. Sunk into the floor, with two steps leading down into the tub, it had gold taps in the shape of fishes. 'Big enough for two,' Jamil said with a smile that made Cassie shiver in anticipation. The whole place gleamed with vibrant colour; it sang with vibrant life.

'You like it?' he asked when they had finally completed the full circuit of the rooms.

'I love it. It's magical.'

'Our own quarters. Yours and mine. I wanted to make a break with tradition, I don't want to spend any more time apart from you than I have to.' Jamil led her back to the fountain. 'This is one tradition—an English tradition—I want to respect, though.' Dropping gracefully to his knees, he took her hand. 'You can do me no greater honour than to be my wife, Cassie. You can make me no happier than to say you will spend your life with me. All I have is yours. I offer you my heart. That, too, is yours, always. Say you'll marry me.'

Cassie dropped to her knees beside him. 'Oh, Jamil, yes. Yes. For you have my heart, too, my dearest, darling Jamil. My own desert prince.'

His kiss was resonant with love. Always, afterwards, Cassie would associate lavender and jasmine with the most extreme happiness. For the first time ever, he kissed her as a lover, as if she were the most precious thing in the world, and the most desirable. Tenderly and passionately he kissed her, as if it were his first kiss, as if he had never kissed, as if he would never leave off kissing. Her lips. Her lids. Her cheeks. Her ears. Her throat. Murmuring his love. Whispering her name. He kissed her, and she returned his kisses, as lovers do, with adoration and fervour, just exactly as if they had never kissed, and always would.

He picked her up in his arms and carried her to the sleeping chamber. Placing her on the divan, he kissed her while he removed each scrap of her clothing. Kisses that coiled their wispy magic around her, raising her pulse, heating her blood, so gradually she did not notice at first. She lay spread before him naked, relishing the reverence in his face, in his touch, on his lips, relishing the way he looked and tasted and touched, anxious to do the same, tugging at his caftan until he lifted it over his head and stood before her proudly erect, magnificent.

He kissed her thighs, then licked into her sex. 'Wait,

wait, wait,' she said, tossing and turning, clutching, trying to hold on, but he would not let her. He kissed her and she came, wildly, jerked into paradise with the force of it, clutching his shoulders for fear of being lost, saying his name over and over.

Even as the pulsing shook her, he pulled her on top of him, easing her down on to the long silken length of him, his face etched with the pleasure of it. Even as the throbbing receded and began to build again, he lifted her, showing her how to sheathe him and how to unsheathe, to move to a rhythm that was just theirs, only theirs, lost in the power of his thrust conjoined with her own, lost in the beauty of him, below her, inside her, swelling and pulsing until he came, crushing her to him, holding her tight against his chest, his heart beating the same wild rhythm as her own.

Her fingers traced the small scar above his heart. The place where he had bled for her. His fingers traced the deeper scar on her arm, where she had bled for him. 'You were right. To embrace true love is a sign of strength, not of weakness. You make me stronger. I love you, Cassie. I will always love you,' Jamil said hoarsely. 'I will never, ever tire of making love to you.'

'I know,' she said. Because she did.

Epilogue

London—two months later

'Henry, haven't seen you in ages.' Lord Torquil 'Bunny' Fitzgerald strode across the salon and helped himself to a glass of their hostess's rather poor claret and plonked himself down opposite his old friend. 'Frightful squeeze this, only came because I heard Wellington was bound to drop by. Didn't realise we'd be subjected to some damned caterwauling female though.'

'La Fionista,' Lord Henry said. 'If you've seen her, you'll realise why Wellington's here—you know how much he likes a good vibrato!'

The two men chuckled heartily. 'Saw your good lady wife somewhere,' Bunny said, flicking open his snuff box. 'Here with one of your daughters—sorry, can't remember her name. The plain one, intimidating gal, bookish.'

'Cressida.'

'Aye, that's the one. Pity she took after your side of the family. T'other one now, she's a fine-looking girl. Cassandra.' Bunny lowered his voice confidentially. 'Last time we met she was in a bit of a spot—assume you got it all sorted, right and tight?'

Lord Henry took a generous pinch of snuff, inhaled it, sneezed twice, wiped a few specks from his coat sleeve and drained his glass. 'I suppose you could say that,' he said, waving the waiter over and telling him to leave the bottle. 'Aye, you could say that, though, by God, Bunny, for a while there it was all hell to pay. After we last spoke, you should know I acted pretty sharply. Sent off a despatch to Cairo; there's a chap there owes me a favour, bit of a bumbler but reliable enough. So I sent him off to fetch Cassandra home.'

'And?' Scenting scandal, Bunny pulled his chair a little closer.

'Well, next thing is, I get a letter from Celia—my eldest, married to Prince al-Muhanna—usually very level-headed gal. Chip off the old block and all that. Anyway, she informs me that Cassandra has taken it into her head to become a governess. For this other sheikh. Al-Nazarri. Something about proving herself, I don't understand it—but all perfectly respectable and above board according to Celia.'

Bunny shook his head. 'And this sheikh, is he…?'

'Rich as Croesus.'

Bunny drew in his breath. 'Tricky.'

'Very. Of course, I sent another despatch to Cairo,

but it was too late, Finchley-Burke had already gone. No post for weeks. No idea what was happening, then I got three letters all at once. Cassandra blithering on the way she does about what a marvellous job she's doing teaching the Prince's brat—dismissed that, needless to say. Then one from Celia telling me that Cassandra has been kidnapped and stabbed and not likely to survive. Well...' Lord Henry drank deep. 'You can imagine how that went down with the other girls. Hysterical, they were. Had to call in Sophia. Bella no use whatsoever, burning feathers and drumming her heels. Took myself off to Boodle's pretty damn smart.'

'My God, I should think so. Another snifter?'

'Wouldn't say no. Then I read the other letter...' Lord Henry chortled '...turns out it's from this prince chappie, Prince Jamil al-Nazarri, demanding Cassandra's hand in marriage.'

'Good lord. But I thought you said she was dying.'

'No, she rallied. She's all right now. Fully recovered. Funny, it took Sophia quite a while before she could laugh about it. So there you are,' Lord Henry said with what in a lesser man would have been described as a grin. 'I've two pet princes in the family now, helped my standing in the Foreign Office no end.'

'But what about the other one—the chap you were so set on Cassandra marrying—Wellington's protégé?'

Lord Henry guffawed. 'Another funny thing. Dead. Malaria. Touch of good fortune for me, because I'd as good as promised her. So there you go, all's well in the end.'

'A toast,' Bunny said, rather sloppily tipping the dregs of the not-so-bad-after-all claret into their glasses. 'To your new sheikh.'

'Prince,' Lord Henry corrected.

'Whatever. Cheers.'

The preparations for the wedding of the Prince of Daar-el-Abbah could not be hurried. Everyone wished to pay their respects and their dues. Men of import and influence, heads of tribes, neighbouring princes, distant kith and kin all wished to take part in the celebrations. Not even Halim could find a way of speeding the proceedings along. They went at the pace they needed to go at. It was the tradition. Jamil, conscious of the fact that he was breaking almost every other tradition, determined to give his beloved bride every possible chance of being accepted by his people, had reluctantly accepted the fact that the wedding would take six weeks to organise. In fact, it took eight. Eight long weeks during which he and Cassie spent an agonising amount of time apart. Eight long weeks in which they both counted the days, the hours, until they were formally united. Eight long weeks of nothing but snatched kisses to fuel their passion.

Eight long weeks, but finally the waiting was over. The betrothal ceremony, the day before the wedding itself, also followed tradition, with the women in one part of the palace, and the men in the other. Celia, who had recently discovered she was expecting her second child, was not present for the celebrations, it being the storm season and Ramiz having too much care for her well-being to allow her to travel. The loving letter she sent was gift enough for Cassie, though. In truth, Cassie would not have cared if they had taken their vows with no one else present at all. All they needed was each other.

The bride-to-be's hands and feet were painted in henna, her hair braided and oiled, and the women danced together. At this point, tradition would end, for the wedding day was to be spent celebrating the future, which meant, Jamil had informed his shocked Council, that the rites would all be new.

The morning saw the bride and groom take breakfast together in the company of their most honoured guests, the women sitting at table with the men, partaking of food from the same dishes. From behind her veil, Cassie's eyes followed her husband-to-be with a longing that was almost tangible—to Jamil, at least. Though this was the most important day of his life, he could not wait for it to be over.

Cassie's wedding gown represented a mixture of east and west. A half-robe of golden silk, with an overdress of gold lace, with long, tight-fitting sleeves, puffed at the shoulder, but instead of an underdress or petticoats, she wore harem pants of gold, generously pleated and caught into her ankles, trimmed with little gold bells that tinkled when she walked. A long cloak of gold lace trailed out behind her, also trimmed with little bells, carried by six little girls at either side, orchestrated by a proud Linah bringing up the rear. On her head, Cassie wore a golden tiara over which another lace veil was suspended, with her long hair brushed into a cloud, cascading freely down her back. On her feet, she wore soft kid slippers edged with diamonds.

Trembling with anticipation, she made the seemingly never-ending journey down the emerald green carpet from the entrance of the throne room. The guests were so numerous that they filled the ante-room at the back, and spilled out into the corridors, but Cassie looked neither to the right nor to the left, for her eyes were focused firmly to the front where Jamil waited for her, wearing a plain silk tunic, a long gold cloak to match her own and a golden head dress. His scimitar gleamed. On his belt was one of the famous yellow diamonds of Daar-el-Abbah. A matching diamond sat on Cassie's finger. As she reached the bottom of the dais, Jamil stepped down to meet her and put back her veil.

'You look like a goddess come down from heaven,' he whispered. 'My beautiful bride. How I have longed for this moment. I can't wait for tonight.'

'Jamil.' She clutched at his hand, grateful for the support, suddenly unbearably nervous. But he smiled at her, his own particular smile, and she took courage and smiled back.

Their vows were said clearly and with a simple sincerity that made the women weep and the men harrumph.

'I now declare you my wife,' Jamil said, gazing deep into her eyes.

'I now declare you my husband,' Cassie replied, dimly conscious of the cheering as Jamil kissed her firmly on the lips.

The wedding banquet was a feast of delights, but she could barely eat. She and Jamil did not dance, but sat watching, their hands entwined, waiting. Finally, Halim stood before them, and informed them that the caravan was ready. 'My very best wishes, Lady Cassandra,' he said, bowing low. Halim was too wise a man to do anything other than accept Cassie wholeheartedly into the palace. In time, he would even begin to think, grudgingly, that the influence she had on Daar, and on its prince, was positive.

Climbing on to the high wooden seat of the white camels, Cassie and Jamil showered the cheering wellwishers behind them with gold coins, and were in turn showered with rose petals and orange blossom. They made the short journey to the Maldissi Oasis in a silence stretched taut with anticipation. The tent stood in the lee of the palms—a huge tent, an opulent tent with an enormous round divan taking pride of place. It was hung with garlands and strewn with more rose petals.

'Darling. My own darling wife. Tonight I will love you as I have never loved you,' Jamil said, scooping Cassie into his arms and carrying her over the threshold. 'And tomorrow, I will love you more.'

He laid her down on the divan and began to do just that. And later, when they embraced naked in the pool of the oasis, they made love again. The cool of the water and the heat of their skin and the velvet hardness of Jamil thrusting inside her made Cassie certain that she had indeed arrived in paradise.

As he gathered her into his arms and spent himself high inside her, as her own climax pulsed around him, she tilted her head back and saw the stars. So close, they were. It felt as if she and Jamil had taken their place among them, where their love would burn brightly for all eternity.

* * * * *

HISTORICAL

Regency

LADY DRUSILLA'S ROAD TO RUIN
by Christine Merrill

Considered a spinster, Lady Drusilla Rudney has only one role in life: to chaperon her sister. So when her flighty sibling elopes Dru knows she has to stop her! She employs the help of a fellow travelling companion, ex-army captain John Hendricks, who *looks* harmless enough...

Regency

GLORY AND THE RAKE
by Deborah Simmons

Miss Glory Sutton has two annoyances in her life. One: the precious spa she's determined to renovate keeps getting damaged by vandals. Two: the arrogant Duke of Westfield—the man assigned to help her find the perpetrators.

TO MARRY A MATCHMAKER
by Michelle Styles

Robert Montemorcy is both amused and exasperated by Lady Henrietta Thorndike's compulsive matchmaking! When his ward pays an unexpected visit, Robert bets Henri she won't be able to resist meddling...only to lose his own heart into the bargain!

**On sale from 1st July 2011
Don't miss out!**

HISTORICAL

THE MERCENARY'S BRIDE
by Terri Brisbin

Brice Fitzwilliam is finally paid his due: awarded the title
and lands of Thaxted, the warrior waits to claim his
promised virgin bride! Gillian of Thaxted will *not* submit to
the conquering knight's powerful physique, or the bold
way his arm drapes protectively over her at night...

Regency

FROM WAIF TO GENTLEMAN'S WIFE
by Julia Justiss

When a destitute governess faints on Sir Edward Greaves'
threshold, chivalry demands that he offer her temporary
shelter. However, the desire Ned feels when he catches
her in his arms isn't at all gentlemanly...

WHIRLWIND BRIDE
by Debra Cowan

Can a hothouse flower bloom under burning Texas skies?
Riley Holt doesn't think so. Susannah Phelps is fair, fragile...
and wholly unsuited for frontier life. And being pregnant
doesn't help matters. What she needs is a ticket back east—
or at least someone to protect her. And damned if fate
doesn't keep volunteering *him* for the job!

On sale from 1st July 2011
Don't miss out!

*Available at WHSmith, Tesco, ASDA, Eason
and all good bookshops*

www.millsandboon.co.uk

REGENCY

Collection

Let these sparklingly seductive delights whirl you away to the ballrooms—and bedrooms—of Polite Society!

Volume 1 – 4th February 2011
Regency Pleasures by Louise Allen

Volume 2 – 4th March 2011
Regency Secrets by Julia Justiss

Volume 3 – 1st April 2011
Regency Rumours by Juliet Landon

Volume 4 – 6th May 2011
Regency Redemption by Christine Merrill

Volume 5 – 3rd June 2011
Regency Debutantes by Margaret McPhee

Volume 6 – 1st July 2011
Regency Improprieties by Diane Gaston

12 volumes in all to collect!

MILLS & BOON

www.millsandboon.co.uk

REGENCY

Collection

*Let these sparklingly seductive delights whirl
you away to the ballrooms—and
bedrooms—of Polite Society!*

Volume 7 – 5th August 2011
Regency Mistresses by Mary Brendan

Volume 8 – 2nd September 2011
Regency Rebels by Deb Marlowe

Volume 9 – 7th October 2011
Regency Scandals by Sophia James

Volume 10 – 4th November 2011
Regency Marriages by Elizabeth Rolls

Volume 11 – 2nd December 2011
Regency Innocents by Annie Burrows

Volume 12 – 6th January 2012
Regency Sins by Bronwyn Scott

12 volumes in all to collect!

MILLS
BOON

www.millsandboon.co.uk

England's Most Ruthless Queen

The story of Eleanor of Aquitaine is vividly brought to life by Anne O'Brien

Praise for Anne O'Brien

"Better than Philippa Gregory"
—*The Bookseller* on *Virgin Widow*

"With this winning book, Anne O'Brien has joined the exclusive club of excellent historical novelists"
—*The Sunday Express* on *Virgin Widow*

www.mirabooks.co.uk

2 FREE BOOKS
AND A SURPRISE GIFT

We would like to take this opportunity to thank you for reading this Mills & Boon® book by offering you the chance to take TWO more specially selected books from the Historical series absolutely FREE! We're also making this offer to introduce you to the benefits of the Mills & Boon® Book Club™—

- **FREE home delivery**
- **FREE gifts and competitions**
- **FREE monthly Newsletter**
- **Exclusive Mills & Boon Book Club offers**
- **Books available before they're in the shops**

Accepting these FREE books and gift places you under no obligation to buy, you may cancel at any time, even after receiving your free books. Simply complete your details below and return the entire page to the address below. You don't even need a stamp!

YES Please send me 2 free Historical books and a surprise gift. I understand that unless you hear from me, I will receive 4 superb new books every month for just £3.99 each, postage and packing free. I am under no obligation to purchase any books and may cancel my subscription at any time. The free books and gift will be mine to keep in any case.

Ms/Mrs/Miss/Mr —————— Initials ——————

Surname ——————————————

Address ——————————————

—————————— Postcode ——————

E-mail ——————————————

Send this whole page to: Mills & Boon Book Club, Free Book Offer, FREEPOST NAT 10298, Richmond, TW9 1BR